MW00938666

Seams

Lori Bell

This book is a work of fiction. Names, characters, places and incidents are the product of the author's imagination or are used fictitiously. Any resemblance to actual events, locales, or persons, living or dead, is coincidental.

Cover photograph by Lori Bell

"Use of barbiturates in the control of intracranial hypertension". *Journal of Neurotrauma* (Mary Ann Liebert, Inc.) 17 (6–7): 527–30. 2000. doi:10.1089/neu.2000.17.527. PMID 10937896.
Jump up . Lee M.W., Deppe S.A., Sipperly M.E., Barrette R.R., Thompson D.R. (1 June 1994).
"The efficacy of barbiturate coma in the management of uncontrolled intracranial hypertension following neurosurgical trauma". *Journal of Neurotrauma* (Mary Ann Liebert, Inc.) 11 (3): 325–31. doi:10.1089/neu.1994.11.325. PMID 7996586.
Jump up. Nordby H. K., Nesbakken R. (1984). "The effect of high dose barbiturate decompression after severe head injury: A controlled clinical trial". *Acta Neurochirurgica* (Springer-Verlag) 72 (3–4): 157–66. doi:10.1007/BF01406868. PMID 6382945.
"What Is a Medically Induced Coma and Why Is It Used?" David Biello. Scientific American. Scientific American, a division of Nature America, Inc. January 2011. Copyright 2011.
Fireworks Over Toccoa. Jeffrey Stepakoff. April 2010.

Printed by CreateSpace

ISBN 978-1496076069

DEDICATION

It seems only fitting to dedicate my first novel to my first readers. From the very bottom of my heart, thank you, I hope you enjoy Seams.

CHAPTER 1

A black skirt, an inch or two above the knee, accented her toned legs as she walked in wedges down the sidewalk in New York City. On a rare lunch break, between interviews, Kelsey Duncan let her mind wander back to the one she had just finished.

The president of a bank adopts a baby after she helps the teenage mother give birth on the Subway. Not just any president. Blair Thompson is a woman in charge. She's thrilling to talk to. Mesmerizing to look at. She's forty-five years old, single, career driven, and now a mother to a week-old baby boy.

When the water broke and gushed from the young black girl's overburdened pregnant body, Blair Thompson was forced to help. She didn't know a thing about what she would do, but she knew something had to be done. Quickly. She had worked until nearly midnight and was so used to riding the subway alone. Not tonight. Tonight she wasn't alone. And the ride wasn't uneventful. She called 9-1-1 from her cell phone, but that baby wasn't going to wait for anyone.

The young girl was clearly panicking and Blair Thompson helped her to the floor and awkwardly lifted up her black ankle-length knit skirt to find the baby already crowning. Blair Thompson encouraged her to calm down and begin pushing. That baby was almost here.

Blair Thompson swears she worked outside of her body to make that miracle happen. The baby was perfectly fine and the subway had stopped in time for the emergency personnel to cut the umbilical cord for a baby boy who didn't have a home.

She couldn't believe how life had just happened to her. The young girl had told her through gut-wrenching sobs how she couldn't keep the baby. She didn't even want to hold him in her arms. She had asked Blair Thompson to find him a home and she walked away refusing medical care when the emergency medical technicians wanted to transport her to the hospital. She didn't have any insurance and barely enough money for food to eat tomorrow. She couldn't take care of a baby. She wouldn't.

It was an unbelievable story and Kelsey couldn't wait to put it into writing back at the newspaper office, after lunch. Blair Thompson, a new mother to a newborn she had helped bring into this world. By taking action and getting help, she had saved that baby's life. But really it was the baby who had saved her. She had told Kelsey so herself. She had worked hard for money and success, but she never had been able to become pregnant. Her marriage didn't survive because of it.

Kelsey pushed open the glass door of the Café on the Corner. All she really wanted was a bottle of water to-go, but when she slid into the corner booth she was glad she had a reason to stay. Kyle Newman was waiting for her right where he said he would be. Mr. Predictable. In that corner booth with a glass of iced water with lemon waiting for her. Life with Kyle was comfortable. After two years together, there were no surprises. There was trust and real love and satisfactory sex.

"Hi there," Kelsey said, smiling at him as she reached for her glass to take a swallow of water. He had ordered a sweet tea and had already given her the lemon from the brim of his glass. She could taste tea in her water which she didn't like but what she did like was how Kyle had thought of her and knew, for her, there was never enough lemon in her iced water. Her thoughtful man. She truly did appreciate him.

"So how did your interview go?" he asked her, but he already knew it went well. Kelsey had that far away look in her eyes which she often had when she began writing a story in her mind before she had the opportunity to get to a computer.

"It was amazing. Kyle, that woman's life changed in just a few short minutes. That was the best interview I've ever had with anyone. I didn't want it to end." Kelsey is twenty-eight years old and has been a reporter for six years. Despite the fact that she never saw herself working in the newspaper business after college, she had found her niche.

"I look forward to reading your story, Kel. We do have to get going here though. I ordered turkey clubs for us - yours with lettuce, mayo and mustard - and I'm going to run up to the counter and grab those because they just called our number." Kelsey thought Kyle looked sexy in his tight dark-washed jeans, cowboy boots, and a white dress shirt, neatly tucked. His work as a police detective allowed him to dress however he wanted. He also had an exciting career. He had admitted to Kelsey a few months into their relationship that he craved routine and a laidback lifestyle outside of work, because his job was anything but predictable and mundane.

She welcomed the consistency that Kyle brought to her life. She always lived vicariously through her writing. Some of the stories she had written and subjects she had met were incredible. She was still thinking about Blair Thompson as Kyle brought their plates to the table. She grabbed the sliced pickle off of the side of her plate and took a bite.

Kelsey was watching how much she ate during lunch, thinking

about Blair Thompson and what great shape she was in had made her want to get back into her workout routine at the gym after work. It had been at least a month since Kelsey packed her gym clothes. Too many late nights in the office. Blair Thompson is a live Barbie doll. She has the long blonde hair, long legs, and a figure that made both men and women look twice. No one would ever guess she is forty-five years old.

Kelsey didn't see it for herself, but she also has a body that stopped traffic. She didn't regularly work hard at staying in shape and looking good, it just happened. It embarrassed her though when someone complimented her. She thought her legs could use a little more muscle and wished her breasts were a little perkier. What she complained about and had wanted to change on her body, most women would have paid to have. She loved clothes and she didn't shy away from wearing short skirts or tight fitting shirts, but she was not quite satisfied with her body and always vowed to work a little harder to make some necessary changes here and there.

One half hour later, Kyle and Kelsey were finished with lunch and walked outside of the restaurant. Kelsey was going to walk back to the newspaper office only a few blocks down the street, and Kyle had paid to park in the lot across from the restaurant.

"I can drive you back to work if you want," Kyle offered, digging his hand into the front pocket of his jeans to retrieve his keys. Kelsey was smiling at him, thinking how cute he looked when the wind took his sandy blonde hair and shuffled it a bit on his head.

"I'm good. I need the exercise, baby." Her own dark hair contrasted his, and yet the two of them were an attractive pair.

In her wedges, Kelsey stood as tall as Kyle's six-foot frame and she took advantage of that when she leaned in for a kiss. Kyle met her lips with his for quick peck, keeping his own lips tightly closed. She rolled her eyes at his conservativeness and smiled at him as she walked away, telling him she would see him tonight at her place.

It was her turn to cook dinner for him. They tried to have dinner together a few times throughout the work week and always on the weekends either at his place or hers. Their jobs were demanding and often meant late nights for both of them but they worked hard at making time for each other.

Kelsey already planned to ask Kyle to stay at her place tonight. She couldn't keep her eyes off of him in his jeans when they were standing outside of the Café on the Corner. She wanted him to kiss her, really kiss her, right then and there, but that wasn't Kyle. Kyle was a lights off, go into the bedroom, type of guy. No spontaneity. But sex was good with him nonetheless. It just seemed like Kelsey's sex drive was always in overdrive and Kyle's was in neutral. Kelsey pushed the warm thoughts out of her mind as she entered the building where she worked and took the elevator up to the newsroom. She had to get that story started.

CHAPTER 2

It was six o'clock when Kelsey saved and filed her story. The newsroom was quiet. Her editor had just left for dinner and would return later to format the paper for tomorrow. A few night interns and the cleaning crew were making little noise as Kelsey leaned back in her chair and stretched her arms in the air. She couldn't get Blair Thompson's words out of her mind. Kelsey always had a fascination for words. She was a bookworm growing up and being able to take someone's words and write a story was a dream job for her now. She was always looking for that 'aha' quote. And this time she had it.

"It feels as if the seams of my life have been let out just a bit," Blair Thompson had told her with a look of serenity on her face. "I've always fought hard for what I wanted and in my career I got it. In my personal life, I couldn't find it. I couldn't reach it. I couldn't find peace." With tears in her eyes, she had told Kelsey, "I thought if I prayed hard enough, God would send me a baby."

God had sent her a baby and he had renewed her outlook on faith, and given her a reason to let out those seams and breathe - and live. For herself. And for Baby Charlie.

That answered prayer came better late than never for Blair Thompson.

***

She was coming down from her writing high as she walked through the parking garage. Time to channel normal again after being wrapped up in such a fascinating story. Kelsey heard the text alarm on her cell phone as she sat behind the wheel of her black Land Rover. She reached into her purse and read the text. *See you soon. Be there by 7.*

Kelsey looked at the clock in her jeep and saw that she had thirty minutes to come up with an idea for dinner before Kyle would walk into the door of her apartment. She could make the drive home in less than ten minutes and she was thinking take-out food, Kyle's choice, would work for tonight. She texted a reply to him as she started the ignition and backed up her vehicle. *I can't wait. Think about what you want to eat. Take-out night. I love you.*

Will do. Me too!

Me too? Kelsey thought to herself, *Me too? What the hell? Would it seriously be too much trouble for the man she's been in love with and sleeping with for two years to reply I love you, too?* Rolling her eyes again made Kelsey feel better as she sped out of the garage and onto the street.

***

Kelsey didn't bother to change out of her work clothes. She just flipped on some lights and the ceiling fan above the table in her kitchen. She slipped out of her wedges and walked barefoot in the kitchen looking for her take-out menus. She was thinking about a salad or pasta and she knew Kyle would be fine with either.

Her cell phone rang at just about the time she was expecting Kyle to walk in. It was Nicholas Bridges, a long-time friend and detective who works with Kyle. Kelsey had his number because Kyle had wanted her to have it stored in her contact list in case of an emergency. She really didn't know him all that well so when she said *Hello* she wondered what he could possibly want.

"Kelsey?"

"Yes…"

"This is Nic Bridges. I work with Kyle. Listen there's been an accident and I need you to meet me at Laneview Hospital on Twelfth Street."

"Oh God - what happened?"

"A car accident. Just meet me soon if you can. Kyle was taken there by ambulance."

Kelsey disconnected the call without saying another word. She pushed her feet back into her shoes, grabbed her purse, and left her apartment. The ceiling fan and the lights were still on inside as Kelsey drove frantically, ignoring speed limits. If she was lucky, it would only take her fifteen or twenty minutes in the evening traffic to get to the hospital. All the while she was driving, she was praying. *Please God… Let Kyle be okay. I can't do this. I can't live without him. He's the best thing that's ever happened to me. Please.*

***

Kelsey moved to New York after college. She was a Midwestern girl, born and raised in St. Louis, and her parents still lived there. She's a writer and the idea of being in New York City had thrilled her. She planned to make the move alone, but it was her best friend Bree Jacobs who suggested the idea for them to move together. Neither of them had a job, but both had college degrees and lofty dreams. Bree has spent the last six years in New York City working in advertising. She's an account executive and every bit as successful as Kelsey. She was not, however, as lucky in love. She dated, but not seriously. The last time Kelsey had dinner with Bree, she confessed to having slept with Nicholas Bridges the previous weekend. Kelsey was stunned and had no idea the two of them even knew each other. Kelsey also knew, from what Kyle had told her, that Nicholas was only separated from his wife. And not yet divorced. Kelsey wanted to get an update on that relationship soon - and warn Bree again not to get too involved with Nicholas Bridges.

***

As she rushed through the emergency entrance, Kelsey spotted Nicholas as he stood up from a chair in the waiting area and waved her over to him. "What in the world happened?" she asked him.

"Kyle was in the middle of a three-car collision on the interstate. Some idiot used the police ramp to switch directions and the car in front of Kyle was cut off. Kyle ran into that car and then a third car hit him from behind. He was sandwiched between the two cars."

Kelsey held her hand over her mouth. She felt sick. And scared. But she wasn't going to cry. She wanted answers. She had to know if Kyle was okay. "Have you spoken to anyone yet? The doctor?" Kelsey was looking at Nicholas and despite the fact that she hardly knew him, she didn't like him. He was arrogant.

He was clean cut, fit, so muscular because she could see his abs through his tight black t-shirt. His head and face were completely shaven. He was sleeping around while still married. Separated. Would he go back to his wife and leave her best friend heartbroken? Kelsey didn't even know if Bree was serious about him. She had hoped not.

"No news yet. Now that you're here though I am going to go take restroom break and grab something to drink. Can I get you anything?"

"No. Thanks. I'm fine." But she wasn't fine. She was falling apart inside as she sat down in the waiting room which was about half full of people who all were there for different reasons. Some, like Kelsey, were waiting to find out if someone they love would live or die. Kelsey put her face in her hands and prayed for good news. She stayed that way for what felt like only a few minutes and when she lifted up her head, she saw a man wearing the traditional blue hospital scrubs that hugged his body in all of the right places. He had a stethoscope hanging around the back of his neck and shoulders, and he was walking toward her.

"Hello. Are you here for Kyle Newman?"

"Yes! Are you his doctor? How is he? Is he going to be okay?" Kelsey was on her feet. Kelsey felt as if her heart would beat out of her chest. The doctor signaled her to sit down and he sat beside her. He didn't sit all the way back in the chair so he could turn his legs toward her and privately talk.

"I'm Dr. Walker, and yes I'm Kyle's physician this evening. Are you a relative of his?" Dr. Walker was expected to ask that question. It was standard procedure, but this time looking at this beautiful woman seated next to him he was thinking he didn't want her to say she was that man's wife and he didn't know why.

"I'm his girlfriend."

Dr. Walker smiled and continued to talk as Kelsey noticed his eyes, bright crystal blue. She felt as if she were looking right through them. "Kyle has suffered a head injury from the accident and he has not regained consciousness yet." Dr. Walker watched a few tears trickle down her face, which again he thought was striking, and he wanted to take her hand and comfort her.

"What does that mean for him? Will he recover? Will he be the same?" Kelsey had heard too many stories about people living normal lives and one day, one accident changed it all. Some were never the same again, mentally and physically. The doctor's heart went out to her and he wanted to reassure her. It was his job to lay the facts on the line, but he genuinely cared about people and healing them. At the moment, however, comforting this woman beside him was also something he wanted to do.

"I know it sounds cliché, but right now all we can do is wait. Kyle is in a coma due to the trauma to his head. Comas aren't as scary as they sound. Sometimes in order to give the brain a chance to heal or to reduce swelling we will even induce a coma. This is just Kyle's body's natural way of resting and waiting it out right now. I'm sure of it." As Dr. Walker said those words he took his hand, a ringless left hand, and patted Kelsey's hand that was resting on her leg and gently squeezed it before letting go.

"When can I see him?" Kelsey asked trying pull herself together, wiping her tears away.

"You can- I'm sorry, I don't think I asked your name?"

"Kelsey Duncan."

Dr. Walker smiled, and Kelsey noticed the cute little dimple on his left cheek."Kelsey, I will take you to see him. I just want you to understand, first, that he looks in really bad shape right now. We may have to do surgery if the swelling on his brain worsens. The swelling could reduce on its own, which would allow him to regain consciousness. We'll just have to keep a close watch to see what happens first."*Oh dear God.* Kelsey didn't know if she could do this. She was feeling queasy, and she needed to check her purse for mints or gum. She wasn't feeling strong enough to see Kyle like that.

As they walked side by side down the hospital hallway together, Dr. Walker was tempted to comfort Kelsey once again. He had always tried to be very kind and compassionate with his patients and their families in distress. This shouldn't have felt new to him, but it did. He wanted to care about this woman. As a man. Not as a physician.

Trying not to stare at her, he moved his legs in sync with hers as they walked. In her wedges, she was only about two inches shorter than the doctor. Her hair was pulled back into a long French braid which made her face look so striking. Her complexion was flawless. Dr. Walker led Kelsey into the Intensive Care Unit. He told her the visitation was restricted to a few minutes at a time. He left her at the door then, and she walked in alone.

Kyle was lying there unconscious and his face was swollen, scraped up, and he had what looked like a white ace bandage completely wrapped around his head. A few machines were set up and sounding off as they monitored Kyle's condition. *What exactly was Kyle's condition? Was this really life or death? Was his life as he once knew it gone forever because of some serious head injury?* He looked lifeless as Kelsey sat down in a chair beside the bed and rooted inside of her purse for a mint. She still felt sick to her stomach, and now light headed. She gave up trying to find a mint, and took Kyle's hand in hers before she composed herself and started talking to him. "Oh baby. What have you gotten yourself into? I know you can hear me. Just wake up so I can see that sweet smile of yours. We should be at home eating dinner…and making love. This shouldn't be happening to you. Don't leave me, Kyle. I love you…" Kelsey turned to find Dr. Walker standing at the foot of Kyle's bed. She hadn't heard him come in and now she was embarrassed that he heard her talking to Kyle. Dr. Walker noticed she was uncomfortable. "I'm sorry. I didn't mean to interrupt."

"No, it's okay. I was just talking to him. I know it's silly-"

"Not at all. It isn't silly. A loved one talking to a patient in a coma is sometimes the best medicine for them. I encourage it. He can hear you reaching out to him." Dr. Walker wanted to say if he personally had been in that bed and heard what she had said, he would will himself to wake up just to be able to be with her. So beautiful. What a lucky man.

"I know you're here to tell me I have to leave now. My minutes are up with him. But I can't. I won't. Please understand, I have to be here," Kelsey was trying to persuade the doctor to allow her to stay with Kyle for awhile longer.

She didn't know if he was so attentive to his other patients and their loved ones, but she could sense how she affected him. She could tell he liked her. She liked him, too. He was a kind person, a gorgeous man with incredible bright crystal blue eyes. His hair was so dark and his face was borderline scruffy. A beard that was barely there was sexy, and this doctor was most definitely that. Kelsey forced those thoughts out of her mind and back to Kyle.

"I came in here to tell you there is a man, a detective, outside wanting to see you. The visitors in here need to be one at a time, but you can stay as long as you like. I will let the nurses know. For you." Dr. Walker smiled at Kelsey and she returned a smile to him.

After meeting Nicholas in the waiting room and updating him on Kyle's condition, he left the hospital and Kelsey returned to Kyle's bedside.

***

The night passed slowly. Kelsey was awake for most of it and never left Kyle's side. Nurses came and went, checking his vitals and asking her if she needed anything. No one seemed perturbed that she stayed way past visiting hours, and Kelsey assumed she had Dr. Walker to thank for that.

***

Kelsey had been asleep in the stiff armchair in the ICU room when Dr. Walker was making his morning rounds at the hospital. As he walked into Kyle's room, he stopped when he saw her. Even asleep, she was striking. She had been there all night long, Dr. Walker knew, and he hoped she wouldn't spend too many restless nights trying to sleep in that chair - especially given the fact that this could be a long road to recovery for her boyfriend.

Kelsey wasn't comfortable enough to sleep sound. Her legs were crossed, as she was still wearing her skirt from yesterday's work day, and her head was against the back of the chair. She opened her eyes when Dr. Walker was checking Kyle. "Good morning, pretty lady. I heard you pulled an all-nighter!" *Pretty lady? Oh my, this guy is awfully sure of himself.* Kelsey was thinking she shouldn't like how that sounded coming from him, directed at her, as she sat up straight in the chair she had attempted to sleep in.

"Good Morning. Yeah, I couldn't leave him," Kelsey was running her hands through her hair because she felt disheveled. She was also feeling terribly hungry. She had not eaten since lunch with Kyle, yesterday, at the Café on the Corner. Kelsey would have given anything at that moment to get back into their routine of life together.

"I understand, but you do need to take a break today. Go home. Take a shower. Change clothes. Make some phone calls. Kyle will be undergoing a series of tests all morning and you really do not have to be here."

"I do need to do all of that, thank you. What kind of tests?" Kelsey felt her body relax around this man and she had no idea why. She enjoyed talking to him and wanted to.

" A CAT Scan to check for anything that could have changed from last night. Since he still hasn't woken up, we are searching for more today. An underlying cause." Dr. Walker was

Laneview Hospital's best doctor. He specialized in brain injuries and he was certain this man would be okay. In time.

"Dr. Walker, can I give you my cell phone number for when I'm not here?" Kelsey started to say more, but she stopped. She could have left her number at the nurses' station, but she wanted Dr. Walker to personally have it. He understood.

"First, call me Brady. And yes I do want your number - in case of emergency or good news for that matter. You will be the first to know when this guy wakes up. I promise."

Brady? The doctor wants me to call him by his first name. What a strong, masculine, modern name."Thank you… Brady," Kelsey felt her face flush as she said his name. His first name. Brady smiled at her, held his eyes on her, and then walked out of the room.

CHAPTER 3

It was two o'clock in the afternoon when Kelsey returned to the hospital. She had showered, and eaten some scrambled eggs and a piece of toast. She was wearing jeans, a loose heather gray sweater with a fitted white t-shirt underneath, and black ballet flats, barefoot. She had planned on spending the night at the hospital again, so she packed a small overnight bag with her toothbrush, a change of clothes, and a few snacks.

When she walked into room 121, in ICU, she saw that Kyle was there. Lying so still again. His tests were complete and when the nurse came into the room while Kelsey was standing at his bedside, holding Kyle's hand, Kelsey spoke first."How soon until the test results are in? I just got back and I'd like to talk to Dr. Walker if he's available." The nurse looked up from checking Kyle's vitals again and told Kelsey with a warm smile that the results should be in later today and she would give Dr. Walker the message.

Three hours had passed and Kelsey was texting her best friend Bree with a "no news yet" update when Dr. Walker strolled into the room, still wearing tight-fitting scrubs.

"Well hello. You're back, looking refreshed, and I have some test results for you," he looked happy to see her there. "There has been no change in the brain since last night. The swelling remains, but is not worsening. What we do now is what we have been doing - continue to wait." Kelsey was relieved and disappointed at the same time. She just wanted this to be over for Kyle. She wanted their kind of normal back.

"Thank you, doctor–"

"Brady. Remember?" Kelsey smiled and quickly looked away from Brady Walker. She turned to Kyle and held his hand again.

"Have you eaten?" he asked her.

"Uh yes, breakfast while I was at home."

"It's almost dinner time. You should eat, and I'm starving. My shift is over and I am going to go grab a bite. Care to join me in the cafeteria?" Brady wanted to ask her to walk across the street to an Italian eatery for some of the best pasta he's ever eaten, but he also didn't want to take her away from the hospital or make her feel like this was a date.

"Dinner? With you? Eating dinner with my boyfriend's doctor might be considered inappropriate. I'm sorry–" Kelsey was about to say *I can't* when Brady stopped her.

"It's just a chance for you to take care of yourself. Refuel with some food. I need to do the same and I would love the company for a change." Kelsey wanted to say yes. She wanted to know more about him. Maybe going to dinner would be the perfect opportunity to find out exactly who Brady Walker is…but why did she care?

"If your shift is over, why don't you go home?" Kelsey asked him rather directly.

"I am on call tonight and most of the time when I'm on call, I get paged, so I have an office on the sixth floor of this hospital that is equipped to live in. Well, it is at least a place for me to take a shower and get some good sleep if I need to."

"Well since you're staying in the building, I don't feel guilty taking up your dinner time. As long as the food is good…" Kelsey teased him and he laughed out loud. His teeth were bright white, his eyes were that bright blue which had most definitely caught Kelsey's attention earlier, and this man had a way of brightening Kelsey's uncertain days right now.

"Give me twenty-five minutes and meet me in the cafeteria," Brady told her as he thought about making a small wish of hers come true. He could at least make sure she ate some good food tonight.

***

Kelsey was waiting in the cafeteria when she saw Brady walk in carrying a bag. She recognized the label on the carry-out bag. It was one of her favorite Italian chain restaurants. It was the same food she had been craving just minutes before she received that emergency call from Nicholas Bridges last night. "What did you do?" she asked him as he sat down across from her and reached into the bag to pull out two leafy green salads with raspberry vinaigrette dressing and two pasta entrees, one with a red marinara sauce and one with a creamy white alfredo sauce.

"Well, the pretty lady wished for good food and this cafeteria doesn't always live up to our highest expectations. So, we have white or red pasta tonight. It's guaranteed to be good." Kelsey was smiling at him and wondering what in the world she was doing there. With him. Her insides were tingling all throughout dinner as they talked and ate their pasta. They ended up splitting the two entrees because they each confessed to loving both sauces.

Their conversation carried on for three hours before Kelsey

realized she needed to get back to Kyle. She was completely wrapped up in this man. This other man. Where he came from, his childhood, who or what had influenced him to become a doctor. They had talked about everything and the time definitely had gotten away from them. He was smart, so good looking, and the most exciting man Kelsey had ever met. His interest in her reached new heights tonight also. He wanted to know more about her. So much more. What she did for a living, with her love of words and all, fascinated Brady Walker.

"I should go. I need to sit with Kyle tonight," Kelsey said checking her phone for any new messages. She was dining with the doctor for chrissake. If there had been a change in Kyle's condition, he would be the first to know. She felt guilty as she acted busy with her phone.

"You know, it's okay Kelsey. It's okay to forget for a few hours. I've told you this could be a long road for Kyle. He is going to need you healthy and strong when he wakes up." Brady reached across the table and touched her hand. And when he did, she melted inside. She felt what she's heard about before. That spark. That initial spark that ignites a full blown inferno in a heart. She saw this coming and she didn't stop it. This man. Kyle's doctor. This available bachelor was touching her and she liked it. She wanted more.

"I need to go. I will see you tomorrow," Kelsey said getting up from the table and fumbling for her purse and Brady was watching her, knowing she needed to walk away because she was uncomfortable with how comfortable things were getting between them. He knew because he felt it, too.

"Thank you for dinner. You didn't have to – but I enjoyed it."

More than I should have.

***

Kelsey didn't sleep at all in Kyle's room. She prayed endlessly for him to be okay, and she talked to him when she could find the words. She also replayed the conversation with Brady in her mind. Over and over.

He had told her about his mother dying of pancreatic cancer when he was six years old. And of his father never wanting anything to do with him after her death. Brady had spent most of his childhood being passed from one relative to another. His mother had three sisters and they all loved him dearly. He loved his aunts, but he missed his mom. He needed his mom and none of the women in his life could fill that void for him. Finally, when he turned eighteen he used the money his mother had left him in a trust fund to go to medical school. It was the last thing he could do for her and he wanted to do it. He wanted to help save lives. Maybe even save a life of another little boy's mother.

***

Kelsey was gone by the time Brady made his rounds in the morning and checked on Kyle. There were no signs of change in Kyle's condition and Brady wondered aloud what in the world was taking so long for this man to wake up. *Open your eyes. You have a lot to live for buddy. She's an amazing woman.*

Kelsey managed to go through the motions of showering, eating a bite, and throwing together another comfortable outfit for the hospital again. She checked in with her editor at the newspaper office and asked for at least a week off. She did suggest doing a few phone interviews, if he was in a bind. She almost wished she could be working from that hospital room. Just to pass the time. And to keep her mind off of the doctor.

She received a text as she was driving back to the hospital. It was from Bree. She had thanked Kelsey for the update on Kyle and told her to call if she needed anything. Kelsey called Bree as she was driving.

"Hey sister, how are you holding up?"

"Okay. I'm worried sick about Kyle."

"I can only imagine how you're feeling. Do you want some company there sometime?"

"You know I love your company and I need it right now. Stop by the hospital when you have time. I'm always there except for a few hours in the morning when I go home to shower and change clothes." *And I'm also unavailable when I'm totally engrossed in a three-hour dinner with Kyle's doctor.*

Kelsey wanted to tell Bree just how crazy life had gotten in the last few days, but she would save that information for when they're face to face.

***

Kelsey didn't see Brady the rest of the day or evening. She wondered if he had already checked on Kyle, or if he had the day off. She thought about what he might be doing. She knew he had an apartment in the city. She knew he worked out at the gym and ran five miles a day in Central Park. A body like that takes work, she thought. She had never seen scrubs look so good on anyone. She couldn't get him out of her mind.

After Kelsey stepped out for bite to eat in the cafeteria, she found herself wandering around the hospital. She was holding and drinking a bottle of water as she walked. She wasn't allowing herself to dwell on what she was doing. She just did it. She got onto the elevator and pushed her finger on the button for floor six. *I have an office on the sixth floor of this hospital that is equipped to live in. Well, it is at least a place for me to take a shower and get some good sleep if I need to.*

Would he be in that office right now? She hadn't seen him since their dinner last night. She was just going to check. No harm in checking on a friend, Kelsey thought as she walked slowly down the hallway on the sixth floor. There were no patient rooms, just labs and offices. The nameplate on the last door on the right read, Dr. Brady Walker. She knocked once and instantly wanted to turn around and run. *What if he was in there? What if he was taking a shower, or sleeping?*

"Come in…" It was his voice. She didn't imagine it. He was in there. *Now what the hell was she going to do? What would she say? Why was she even up here?*

Kelsey opened the door and peeked inside. Brady was sitting behind his desk, still wearing his scrubs, and punching keys on a desktop computer. He slid his chair back when he saw her, and he stood up from behind his desk. "Kelsey… Hi. It's nice to see you. Please, come in."

"I'm sorry to bother you. I don't even know why I'm here." Kelsey was looking around his office. He had a black leather sectional, a TV larger than the one she had in her apartment, and the place just looked comfortable enough to live in. She thought of it as more inviting than any other office she had ever seen, and she had walked into offices of many different varieties for interviews over the years. Maybe the inviting part was having him there. She felt like she followed him tonight, knowing he would be in there. She felt, at that moment, like she could follow him anywhere.

"You're not bothering me. I'm glad you're here. I'm glad you checked to see if I was in here. I'm not working the ER or the floors tonight, just catching up on some research."

"I can let you get back to that," Kelsey said backing away from the front of his desk where he had walked around to meet her, and they were both standing close together. *Too close.*

"Absolutely not. Come sit." Brady sat first and she followed him over to his couch. It was completely dark outside and she could see what looked like the entire city from the open blinds on the wall behind his desk.

"Nice view," Kelsey said not knowing what else to say and wishing she hadn't been bold enough to look for Brady tonight. She was not herself when she was with him and that had both scared her and intrigued her.

"Yes, very nice from where I'm sitting," Brady said inching closer to Kelsey. His lips were close enough to hers where she could feel him breathing.

"Brady…" She knew she should move. Resist him.

"I can't stop how I'm feeling right now. I know you are feeling it, too. You wouldn't be here if you weren't." That was all he said before he met her lips with his as he took her bottom lip first and lightly kissed it, holding it between his own lips. He did the same with her upper lip. So slowly. So tenderly. Her mouth was open for him and she wanted to feel more of his lips on hers. He continued to kiss her so lightly and she moaned out loud as their tongues met more aggressively than their lips had. She was losing her mind kissing this man - and allowing him to kiss her.

She was savoring how it felt to be with this man. His whiskers on her cheeks felt so soft, almost tickly. She was running her fingers through his dark hair as he made his way down her neck and then to her earlobe. She grabbed the back of his scrubs, pulling his shirt out of his pants and over top of his head. She ran her fingers over him - his chest was tight, fit, so hard - as he undid the zipper on the athletic pullover she was wearing. He helped her out of it, over her head, and couldn't keep his eyes off of her breasts. She reached for the clasp in the front of her bra, undid it, and her full breasts sprang out for him. He was there touching them, sucking on her nipples, gently and then aggressively. Kelsey had never been so turned on in her life. No man had ever had this effect on her. She could feel how hard he was through his pants. His erection was growing and fighting to be free. She reached down and pulled his pants off of him and he kicked them off of his ankles, as his boxers went right with them. Kelsey scooted beneath him on the couch as he kneeled over her. She touched him, stroked him, and then pulled him into her mouth. With pleasure. With desire. She had never wanted this so badly before. Brady was moaning aloud as he rocked back and forth on his knees. He wanted this moment. This woman. More than he ever wanted anyone, body and soul. Brady pulled himself out of her mouth. She knew he didn't want to come that way. Not this time. She spread her legs as he explored her with his tongue. She was losing her mind again as he found her clitoris, and he sent unbelievable sensations through her body and he pleasured her until she came into his mouth. He was tasting her, couldn't get enough of her, as she pulled him up to kiss her full and hard on the mouth. Then he entered her with a force that threw both of them into a rhythm that continued indefinitely. She eventually moved to sit on him and she rocked her body over him. Finally, after he had entered her from behind - with her back up against his chest - he pushed himself deep inside of her and climaxed.

As they lay spent in each other's arms, Kelsey could not believe what had just happened. She had never experienced an orgasm like that. She had never tried so many different positions. She was used to missionary style, good sex. Not explosive sex. Not dirty sex. Not this amazing feeling she felt lying naked in Brady's arms.

He propped himself up onto one elbow and slid his other hand down her body. He circled her nipples with his finger tips and down to her navel, and then explored lower. Much lower as he slid his finger up inside of her, in and out, repeatedly. Neither one of them said the words *I want you again,* but they certainly felt it, and minutes later they were finding that very same passion again. This time, Kelsey wouldn't stop until she had pleasured him the way he had her, before.

Afterward, they were spent in each other's arms, and slept until the sun came up through the open blinds of that sixth floor office.

***

Kelsey woke up with a much clearer head than she had the night before. She was full of guilt as she sprung out of Brady's arms on the couch and into her clothes that were strewn across the floor all night long.

"I can't do this. I can't believe I did this!" Kelsey was in sheer panic mode as Brady stood up and slipped into his boxers and scrub pants at the same time, and he tried to talk to her.

"You need to calm down. You know as well as I do that we could not control ourselves last night. Kelsey we have something here. Something very real and unique. I know I can honestly say I've never felt this way about anyone in my life. I love being with you, talking to you, eating with you, holding you, and touching each other the way we did last night. I love you. Yes, already, after having only met you a few days ago – I love you!"

Kelsey listened to Brady's heartfelt words with tears in her eyes. "I know you mean every word of that, Brady. I know you are a good man. I feel what's between us. It's explosive. It's like nothing I've ever experienced before. This isn't me though. This isn't *who I am*. I just cheated on Kyle, the man I imagined spending the rest of my life with. The same man who is fighting for his life right now in a hospital bed five floors below. It's like I'm having an out of body experience or I'm caught up in a whirlwind. I'm free falling and I need to catch myself and get it together and walk away now before it's too late."

"Too late for what? Too late to live a life you're meant to live? Kelsey, Kyle is your *boyfriend*. People change. People grow apart. You do not have to follow some life blueprint of having to marry a serious boyfriend. If you ask me Kelsey, I think you settled with Kyle. Life was comfortable with him so why change it? Why look for more? I get that - but something more, something amazing, has come along. Us. We can't ignore this. I can't let you walk away from what feels so meant to be."

"I need some time to think." Kelsey grabbed her purse off of Brady's desk and walked out of his office.

CHAPTER 4

Kelsey could feel her face was stained with yesterday's makeup, and now wet with tears. She tied her hair up in a knot on top of her head while inside the elevator alone. She needed some time to process everything that was happening. She went directly to Kyle's bedside because whether her choice was right or wrong last night, being there with him is where she knew she was supposed to be right now.

She held his hand, but she couldn't find the words to say to him. *How long will he be in this dreadful coma and when he does wake up, how in the world will she ever be able to face him after what she has done?*

Sitting there, Kelsey let go of Kyle's hand and bent over his bed and cried. Her head was down, pressed into the sterile smelling hospital sheets, when she heard the door of room 121 open. She looked up, trying to compose herself and that's when she lost it again.

"Oh thank God you're here, Bree!"

Kelsey was sobbing as Bree opened her arms and Kelsey walked over to her and fell into them. There was not a better hug in the world than those from her best friend. The two of them shared everything. They bonded through their similarities and their differences. Kelsey, the brunette, played by the rules. And Bree, the blonde, didn't think twice about breaking them. There wasn't a single secret between them and never would be.

"Oh my gosh, honey, you're breaking my heart," Bree said holding her best friend in a tight-locked embrace and looking over at Kyle for the first time since she walked into the room.

"Come here, sit down, talk to me. You've been cooped up in here too many days. This is bound to make you dial crazy sooner or later."

"Please take a walk with me so I can talk to you," Kelsey said reaching for the hand of her dearest friend as they walked out of the room, down the hallway, and into the cafeteria. They each took sips from their coffee cups while sitting alone in the cafeteria, which had already seen the breakfast crowd come and go for the morning. A few people hustled in and out for a quick coffee or a snack.

"Jesus, Kel. You look like hell…"

"Thanks a lot Bree."

"Well I could have said you look *tired* but we both know how bitchy you get when I say that to you." It was a simple observation and an honest comment, Bree thought, to tell someone they looked tired. Kelsey often did work too hard and never got enough sleep. Kelsey would always take offense and believe Bree was referring to her looking a mess. *It's just the look in your eyes sister, that's all I mean by that,* Bree would always say, defending herself, but Kelsey always became grouchy.

Kelsey smiled at her. It was so good to have her sitting there, talking to her. Life always felt unbelievably comfortable between them. "I know you called, wanting to come visit me here, but you have no idea how perfect your timing is this morning."

"Actually, I came by last night and asked for you at the nurses' station, but they told me you had gone for a walk and probably went home."

Kelsey raised her eyebrows, thinking of her walk and where it led her, and what had been happening a few floors up as Bree stopped by. "I didn't go home last night. I was here."

"I checked the bathroom on this floor and the cafeteria just in case but–"

"I was with Kyle's doctor. He has an office on the sixth floor of this hospital. I hadn't seen him yesterday when he made his rounds and I went looking for him last night to see if he was still here after his shift had ended. He stays here sometimes. His office is like a hotel room, and I guess you could say he's a workaholic."

"Sounds like you've gotten to know him a little bit. I guess that happens being here, day and night."

Oh I've gotten to know him alright. Every inch of him. "Bree, my life is such a mess right now. In just a few days everything has spiraled out of control."

"I cannot imagine, but it's going to get back to normal. Kyle is going to wake up, right? I mean, what does his doctor say? You've been texting me that his brain looks good and eventually he will heal and wake up, right?"

"I hope so. Brady thinks so."

"Who's Brady?"

"Kyle's doctor. The thirty-year-old Dr. Brady Walker."

"Oh, um, is there something you're not telling me here?" Bree noticed a tone in Kelsey's voice and didn't recognize the look on her face as she spoke about Dr. Walker. "Is he hot?" Bree laughed out loud at the idea of Kelsey getting all hot and bothered over another man. It just didn't happen. She was with Kyle, she loved Kyle, she enjoyed - or was content with - the same ole sex routine with him once or twice a week, if that, and that was that.

"I don't know where to start. Bree, I've never felt like this before. I feel like I've known him all of my life or even in another life. He's so easy to talk to, he's incredibly smart and exciting. Last night I went looking for him because I couldn't fight this need to be with him. I found him and he knew why I was there. He felt it, too. We started and we couldn't stop. We had mind-blowing sex all night long on his couch. All of the oral sex, orgasms, and positions you've experienced and told me about as I just nodded my head wondering when I'd ever get to the point of experiencing that, if ever. I've told you how Kyle is when it comes to sex. It's the same every time. It's missionary style and it's over before it even really begins. It wasn't like that with Brady. God, I'm such a whore…"

Bree was speechless. Absolutely speechless. Her eyes were wide as she listened to her best friend tell her a story that she *never* would have believed were true if she had not heard every single word directly from her. She pushed her coffee cup aside, and leaned forward with her elbows resting on top of the table.

"Kelsey Duncan, are you fucking kidding me?"

Kelsey shook her head and looked down at her own coffee cup, appearing embarrassed, but she felt better having told someone. Not just anyone though. Her best friend always had words of wisdom. Bree had never let her down when she needed to hear the right words, often times inspiring words. Kelsey had told Bree numerous times how she should have been a shrink instead of an ad executive.

"Look at me, Kel..." Kelsey looked up through her tears and Bree reached for her hand on the table. "This is not you. I know that because I know you better than anyone, and you know that because you've lived your life a certain way - the same way - forever. With that said, I think you should open your eyes and especially your heart to this. I know you love Kyle and I think he's a great guy. He may not be the guy for you though. He lives every day the same way. Other than his job, he is a routine robot. That's okay if your eighty years old, but come on Kel, get yourself out of that box. You know how I always say you were drawn to Kyle because he's safe. He's just like you thought you needed to be but what I'm seeing and hearing from you right now, about what you experienced last night, I think you know you want more in your life."

"It was incredible sex, Bree. What if that's all it was though?" Kelsey knew she and Brady had bonded days before they became intimate, but she also wanted to be realistic. One night stands, hot affairs, happened - but didn't last.

"It could be more than that," Bree wanted it to be more than that for her best friend. She herself was looking for more than that. She had her share of one night stands and torrid affairs. What she was doing right now with Nicholas Bridges, a man who was still married, was another example of how she lived in the moment and hoped for something more. Something long-lasting. She wanted the packaged deal - physical attraction and love. Someone to share her life with, forever.

"I love you, Bree. You have no idea how much I need you right now."

"I love you too, and I'll always be here for you." Their relationship was rock solid. So secure. Neither of them ever hesitated to be direct. To be honest. And they respected that about each other.

"I have to say this, and I don't mean to be hurtful with my word choice here but… I don't want to be you, Bree. You can handle wild and crazy. I can't. I need normal. I don't know if I have it in me to break Kyle's heart *when* he wakes up. I don't know if I can give him up to take a chance on someone who I am falling in love with, but hardly know. What if I am doing this because Kyle is so helpless and out of reach to me right now? What if I take one look at him when he's awake and fall back into that comfort zone again?"

"I think you need to talk to Brady. What did he say to you this morning after the two of you got together last night?" Bree was so used to men who didn't communicate, or the ones who made empty promises.

"I want to believe what he said to me was heartfelt because it sounded so damn intelligent - which is so Brady. He told me that I do not have to follow some blueprint of committing my life to a man just because I've loved him and shared a life with him as my boyfriend for a couple years. He wants me to take this chance and grab his hand for the ride of my life, so to speak," Kelsey smiled and Bree's response was exactly what she had expected.

"I think you already had that ride last night!" They both laughed and Kelsey blushed.

"Tell me how amazing it was..."

"Oh p-l-e-a-s-e, like you don't already know!"

"I do know I've always wanted you to experience that kind of intimacy. I've always worried that Kyle has some sort of problem. I know you are a sexual person. You look sexy as hell no matter what you're doing or what you're wearing and I know from our private talks all of these years together that you need more. You've told me how you feel when you want to be made love to - really made love to - and Kyle just goes through the motions or asks for a rain check. Jesus Kel, you're both in your late twenties, you should be all over each other. What man that age isn't looking for that, and thinking about sex 24/7?"

"I love Kyle. And I've always believed that a relationship doesn't have to be all about sex."

"No it doesn't, but sex should be a big part of being in love and sharing your lives together. For chrissake what happens if you do marry him? I hear married people never get it on." Kelsey laughed again and it felt good.

"I don't even know if Kyle wants to get married. We've never made those plans. We just live with the assumption that we will always be together - and maybe one day get married and have kids. I know he wants to be a dad. I just never thought I'd be facing the decision of whether or not to stay with him. And now, could this be any crazier with him in a coma and me contemplating walking away?"

"We both know you won't do that. Not now. Not until he's well again." Bree's cell phone was buzzing inside of her Louis Vuitton bag and she looked to see who was calling. Bree promised to just be a minute after Kelsey told her to *go ahead and take that call.*

"Hi sweets. I am in the middle of something right now with Kelsey, and I have a client meeting this afternoon. No, there's been no change yet. Still mending. Okay, I will tell her. See you later. Me too." It was obviously Nicholas Bridges and Kelsey sighed when Bree ended her call and set her phone down on the table.

"I was hoping you weren't still tangled up with him, Bree."

"Of course you were - but I am. Why don't you like him? He thinks the world of Kyle and is worried sick about him."

"He's on my group text list for updates. I'm keeping him in the loop. The guy is married with a three year old, what could he possibly offer you right now?"

"No, he's separated, and what we bring to each other's lives right now is enough. I don't care about the rest yet."

"Yes. Yet. But you will. Don't let him break your heart, honey. Just be careful. He rubs me the wrong way every time I see him."

"Well as long as he continues to rub me the *right* way I'm good." The two of them laughed out loud in unison as Bree stood up and opened her arms. They stood there hugging like no one else existed in the room, or in the world.

Bree left a few minutes later, after she reached into her bag again and pulled out the newspaper issue in which Kelsey had written her most recent story. She had picked up a copy, read it with pride for her dear friend, and saved it. It was the story about Blair Thompson and the baby on the subway.

Kelsey had not seen the article since she had written and filed it the night of Kyle's accident. She had not been back to the office yet, but her editor had called to commend her on the story and to tell her that Blair Thompson had sent her a huge bouquet of flowers, which was waiting on her desk for her.

She obviously had been so pleased with the wonderful story Kelsey had written. Kelsey sat back down at the table in the cafeteria and unfolded the newspaper to the read the front page. Her story was front page news. Again. She never tired of seeing her by-line and she already missed reporting and writing. She missed a lot of things, like the simplicity of her life before Kyle's accident. Now so much had changed in her mind and in her heart, and she didn't know if she could ever go back to being who she was *before*.

Kelsey was reading and thinking the headline was awesome. Her editor had pulled Kelsey's favorite quote from the story and used it to write: **Bank President Is Bursting At The Seams After Delivering Baby On Subway**

Kelsey remembered Blair Thompson saying, *"It feels as if the seams of my life have been let out just a bit." You can say that again,* Kelsey thought.

Given all that was happening to Kelsey with the uncertainty of Kyle's life - and his place in hers if and when he does make a full recovery - Kelsey couldn't help feeling different.

Sure there was so much sadness and fear about Kyle consuming her. But, it wasn't until last night when the connection between her and Brady deepened that Kelsey actually felt like she had found herself letting go and relishing the feeling of being free. Feeling seamless.

CHAPTER 5

Kelsey was back in Kyle's room again. She had gone to her apartment another time to take a shower, put on some clean clothes, and make phone calls to her editor and to her parents in St. Louis. Everyone wanted updates on Kyle, everyone kept sending their positive thoughts and prayers.

"Come on baby, this is getting ridiculous. Wake up so we can get out of here," Kelsey wanted to say and *get back to our lives,* but she couldn't. Not yet. She needs to be sure of what she wants. And right now, she just wanted Kyle to be okay again. He deserves to get out of that hospital bed and live again.

"Knock, knock…" Brady was back and Kelsey was feeling uneasy seeing him for the first time since they had slept together.

"Hi there… um, I can go if you want to examine him."

"I want you to stay while I do please, and then we need to talk," Brady's voice was deep and quiet at the same time. It always sounded like that. He sounded sexy, Kelsey had thought. He looked amazing again to her as he made his way around the room in his scrubs. Kelsey was so attracted to this man. Brady could relate. He was watching her as she walked over to the window and stood in front of it with her back to him. She was wearing a pair of dark-washed flare legged jeans with black heels, and a fitted white v-neck cashmere sweater.

She looked dressed for somewhere to go. She looked more put together than Brady had ever seen her. Her dark hair was pulled up on top of her head in a loose bun and strands of hair hung down alongside of her face. That face. Those lips. Brady had completely fallen for her. She was the one. She was *it* for him. He would never look at another woman the same way again without comparing her to Kelsey Duncan. He didn't want to lose this feeling. Ever. And he certainly was going to do everything possible not to lose her.

They walked together again through the hospital halls. Brady suggested a bite to eat or something to drink, but Kelsey wanted to avoid the cafeteria. He mentioned going up to his office, and Kelsey shot him a look. "We probably shouldn't – if you know what I mean. I need some air. Do you want to go outside?"

"I know just the place." Brady took her hand, led her to the elevator, and up to the rooftop of Laneview Hospital.

"Do people really come up here?"

"No but I do. It's become a place for me to think and not feel so cooped up inside the hospital. Day or night, whenever I feel like it, I come up here."

Kelsey crossed her arms over her chest as the wind picked up. It was September and the air was unseasonably cooler, but she had found it refreshing and the feeling of peace that had overcome her on that rooftop was simply nice.

"Talk to me. What are you thinking right now?" Brady walked over to her, faced her, and took both of her hands in his.

"I'm thinking how you keep telling me Kyle is going to be alright. He's on the mend, but he's just not ready to wake up yet. When will that change? And when it does change, how am I going to handle walking out of this hospital with him and never seeing you again?" Brady swallowed hard. She was planning on staying with Kyle. She was questioning the relationship they were building.

"As a doctor, I know the day will come for Kyle to wake up. He just needs time. As a man in love with the most incredible woman I've ever laid eyes on, I can't let you walk away from me. We are just getting started, babe. Let's love each other for the rest of forever." Brady pulled her close and held her. He was warm and she was shivering in his arms. He smelled so good to her. His cologne. So delicious. She held him tighter and she could feel herself unraveling again. He pulled out of their embrace and moved her face to look at him. Before either of them spoke, he kissed her full on the mouth. Their tongues met, their heart beats quickened, and they couldn't stop themselves. Still kissing her, he moved and guided her over to the elevator door on the rooftop. He pinned her against it. Gently, yet seductively. He kissed her hard and moved his hand up inside of her sweater. She slid her hand inside of his pants and moved the elastic waist band down a bit farther as he sprung up into her open palm. He quickly unzipped her jeans and squatted down to slip them halfway off of her. She was wearing a lace cheetah thong and he smiled up at her when he saw it, moved it to the side, and then pushed himself inside of her. It was all happening again. She was moving her back up and down the elevator door as he plunged deeper inside of her.

Moments later, they quickly separated their bodies from each other and slid down to the ground, sitting there partially undressed and totally satisfied. Again.

"What in the hell just happened here?" Kelsey asked trying to catch her breath. Please tell me you've never done this before - up here. Kelsey laughed out loud as Brady stood up, pulled up his boxers and his scrub bottoms, and then helped her with her jeans.

"No there's a first time for everything and this definitely was my first on a rooftop, babe." Brady was still laughing as he kissed her sweetly on the mouth. "Are you okay?"

"I think I'm crazy," Kelsey said feeling the whiskers on his face and under his chin with her fingertips. "I love you, Dr. Brady Walker."

Brady had tears in his eyes as he looked directly at her. "I love you more, Kelsey Duncan. More than I ever thought possible. I think it's quite obvious how attracted I am to you, but you also have to know I truly do love you. I love everything about you. How you talk, how you walk, how you taste, how you smell, how you think, and how you love big. I know you love Kyle Newman. I know you love your parents, your best girlfriend Bree, your job. And I can't tell you how it makes me feel inside to hear you say you love me, too. I feel honored and blessed to be with you."

Kelsey was crying as he said those words to her. This just didn't happen to her. She'd never known a man more exciting, more grateful, and more willing to seize life. "That's so beautiful, thank you. I could say all of the same to you. I hope you realize that. You are the amazing one. God, Brady, what are we going to do now…"

Brady smiled at her as his bright blue eyes sparkled in the daylight. He held her close, touched her face, and then warmed her hands in his. "We are going to take this one day at a time. Together."

When Brady's pager buzzed, the two of them went back inside of the hospital. Brady was needed in the ER and Kelsey was going to check in at the newspaper office. They agreed to meet back at the hospital after Brady's shift was over.

***

Kelsey met with her editor and they discussed what he could expect from her. She suggested doing a few phone interviews within the next week and she would write her stories from her laptop in the hospital room. Her boss was an understanding man. He sympathized with Kelsey's need to be at the hospital, and with her desire to slowly get back to work.

On her drive back to the hospital, Kelsey was talking to Kyle's insurance company on speaker phone. They informed her that if Kyle's condition didn't change within a month, he would have to be moved to a facility equipped to handle him. Kelsey snapped and told the person on the phone that *it was barely a week since his accident and he will be awake before moving him even becomes an option!* All Kelsey wanted to do was get back to Kyle's bedside and make him listen to her. It was high time for him to wake up.

Two hours passed in Kyle's room and nothing had changed with him again. Another day of the same. It was almost six o'clock when Kelsey walked out of his room and down the hallway to use the restroom. She hadn't eaten much all day, she just kept buying and drinking bottled water. She was planning to eat dinner with Brady when he was done working and she was thinking about being with him again as she walked back toward Kyle's room. The door was open and two nurses were chatting, one on each side of Kyle's bed. They were changing out his IV and resetting a few machines when Kelsey stopped in the doorway to listen.

"She's been here day and night for the last week waiting for her boyfriend to wake up while she's openly sharing coffee and take-out dinners in the cafeteria with her boyfriend's doctor. Have you seen the way Dr. Walker looks at her?"

"Shh… Mary Sue, someone is going to hear you. She's here in the hospital you know." One nurse told the other and then had something of her own to share.

"You do know she went up to his office the other night?

"Shut the front door!"

"People see things around here."

"Did anyone hear anything?" The nurses laughed out loud and finished working in Kyle's room as Kelsey stepped away from the door. She was feeling awful and hearing the nurses talk about her and Brady angered her. They had no idea what was going on between them. It was real. It was surreal, too. She and Brady needed to be more careful. Tonight they had to talk. Really talk about what they were doing.

Kelsey had already turned the corner and was out of sight when the nurses came out of Kyle's room. Around that corner, she saw Brady. For the first time, he was wearing real clothes - jeans and a hunter green short-sleeved polo shirt that accented his biceps. "Hey there. I was just coming to get you. I took a quick shower and changed. I hope you're hungry."

Kelsey smiled at him. "I am hungry and I want to have dinner with you, but do you really think this is a good idea to be seen like this, here and together?"

"First of all, I don't care who sees us in this hospital. And second, I want to get out of here tonight. I would like to take you to a restaurant to really wine and dine you for a change."

"Brady, listen, I heard the nurses talking. They know."

"Of course they know. They don't miss much around here. Let them talk and let them think that they know what is going on between us. You've been by Kyle's bedside all afternoon again and I'm done working until tomorrow morning. We both need a break, we both need to eat. Let's go…" He put his arm around her and led her to the elevator. While they were waiting in front of it, one of the nurse's loud voices carried all the way down the hallway.

"Dr. Walker, I'm glad I caught you! Hurry! Kyle Newman is waking up."

CHAPTER 6

Brady told Kelsey that it could be anytime. Kyle was moving his hands and fluttering his eyelids. The nurse had seen him open his eyes and stare at her for a few seconds before closing them again. It was happening. Kyle was coming out of his coma after nine days.

They were talking openly at the foot of Kyle's hospital bed when Kelsey began to cry. She was carrying so much guilt. She wanted to be with Brady. She knew it was wrong to agree to go out to dinner with him when Kyle was all alone in his room again. He was counting on Kelsey – and she was letting him down.

"Hey, hey, what is it? Come here babe, it's okay, let me hold you," Brady pulled Kelsey close as she cried into his neck.

"I'm a horrible person, Brady. I'm carrying on this affair with you when Kyle is fighting to come back to me," she was whispering in fear of Kyle actually being able to hear her.

"Kelsey, please, stop this. You're not married to this man. I don't have a wife and kids at home. This isn't wrong. Life happens. Love happens. And I'm not about to let you give up on us." Brady kissed Kelsey lightly on the lips as Kyle laid there, in a coma. A coma he would soon come out of. And when he does, Kelsey prayed he would be healthy and able to pick up his life where he left off. She just didn't know if she still wanted to be a part of the equation. With him.

Her monotone world with Kyle was hanging in the balance as Kelsey had now been jolted into the sheer electricity of life. It was the complete opposite of finding peace. She was both conflicted and drawn to living with this newfound excitement she had found with Brady.

CHAPTER 7

Almost three weeks had passed since Kyle showed signs of emerging from his coma. Kelsey had gone back to work part-time. She handled her phone interviews in Kyle's room, wrote her stories by his bedside, and stopped in at the newspaper office a few times a week. She also was back into the routine of going to the gym. Her mind and her body needed a release. She spent hours talking to Kyle, willing him to wake up, but there had been no change in weeks. By now she was even used to his involuntary movements. She did see his eyes flutter several times but he had never opened them for her, like he had once for the nurse. Kelsey was frustrated, exhausted, and still reeling from her affair with Brady.

The two of them were connected in every way. They talked endlessly every day and managed to sneak away almost as often to be together. His office became her safe place. She cried there. She laughed there. She slept there. She ate many dinners in there. And she and Brady made love there, time and again. They were very much in love. They knew everything about each other now. Their families. Their friends. Their pasts. Their quirks. Their strengths and their weaknesses. Their hopes and dreams for the future. Brady had talked about everything he wanted to do with her. Places he wanted to see together. Children he wanted to have together. Kelsey pulled back from that conversation every time with the same look in her eyes. She couldn't commit to anything, or to Brady. Not yet. Not until she knew where Kyle's life was headed. Was he going to die in that hospital bed? Would he spend the rest of his life in that bed, in a coma, having her watch his body age just lying there? Life was cruel and unpredictable sometimes.

Kyle's visible cuts and scrapes had completely healed. He no longer laid there with any bandages or machines beeping. He was still in the intensive care unit and had an IV in his arm which was taking care of feeding him for the past month. He had lost weight and looked pale. All of his tests showed positive signs that there had been no brain damage from the car accident. So why was he still not waking up?

Exactly a month to the day of the accident, he did.

Kyle Newman opened his eyes and forced himself to focus clearly on the woman sitting by his bedside punching the keys on her laptop while she transcribed an interview through earbuds. He weakly cleared his throat, but she didn't hear him. He wiggled his fingers but she didn't see them. It was when he managed to raise his hand in the air and then awkwardly drop it back down onto the mattress that Kelsey was startled and hurried to push the laptop off her lap and quickly placed it on the floor as she stood up.

"Oh my God! Kyle! You're awake. This is really happening!" Kelsey sat on the bed and held his hand and looked into his *open* eyes. "It's about damn time!"

Kyle managed to smile. His lips were so dry and cracked, despite the fact that Kelsey smeared Carmex on them every chance she got. "What happened to me?" Kyle's voice was hoarse, but his words were clear.

"You were in a car accident. A month ago! Do you know who I am? Do you remember anything?"

"I remember my life with you. I remember how much I love you." It took a few minutes for those words to come out and when they did Kyle squeezed Kelsey's hand and tears streamed down both of her faces. God how she loved this man.

"I gotta call the nurse - and page the doctor!" Kelsey alerted the medical staff and the doctor was on his way.

***

Brady's eyes were wide as he sprinted into room 121. He looked directly at Kyle lying in bed with his eyes open. He quickly glanced at Kelsey and *his* eyes said it all. Was this really the moment they had been waiting for the past four weeks, or was this something they both secretly dreaded? Kyle played a huge role in whether or not Brady and Kelsey would see happily ever after. They both knew that.

Kelsey watched as Brady was in complete doctor mode. He checked Kyle, physically and then mentally he quizzed him for signs of damage to the brain. Kyle passed the tests. He remembered everything prior to the car accident. Even more vital things would come in the next twenty-four hours. Could he feed himself? Could he walk? Would his speech continue to be drawn out and downright slow at times? A complete recovery would take time, but Brady expected one from Kyle and told him and Kelsey as much.

"I can't believe I've been lying in this bed, dead to the world, for an entire month," Kyle sighed as he tried to lift his head up off of the pillow but couldn't find the strength. He was overdoing it and needed to rest.

"You have, believe me I know. I've been here most of that month." When Kelsey said *most of* Brady caught her eye and gave her a soft smile. Sort of his way of encouraging her that she was supportive of Kyle. She was there for him. Despite what they were doing when she was not sitting by his bedside.

Kyle took Kelsey's hand and kissed it. "I know you wouldn't be anywhere else, Kel. Thank you. I love you." That was the second time Kyle had told her he loved her since he woke up. He already had come out of the coma a changed man. He rarely said those words to her, it was always *ditto* or *me too* after Kelsey had said it first.

Kelsey was about to say, *I love you too baby,* when Brady interrupted. "I don't want to be the bad guy here, I know we've waited a long time to see this guy awake - but he needs to rest. We need to get out of here so he can." Brady looked at Kelsey and she glanced back and Kyle. She told Kyle the doctor was right, kissed him on the forehead, and said she would be back soon.

***

Back up on the sixth floor, Kelsey stood in front of the window in Brady's office and watched it raining outside. With each passing second, the rain fell harder and the wind picked up stronger. The stormy weather mirrored Kelsey's life at this exact moment in time. Stormy. Unpredictable. And a little bit scary. She watched lightning crack across the sky and jumped when the thunder rumbled louder than she had anticipated.

"Hey, it's okay," Brady came up behind her and held her. She leaned her back against him and wrapped her arms over his, folded around her middle. "I know what you're thinking and it's all going to work out. Kyle is going to make a complete recovery. He will walk out of this hospital and never look back."

And what if that's what I'm supposed to do too? "I hope so. He deserves to get his life back. He's a wonderful detective. I know they miss him at work." Small talk. They were both avoiding the one question on each of their minds. What did this change of events mean for *them?* When would *they* get a chance to get on with *their* lives? Or would they?

Kelsey turned around in Brady's arms and he continued to hold her. Their silence fueled the tension inside of them, but being alone together right now was all they wanted. Talking and making decisions would come later. Brady hoped and prayed to God, and to his mom in heaven, for help with that feat. He needed Kelsey in his life. He had never wanted anything or anyone more. Except for all the times he wished on a star for his mom to come back home after she had died. He still looks up at the stars and thinks of being a boy and wishing it was that easy to bring her back.

"I don't know how long I should stay up here, away from Kyle," Kelsey was scared. She knew this had to come to an end now. One man was going to have to be told that it was over. She couldn't continue this affair with Brady now that Kyle was awake. She would have to wait until Kyle was back on his feet again – and then tell him. Or, she would walk away from Dr. Brady Walker forever. The life that Brady had to offer her now was exciting, happy and fulfilling. Her life with Kyle was comfortable. And happy. She loved Kyle. She always knew what to expect from him, from them. She loved Brady, too. She knew what to expect from him as well - but it was different. Life with Brady was seamless - or at least that is how their days and nights together have been thus far. With him, she felt like she could spread her arms wide - and still reach farther. She wanted to reach farther. She wanted to find parts of herself that she never allowed to surface. There was more to Kelsey Duncan than Kyle knew. Brady had brought that out in her. He had shown her how to be adventurous and still feel secure.

"He should probably rest for awhile," Brady said hoping Kelsey wouldn't rush back to his side. He told the nurses where he would be if they needed him, but right now he only wanted Kelsey to need him. Brady pulled her closer and softly kissed her on the lips. She responded, as she never could resist him, but then she pulled away. "We can't do this now."

"I think you're wrong. I think we need to do this right now. We need to reassure each other that *this* is where we should be. Together. I love you so much, Kelsey. Don't walk away." Brady kissed her again she responded.

"If you keep kissing me like that, we are going to end up how we always end up," Kelsey said to him with a flirty expression that made him want her more. Right then. Right there. "I won't do this now, Brady. It's time now for me to sort out all of this, in my head and in my heart. Kyle is going to be awake from resting soon and he'll be waiting for me - and he deserves to have me there. I at least have to give him that." *For now.*

"I understand, and I love you even more for being such a good person."

"I'm not a good person. I've been cheating on Kyle and I don't feel good about that at all. That's not me, Brady. I wasn't raised that way. I have values for chrissake – and those seem to have flown out the damn window in the last month."

"I know, I know, you used to be a good Catholic girl until I got my hands on you…" Brady attempted to touch her again and Kelsey tried not to laugh at him as she pushed his hand away from going up the bottom of her shirt.

"Stop. Please. This isn't funny. This is far from funny. I love you and I don't know what to do about that." Brady's eyes were locked on her. "You hold onto that feeling. Don't ever let an ounce of that love you're carrying for me escape your body. And please never doubt that I love you every bit as much, if not more. Take my hand and don't look back," Brady reached out his hand to her and Kelsey took it. She intertwined her fingers with his. She had never felt this way about another man before and she wasn't sure she ever would again. A few minutes later, she was walking out of Brady's office and back downstairs into room 121, where Kyle was awake. Again.

***

"Hey where've you been? I can't sleep without you here with me." His speech had already sounded better, not as slurred, as he was sitting up in bed with a few pillows propped up behind him. The nurse had brought him some broth and a few crackers to eat. Kelsey sat down in the chair beside his bed, still finding it unreal to have him awake. Finally.

"What do you mean you can't sleep without me in here? We've all been trying to wake your ass up for a month," Kelsey laughed as Kyle slurped the broth off the spoon and winked at her. "I knew you were sitting right here with me, the whole time. I could feel you, baby." Kelsey smiled, but feeling ashamed, she looked away from him. She had cheated on Kyle, time and again and now she was considering breaking his heart – for excitement, for adventure, for that seamless feeling, for amazing sex, and for love. She truly did love Brady Walker.

CHAPTER 8

Five days later, Kyle was going home. He was feeling more than ready, and all of his test results showed no sign of brain damage. He was having occasional headaches for which Dr. Walker prescribed painkillers, and advised him to take it easy before going back to work and hitting life hard again.

It was Friday afternoon and Kelsey was writing a story at the newspaper office. She wanted to get it filed and arrive at the hospital to pick up Kyle within the next hour. She looked at the time and it was already fifteen minutes past four. She sent Kyle a quick text, *I'll be there by 5*, and resumed typing on her computer.

She had seen very little of Brady the past five days. She had gone back to work full-time at Kyle's urging, and she visited Kyle for a few hours each evening before going home to her apartment. Brady was texting her daily and nightly and she was responding to his *I miss you, I love you,* messages. She wanted him in her life. She wanted a life with him, but first she had to get Kyle well.

Kelsey was walking out of the door when she received another text from Brady. *Please come see me before you check Kyle out of this hospital. My office before 5:00. I love you.*

Kelsey arrived at the hospital and went directly to the sixth floor. She didn't knock on his office door. She just walked in like she had so many times before. And Brady stood up from behind his desk. *God, that man, and the way he looked in his scrubs.* "So he's going home. He told me he wants to stay at his place but you insisted he come home with you for awhile..." Brady didn't want to think about Kelsey nursing Kyle back to health. Or how he would be in her bed - with her.

"Yeah...I thought it would be better if he wasn't alone, at least for a few days." The mood was awkward between them as Kelsey went over to the couch and sat down. Brady followed her and sat close.

"It's okay, babe. He's going to need some care until he has his full strength back. I just, well to be honest, I just wish I could get this picture out of my head of him in your bed," Brady touched her knee. She was wearing her short black skirt again with a thin pale pink sweater and a white camisole underneath. Her stiletto heels made her legs look amazing, Brady thought.

"Don't Brady - I owe him that much. I do love him. I just don't know if a life with him is what I really want anymore. You have shown me that there's more to me, if that makes sense. You have brought me to life in ways I didn't even realize were possible."

Brady kept rubbing her knee and she spoke to him. "If you're talking about the rhythm you discovered in yourself on the dance floor that one night with me, that was all you babe," Brady laughed out loud as Kelsey blushed remembering the night he talked her into going to a club. She hadn't danced like that since college, hanging out with Bree. With Brady she also had had five glasses of wine that night so she was feeling loopy. Kelsey was also remembering how he brought her back to his apartment near Central Park that same night and made love to her on the wood floor of his living room. It was the first and only time she had been to his apartment.

"Thank you, Brady."

"For what?"

"For being you."

"I've never felt more like me until I met you, Kelsey. This may be the end of a road today with Kyle and his hospital stay but it's just the beginning for us. Believe that. We can make it happen," Brady leaned toward Kelsey and pressed his lips on hers. She opened her mouth and the two of them were sealed together and consumed by pure passion. He lifted her onto his lap and moved her skirt up around her hips.

"Brady – I can't do this. I will never be able to walk downstairs and look Kyle in the eye if we do this right now. I told myself and I told you, I wouldn't do that again until I talked to Kyle and figured things out." Kelsey got off of his lap and stood up to put herself back together. Brady met her with a long, close hug, and neither one of them wanted to let go.

***

Kyle was dressed in jeans and a gray t-shirt that said POLICE in bold black print on the front. He was slipping into his gray and black NIKE tennis shoes with no socks when Kelsey and Brady walked into his room together. He was no longer in room 121, in ICU. He had been in a regular hospital room on the second floor for the past five days.

"Oh hey, you're both here at the same time," Kyle was smiling as he bent forward to tie his shoe laces, squeaking his tennis shoes on the floor. *Yes, we're both here together. We are together. In every way*. Kelsey was feeling so ashamed. She couldn't keep this up much longer. Kyle had to know.

Kyle did know that she and Dr. Walker became friends during the last month. Kelsey had slipped and called him Brady too many times in front of Kyle and he had asked her why they were on a first-name basis. *Friends. That's all.*

***

Kyle laid his head back on the passenger seat as Kelsey accelerated out of the parking garage. *He will wear out quickly and will need a lot of rest in the days ahead,* Brady had warned them. Kelsey picked up her phone to retrieve a text as Kyle was resting his eyes next to her.

"Don't you think you should wait to get that? Texting and driving, it's dangerous, Kel," Kyle kept his eyes closed. He knew he would be paranoid for awhile about being in a car, and especially driving.

"I've got it baby. You're in good hands." Kelsey read the text, *You're amazing…and I want to be with you forever,* but she didn't reply until they were a few miles down the road and Kyle was completely asleep. *I feel the same way,* and she left it at that.

***

Kyle was settled in at Kelsey's place. She had gone to his apartment and gotten some lounge clothes for him to wear the next few days while he was staying with her. He already kept a toothbrush and a razor there for when he spent the night. It was different now though. Kelsey was feeling uncomfortable around him, and Kyle could sense it.

"So when are you going to relax?" Kyle asked her from across the room. He was reclining on her couch and she had just walked into the room from the kitchen, carrying two bottles of water.

"I will sit down. I just wanted to get us some water."

"That's not what I meant. It's how you've been acting lately. You seem tense, like something is bothering you." Kelsey sat down next to Kyle. She didn't put her feet up on the recliner with him. She crossed her legs and turned toward him. She didn't know how to answer him. It was just too soon to be honest with him considering how he was still recovering from the car accident.

"I have spent the last month worried sick about you, wondering if you were going to live or die. The doctor and the nurses kept telling me you were getting better. You just needed time. Well the whole idea of you being in a coma that long just threw me for a loop, Kyle. I just want you to be okay, you know, get back on your feet again."

"I am fine baby… I promise you, everything will get back to normal for us really soon," Kyle leaned over and kissed her on the cheek. But Kelsey didn't want their kind of normal back again. She loved Kyle with all of her heart, but settling for a relationship that was just okay day after day and year after year wasn't something she was entirely sure she still wanted. Not since she had been with Brady, and she had found room in her heart for him, too.

She was dying to talk to Bree, the only person who could help her sort this out. So after she helped Kyle into the shower and later into bed, she waited for him to fall asleep before she went into the kitchen and called Bree.

"Is this a bad time, Bree?"

"Of course not. What's going on? How's Kyle doing at your place?"

"He is sleeping for the night. He will get stronger each day so for now he just has to rest until that happens," Kelsey was purposely keeping her voice down, not to wake him.

"And that's when you're going to tell him that you're leaving him?" Bree and Kelsey had talked every day while Kyle was hospitalized. Bree knew how serious Kelsey was about Brady and how quickly their relationship had progressed. It was clearly more than just about sex and Bree envied how Kelsey had found a man who wanted to sign up for forever. Bree was struggling with Nicholas Bridges and the fact that he and his wife still were just separated and not yet planning for a divorce.

"That sounds awful. I don't know how I'm going to make that decision to break his heart. I don't know if I can," Kelsey realized she was being honest for the first time - with herself.

"So what are you saying? Haven't you and Brady discussed what comes next? He wants a life with you, and now you don't?"

"I do want him. I'm in love with him. I'm sucked into his world. All of the time we spent together was amazing. I could talk to that man all day and all night, mentally and physically we've already formed an unbreakable bond."

"God Kel, listen to yourself. I am so jealous. I've waited years for a man to love me like that and want me like that - and for myself to feel the same way. It has to be a two-way street and it's never been for me."

"Oh Bree… it will happen for you. Just stop screwing that married man and maybe you can help speed up the hunt for Mr. Right."

"Oh shut up. He just needs to get a fucking divorce." The two of them laughed, but Kelsey wished for so much better for Bree. She deserved better.

***

Kelsey was turning off the living room lights when her cell phone beeped. She sat down on the couch and read the text. *Going crazy without you in my arms. What are you doing right now?* Words on a phone, Brady's words, sent tingles throughout her body. She almost wished he didn't have that effect on her. She almost wished she could have gone through life with Kyle never knowing that a part of her wanted and needed more from a man. Trying to be strong, trying to do right by Kyle, she turned off her phone and went to bed.

CHAPTER 9

On Saturday morning, Kyle was awake before Kelsey. He already had a pot of coffee made when she came walking into the kitchen to find him cracking a half a dozen eggs. "What are you doing?" Kelsey was concerned that he was overdoing it, less than twenty-four hours after he was released from the hospital.

"Making breakfast, scrambled eggs, toast, and coffee. Sit down. It will be ready in a few," Kyle winked at her and turned back to the stove top to prepare the food. He was barefoot, wearing pajama pants and a navy blue t-shirt. Kelsey could tell he had lost weight because his t-shirt looked boxy on him.

"Are you sure you're feeling up to doing all of that?" Kelsey knew fighting a man like Kyle to rest was a losing battle. He wanted to be back on his feet and productive again.

"I want to do this, Kel. I'm feeling good. No headache since last night before bed." A few minutes later they were eating together and talking about nothing at all. It was just like old times and Kelsey was glad it was Saturday and she didn't have to rush off to work, but she did want to leave her apartment when Kyle told her Nicholas Bridges was coming by with some files for him to catch up on while he is on sick leave.

"I am going to take off for awhile when he gets here. You know I can't stand that guy – especially now that he's messing with my best friend's heart."

"I know how you feel about him, but I don't think Bree is innocent in this either," Kyle was not fond of Bree. He thought she was too wild, acted sexier than she was, and needed to grow up.

"Let's not even get into this. Our best friends are in a relationship, or at least having hot sex every chance they get, and neither of us approve of them together."

"Did someone say hot sex?" Kyle slid his chair over to Kelsey's and brushed his lips on hers. She kissed him back softly with her lips closed.

"I don't want to get you too hot and bothered big boy, you're not recovered yet," Kelsey smiled at him but inside she felt nervous. What if Kyle was ready? Could she really give herself to him after everything she and Brady had shared - and promised each other?

"Oh no worries there, Kel. I don't want to do anything to make these headaches come on any stronger than they already do," Kyle walked over to the counter, opened the prescription pill bottle, and popped a pain pill in his mouth and took a drink of water from a glass.

"You're getting another headache?"

"Yes. I can see myself getting addicted to painkillers if this continues."

"Oh stop it. Considering what you've been through, I'm sure those headaches are perfectly normal and will be gone soon."

Those headaches were a part of Kyle's days and nights as time progressed. A week had gone by and he didn't tell Kelsey how bad they were because he wanted her to go to work and not worry about him. He was planning to return to his job on Monday and he told Kelsey as much over their pizza and wine dinner.

"Are you sure you'll be ready by Monday?" It was Saturday night, and Kelsey wasn't sure if Kyle would be strong enough so soon. She picked a fresh mushroom off of her slice of pizza and ate it as she looked at him, hoping he was feeling well enough to return to work.

"I'm going to take it one day at a time, or even work half days if I need to. I'm just ready to get out of this apartment."

"Gee thanks."

"You know what I mean. I miss being productive, I miss work, I miss my own bed." Kelsey looked at him with another look of *gee thanks*, and Kyle responded, "You know I want you in my bed, I do, but I've already decided that when we get married we are using my bed as *our* bed," Kyle took a swig of red wine and Kelsey did the same after him.

Married? Why is this subject coming up now? He had never uttered the word in the two years they have spent together and now Kelsey was hearing it and feeling more confused about her life by the minute.

"I have no idea what you're talking about. My bed is comfortable," Kelsey was hoping this would turn into a play fight with a little bit of back and forth banter so she wouldn't have to address the fact that Kyle had just brought up marriage.

"You heard me, Kel. I think we should get serious. Let's go ring shopping this weekend. Just browse a little. Show me what you like…" That was so like Kyle. He wasn't going to surprise her with a proposal. He wanted to plan ahead, tell her, and have her pick out the ring. Spontaneity wasn't in his blood. A few months ago, that would not have mattered so much to her. She would have been elated to *plan* their engagement. But, since Brady, everything had changed.

She missed Brady. They had exchanged a few texts this past week, while she was at work, and that was all. He was being very patient and truly trying not to bother her every single time he thought of her."I don't know what to say…"

"Say that you love me and you want to be my wife."

"I do love you, Kyle. Let's just take this one day at a time, okay?" Kelsey got up from the table. She didn't want to eat anymore. She didn't know what she wanted. She was upset with herself for making a mess of her life. If she was supposed to be with Brady, then why did it hurt so much knowing she was going to break Kyle's heart? It was breaking *her* heart to imagine it. Imagining Kyle's reaction to knowing the truth about her - and Brady - made Kelsey feel sick to her stomach. She started to place some dishes in the sink when Kyle wrapped his arms around her.

"Come here… it's a huge step, I know. I also know that I want to spend the rest of my life with you. I love you." Kyle's words brought tears to her eyes and she cried in his shirt.

"I'm sorry, I'm just stressed. You know I love you, too. Never forget that." She didn't know what came over her after that but she kissed him, long and hard on the mouth. It was their moment and a part of her truly wanted to know if what they shared was worth giving up. She wanted to feel everything with him as she had felt with Brady. If being in Kyle's arms and Kyle's life could compare, then she wouldn't have to confess her sins and break an innocent man's heart. Kyle kissed her back and when she began to reach for the button fly on his jeans, he stopped her. With his hands on top of hers, he told her he couldn't.

"I just want to get some sleep tonight, baby. I was thinking about going back to my place, you know, to give you some space, and I need to get settled in again, in my own bed and all." Kelsey wasn't just disappointed, she was crushed. That's the way it always was with Kyle. He was never turned on enough by her, or he wanted to sleep, or read over a case. She had once shared with Bree that she had developed a complex in the bedroom. Kyle was a man who didn't want her for sex. They were like an old married couple kissing hello and goodbye with their mouths closed and cuddling on the couch before bed.

When Brady came along, everything changed for Kelsey. He woke up the woman inside of her - and she didn't know if there was a way to turn back now. Or if she wanted to.

***

Kelsey drove Kyle back to his apartment, made sure he was settled in, and told him to call her if he needed anything throughout the night. Her feelings were badly hurt, but she was hiding that pain from Kyle. That was just him. How he was. He wasn't a very sensitive man and Kelsey had been used to being with a man like that - until she met Brady. She hadn't heard from Brady since he sent her another late night text two days ago. She had not replied to that text and wondered if she should just leave things as they are with him. Untouched. As she was driving home, she called Bree. She told her everything that had happened - and not happened with Kyle. She admitted to wanting to be with him, but again he turned her away. He seemed well enough. And she wanted to be close to him again.

"Go to him, Kel."

"What? I just dropped him off and he said he wants to be alone tonight."

"I'm not talking about Kyle. Go to Brady. Talk to him. Tell him what's going on, what you're feeling, and just be with him. You are not going to know what you really want unless you keep the communication lines open with him."

"He's just giving me time to tell Kyle…"

"Tell Kyle? You just told me you wanted to sleep with Kyle tonight. You are so confused and it doesn't have to be that way. Make up your mind to start living. Start a new life. With a new man."

"And what if it's not what we both thought it would be? What if our time together was some kind of fairytale and we can't get that back after we try to move forward together?"

"From everything you've told me, I don't see you regretting anything. And yes things are going to come up, life will get in the way of always being happy, but you just deal - and overcome those things."

Kelsey drove past the exit to her apartment as she listened to those wise words. "You are so amazing. Tell me again why the hell you aren't married with eight children yet?"

Bree laughed at her comment and replied, "Because I keep picking the wrong guy for me."

"Oh Bree, I've been so wrapped up in my own drama that I haven't even asked how things are going with Nicholas..."

"I don't want to get into it right now. It's Savannah's birthday today, she's four, so he's spending time with her - and her mother. We had a pretty nasty fight about that earlier so I'm feeling kind of pissy about love right now. Cheer me up by going to Brady tonight. Just do it."

"I want you to keep me in the loop about your pain, too. Do you hear me? I am here for you. Anytime. You know that. And yes I've already passed up my apartment. I'm going to call him in a second."

"Call him now. I'm hanging up."

***

Kelsey drove around Central Park three times before she sent him a text. *Hi. Are you busy right now?* It was all she could think of to say. She didn't want to disturb him if he was working, or out with friends, but she had hoped he was at home right where she was driving around in circles for the past fifteen minutes.

Never too busy for you. Just got back from a run and fresh out of the shower. Wish you were here.

I am. Been driving around Central Park. Can I come up?

Yes please do!

Kelsey parked her jeep, fed the meter, and met the doorman who Brady had already told to let Kelsey in. She knocked once and Brady flung the door open before she had the chance to pull her hand back from it. He had wet hair, damp skin, and she was staring. He was wearing a pair of gym shorts and that is all. He smelled amazing from where Kelsey was standing as he pulled her by the hand and into his apartment. She was wearing black yoga pants and a tank top underneath a fleece jacket. She hadn't bothered to change into anything special just to bring Kyle home. She hadn't planned on seeing Brady tonight.

"It is so good to see you," Brady pulled her close, against his bare chest, and she hugged him back. "How's it going?" He felt like it was a good sign that she was there tonight. Kelsey pulled away from him and walked over to sit down in his living room. She chose the loveseat and he followed her.

"Kyle is doing much better. He's going back to work on Monday. He is still having headaches and taking pain pills, but he's strong enough to go back to his apartment and take care of himself apparently."

"That's where he's at now?" He thought it was unbelievable how a man would not want to be with a woman like Kelsey. It was Saturday night and if she was his, and only his, the last place Brady would want to be is anywhere without her.

"We need to talk, Brady. Please just let me explain something and don't say anything until I'm finished."

"Okay, tell me what's going on…"

"Things are good with me and Kyle." Brady exhaled. He had not prepared himself for this. He didn't want Kelsey falling back into the life she had with Kyle. It had taken everything in him not to contact her and beg her to be with him. "Things are beginning to get back to normal. Our kind of normal. I never wanted out of my relationship with Kyle. We're good together. Then you came along and I felt like you released a part of me that I didn't know existed, or I was too scared to find. I just don't want to lose who you taught me to be. I need to be that person. I feel like I deserve to be that person."Kelsey reached for Brady's hand and held it. "Kyle wants to get married. He wants to go ring shopping this weekend and seal the deal between us."

"And what you do want?" Brady held his breath.

"When he suggested we take our relationship to the next level, a part of me wanted that. That same part of me kissed him tonight. I mean, really kissed him. I wanted him to make love to me." Brady pulled his hand out of Kelsey's grip. "Just please listen before you get upset. Part of me wants to know if what he and I have is worth giving up, but more than that I wanted to feel everything with him as I've felt with you–" Brady stood up from sitting next to her. He was angry, he walked away and swiftly turned back around in the living room. "So you let him touch you? Goddamit Kelsey, was the fuck worth it?"

"Stop it, Brady. I asked you to let me finish talking before you interrupted. Brady held his hands up as if he was surrendering and Kelsey continued to explain. "I came onto him and he rejected me. Again. I was bluntly reminded that this is Kyle. That is us. We're not about sex. I don't turn him on like–"

Brady suddenly had a realization when Kelsey didn't finish her sentence. She had never been physically desired, not in the passionate way that he wanted her. Brady now understood that this wasn't totally about love. This, for Kelsey, also was about feeling desired and having confidence. Kyle had slowly taken away the confidence Kelsey had in her sexuality and Brady had given it back to her, and so much more.

"I was hurt. The man was in a coma for a month and living with me for the past week and he doesn't even want to make love to me. What is wrong with me?"

"There's nothing wrong with you. It's Kyle. As a doctor, I really think he needs to have his testosterone levels checked. As a man in love with you, I don't care if he has a problem. All I care about is you and loving you and my God wanting you. Kelsey Duncan you are the sexiest woman I've ever laid eyes on. You make me feel things for you and want to do things to you that drive me insane to think about." Brady walked over to her and pulled her onto her feet. She didn't speak and neither did he. He just kissed her and she responded with the passion and desire and intensity that only they shared.

When they caught their breaths, Kelsey spoke first. "I'm here tonight because I need you. I want you, like this - and in my life. I can't stay away from you anymore. I can't pretend I want to live the life I was so comfortably settled into the past couple of years. I want to be in your world, Brady. I know I said I wanted to think this out, I thought I needed time and it's wrong of me not to be honest with Kyle before coming here tonight but I had to see you."

Kelsey put her hands on his bare chest and he closed his eyes, smiled, and inhaled through his nose. "Jesus, do you have any idea what you do to me when you put your hands on me like that?" Brady put his hands around the back of her neck, underneath her long hair that she was wearing down tonight and he pulled her into a kiss. Afterward, he swooped her up and carried her to his bedroom. He put her back onto her feet and they were standing at the foot of his bed. There was a lamp on, on his nightstand, and Kelsey was thinking how romantic his bedroom looked in the dim light. He had an oak wood sleigh bed with all white bedding. The sheets, the pillows, the comforter were immaculate looking. The last and only time Kelsey had been there, in his apartment, they had made love on the wood floor in the living room. They never made it to the bed. Tonight she wanted to be in *his* bed.

The passion was back, the desire was almost overwhelming at times as they peeled their clothes off and made it into the bed. Awhile later the sheets were wrinkled, disheveled, and damp as their bodies were spent and lying together, completely satisfied in each other's arms. Shutting out the world and making love was a dream come true again. For both of them.

Kelsey rolled over onto her side and propped herself up on her elbow. She ran her finger up and down his bicep as he smiled at her and that smile lit up his eyes. *Oh God those eyes.* "Thank you…"

"No. I should be thanking you, I should be telling you and I am telling you right now that you are stellar in bed. You are beyond sexy and you make me want to make love to you repeatedly all night long. I don't ever want you to forget that you are incredibly desirable and I am honored to be with you." Kelsey had tears in her eyes. She had never felt so loved and desired.

"Did you say repeatedly?" Brady laughed at her and did exactly as he had said he wanted to do. Repeatedly. All night long.

Kelsey woke up to a bright room. The sun had completely come up. She had spent the entire night with Brady. He was still asleep next to her. The white sheet was barely covering him at the waist and he was still completely naked. God how she loved this man for all he brought to her life. Her heart was bursting at the seams.

Brady woke up when he sensed her staring. "Didn't your mama ever teach you it's rude to stare?"

"Of course she did, but sexy people don't count."

"And why is that?" he asked, smiling at her, so happy to wake up with her.

"Because I simply cannot help myself," Kelsey said as she kissed him and he pulled her on top of him.

"Waking up with you like this is something I want to do for the rest of forever," he said.

"Me too. And what we did last night, all night, put that the on the list for the rest of forever too," Kelsey intended to be funny but she meant every word. There was no turning back now. But it was time to face reality and the reality is… she needs to be honest with Kyle. It's time to let him go no matter how painful and how hurtful it will be for him - and for herself.

It was Sunday morning and neither of them had anywhere they needed to be. Brady had a rare weekend off from the hospital and Kelsey wasn't thinking about anyone needing her other than the man lying beside her. They made love again and showered together before Kelsey put last night's clothes back on and tried to leave Brady's apartment.

"I really need to get back to my place and check in with Kyle. Not to mention I need to go see how steep my parking ticket is from running over the meter all night long."

"I don't want you to go but I know you have to, and I will take care of that ticket if there is one babe. I should have pulled your jeep into the garage last night. I didn't even think of it, I'm sorry." Neither of them had thought of anything or anyone else. That happened when they were together. It was a surreal feeling. It was more than just being new to each other. It defined how they were meant to be together.

Kelsey finally tore herself away from Brady and promised to call him later. She got back to her apartment at noon and as she was flipping on the switch to the ceiling fan in her living room, she heard a text come through on her phone.

I've decided I sleep better with you. I'll pack a bag and come back tonight if you'll have me.

Kelsey stared at the text. This had to end. She couldn't have two men in her life. In her heart. She had to tell Kyle the truth tonight.

CHAPTER 10

Kelsey talked to Brady again after she said yes to Kyle coming over. She explained to Brady how she needed tonight to tell Kyle everything. And then the two of them could begin their life together. Neither one could wait but they knew it wasn't going to be easy for Kyle to find out the truth - and eventually, hopefully, accept it. Kelsey's phone conversation with Brady was interrupted when he was paged to the hospital for an emergency. They were short-staffed for the weekend and Brady was needed.

A few hours had passed after talking to Brady, and Kelsey's nerves were wearing on her, so she got into her jeep and drove to the hospital. She didn't know what kind of excuse she was going to use if anyone were to ask her why she was there. She just took the elevator directly up to the sixth floor with hope of finding Brady in his office. She needed one of his pep talks to get through tonight. She needed reassurance that she wasn't an awful person.

Kelsey was wearing a lilac tunic sweater and skinny jeans with knee-high black boots. The two-inch heels on her boots were echoing through the empty hallway as Kelsey reached Brady's office door. It was slightly open and she looked in before entering. She stopped herself when she saw another doctor, in scrubs, who was older than Brady. Brady's scrubs were always tight fitting and clung to every muscle and curve. The other doctor had the standard baggy look. Kelsey started to back away. It was obvious they were in the middle of a discussion as the two of them were looking over a file in the other doctor's hand and referring to Brady's laptop on his desk. Just as Kelsey was carefully and quietly going to step away from the door, she heard the other doctor's words.

"So your patient is completely recovered? No signs of brain injury or reactions at all from the thiopental? Keeping a patient in a medical induced coma for that long of a time, without brain swelling, is risky, Dr. Walker. I'm still baffled why you did it."

Kelsey started to assume the patient they were discussing was Kyle but then she knew it couldn't have been. Kyle was not in a medically induced coma. It had just taken Kyle forever to wake up. One week after his accident Kyle had shown signs of wanting to wake up, but he had slipped back into a full coma for an additional three weeks.

"Yes the patient is fully recovered. I will see him for a follow up next week but as of right now he is experiencing some headaches, for which he is taking prescribed painkillers, but rapidly getting his strength back. He's ready to resume his life." *Just not with Kelsey. Not with the woman who wants to be with me as badly as I want her. Thank God for answering my prayers. This time.* "And the thiopental is completely safe on any patient. Despite the fact that the brain swelling had diminished, you know that any severe trauma to the brain requires rest and thiopental allowed my patient to recover while comatose. The areas at risk in his brain were therefore protected and his brain completely healed."

"Medically, I know you're right. It all makes sense. It's just unusual for the family or loved ones to agree to intentionally keeping someone under when all signs pointed to healing to begin with. There was no surgery, no swelling after a few days, and your patient had even showed signs of wanting to come out of the coma. A patient being under general anesthetic for that long of a time could have, again, been risky."

"I used this option for as long as I needed to. My patient will make a full recovery. I know I made the right decision so why rehash it?" Kelsey had thought Brady sounded abrupt with his colleague. The other doctor accepted Brady's explanation and after a handshake later, they were closing their private meeting.

That doctor may have been satisfied with Dr. Walker's explanation, but Kelsey wasn't. She had backed up and walked quickly and quietly this time down the hallway. She turned a corner and waited for the doctor to get on the elevator before she headed back to Brady's office door. She didn't knock. She just pushed open the door and Brady looked up from sitting at his desk. He looked surprised at first but then that wide smile of his came across his face for her.

"Hey… what brings you here, babe? Close the door behind you and come in." He rolled back his chair from behind his desk and offered her a seat, on his lap.

"I wanted to see you. I guess you could say I couldn't stay away," Kelsey walked over to him and just as she was about to ask him if Kyle was the patient he had been discussing a moment ago, he was paged over the hospital intercom.

"Oh damn, I will be back soon. Sit tight. Stay here. Please?" As Brady exited the room, he looked back at Kelsey and she assured him she would be there when he returned.

She sat down in his desk chair and pulled up the Internet on his laptop. She wanted to Google thiopental.

A barbiturate-induced coma, or barb coma, is a temporary coma brought on by a controlled dose of a barbiturate drug, usually pentobarbital or thiopental. Barbiturate comas are used to protect the brain. The hope is that, with the swelling relieved, the pressure decreases and some or all brain damage may be averted. Several studies have supported this theory by showing reduced mortality when treating brain injuries with a barbiturate coma.

Everything she read online made sense, but had Kyle's condition called for an induced coma? It didn't seem like it. He had continued to improve, she was told his brain was healing and the swelling had decreased and the tests showed no signs of damage to the brain. Why didn't Brady tell her he was intentionally keeping Kyle in a coma?

Kelsey scrolled down the page for more information. Had Kyle's life been in danger?

How safe are drug-induced comas?
A drug like this is used every day in the operating room. It is probably the most used drug in all of anesthesia. Every day essentially, when patients go under general anesthesia that whole state is a reversible coma. It's a difference in dosage.

Are there after effects?
It's hard to sort out, because if you're going to these extremes you're already dealing with a very dire situation. If there are effects later on, it's an extremely difficult distinction to make whether it is an effect of the drug-induced coma. People who do this are very mindful of watching and monitoring. They make every effort to only use this option for as long as they need to.

Kelsey's mind was reeling. *And just how long did Brady intend to keep Kyle under? Had Brady stopped giving Kyle the drug after he had enough time to win me over? We were talking about a future together. Is that what he wanted before Kyle woke up?* Kelsey had questions. And one very serious accusation.

When she clicked out of that page online, she logged off the Internet and found herself staring at the file which Brady had just been discussing with the other doctor. At the top, it read, Kyle P. Newman. The entire report was there from mid September to mid October. Every test was documented, every drug was listed. Daily, after Kyle's ninth day in the hospital, thiopental was injected into his IV. It was administered at the same time each evening, and initialled by Dr. W. Not a single nurse had ever given Kyle thiopental. Every other drug they had. This thiopental was Brady's doing and it looked as if he had made sure no one else had to bother with it. Or know about it. Including her. Kelsey was never told about Kyle being medically induced into a coma for all of those weeks. He had been drugged for three weeks – following that one night when Kyle had started to wake up. Kyle had repeatedly been put into that coma while Brady and Kelsey continued to get to know each other, to sleep together.

Kelsey's reporter instincts had kicked in and she didn't like this at all. What she was investigating was looking like Brady had purposely kept Kyle under so he could continue his affair with *her*. He was buying time. Or was he? Was Kelsey misunderstanding something? Surely there's a medical explanation that will clear up all of this, she hoped. Kelsey backed away from the computer, stood up, and walked over to the window. She cracked it. She needed some air. *Please God don't let this amazing man be a liar, a conniving son of a bitch. Was he too good to be true? I am about to change my life for him. I am about to shatter a good man's heart for him.* Kelsey closed the window and turned around to find Brady walking back into the room.

"Okay babe, sorry to keep you waiting. I'm just on call for the rest of today so we can get out of here if you want." Brady walked over to the window where Kelsey was standing and he noticed her eyes. She seemed distant, reserved. He wondered then if she had told Kyle the truth and if she was feeling guilty and hurting from it.

"I don't want to leave right now. I need you to explain something to me," Kelsey walked over to Brady's desk and picked up the file. "What is this?"

"It's Kyle's file. I just had a meeting with Dr. Jonas and we went over Kyle's case."

"I know you had a meeting, I almost walked in on it and I didn't mean to overhear you but I did. Were you truthful with me the entire time Kyle was here in this hospital? Why were you discussing a medically induced coma and why does it say right here in Kyle's file that you purposely put him under for three weeks? And you did it right after he had shown signs of coming to!" Kelsey's anger surfaced.

She is a smart woman. She had investigated many stories in her journalism career. She knew exactly what this information meant. Only she was able to read between the lines as to why Brady actually did it. He did it because of her. Because of them. He wanted to steal some time to be with her - without Kyle being in the way.

Brady remained calm but his heart felt as if it were about to beat out of his chest. "Hey, calm down. I can explain drug induced comas to you. I know we already talked about how Kyle's brain needed to heal and it was healing. It was my decision to begin thiopental and as I administered it, Kyle's condition remained the same, unchanged and out of danger with rest, which contributed to his complete recovery. I believe that I averted any brain damage with that method." Kelsey was studying Brady's face as he spoke to her. He never told her any of this before, exactly what he was doing, and now he was speaking to her as a doctor - not as a woman in love with him who wanted answers.

"You lied to me. Do not stand there and tell me you put Kyle into a coma because you wanted to save his life. He was recovering, you told me so yourself! And he was beginning to wake up. You did this on purpose so you could have me!" Kelsey was yelling at him and he walked toward her and calmly asked her to keep her voice down. "Answer me, Brady. Admit that you kept this from me."

"I did not lie to you. I told you repeatedly that Kyle was going to wake up and make a full recovery. All of the tests–"

"Oh fuck the tests! And fuck you!" Kelsey wanted to walk away and when she started to, Brady stopped her. He put his hands on her shoulders and made her face him.

"Listen to me. I am a good doctor. I would never harm a patient. I would never harm anyone. I save lives Kelsey, and I did what I needed to do for Kyle. I would have medically induced his coma at that stage in the game whether you and I were involved or not. I didn't tell you because you were struggling with what had happened to Kyle and with what was happening between us. The guilt was killing you, and I knew that. I also knew that you would question my motives. Did I want Kyle in a coma so we could be together? Was I hoping he wouldn't survive so I could secure a future with you? Don't think those things. I'm a doctor first, Kelsey. I would do the same thing again, for any patient, if I had to do it over."

Kelsey was crying. His hands were still on her shoulders and she was crying for how stupid she had been. This man was dishonest. This new, amazing man had her fooled into believing that she had found her soul mate. He had said all of the right things to her and she had fallen for him, heart first.

"I know you're angry and I am so sorry you feel like I was being dishonest. I would never hurt you, Kelsey. Please believe that." Kelsey backed away from his grip and wiped the tears off of her face with the back of her hand. "Healthy people do not step toward a relationship with the intention of hurting each other. What you did may have been right for Kyle, but it was wrong of you to do it on the sly. I read the medication charts, I read the files. You were the only one who gave Kyle that drug, every night. None of the nurses were aware of it. No one was. And you wanted it to be that way. So whether you were protecting me or wooing me, it doesn't matter now. This hurts like hell, Brady. You are not the person I thought you were. And this, I can assure you, wasn't my intention either - but now it'll be me who ends up hurting you."

"No! What are you saying? This is it? It's over between us?" Brady spun Kelsey around to face him again. "Stop turning away from me. Just stop and think about this. You and I belong together. We need each other. We need this–" Brady attempted to pull her into a kiss, but this time she was strong enough to fight her emotions. This time she pulled away. In anger. "I can't and I won't do this anymore. I don't trust you."

"I love you, and I know you love me. Let that be enough to help you trust me again, Kelsey. I'm worthy. Just give me the chance to prove it to you. I truly believe that I did what I had to do - for all of us."

And there it was. He had said it. *For all of us.*

Brady had taken Kyle off of thiopental three days prior to him coming out of the coma. He had been pleased with the test results again that week and he also knew that he and Kelsey had a chance, a real chance to be together. She had changed his life, he had finally found a woman he wanted to call his wife. And he had won her heart.

"Oh you proved something to me alright. You proved that you're not the man I thought you were. You are not the man I wanted you to be. And you're right, I do love you. I love you more than I ever thought was possible to love a man. You brought something to my life that I thought I could never walk away from. Never live without. Well you shattered that dream by being a sneak and a liar. I don't ever want to see you again!"

Kelsey was sobbing as she made it all the way to the door before Brady spoke to her. He was still standing across the room and when she looked back at him there were tears streaming down his face. Those bright crystal blue eyes confirmed so much pain. She could hardly continue to look at him. "Kelsey- I can't lose you. We can't lose us. Please don't leave."

When she closed the office door behind her, she didn't slam it. She didn't have the strength. It was as if the anger was already gone, and now the pain of heartbreak had surfaced. And it was killing her. Walking away from Brady Walker took everything she had. But she did it. She did it for herself. And she did it for Kyle.

CHAPTER 11

Bree missed the phone call from Kelsey. She and Nicholas were back together and in her bed ignoring the interruption when the call came through. Kelsey was crying and driving and needing to talk to her best friend. She was the only person who knew about her affair. She was the only person Kelsey could confide in and now the support she needed would just have to wait.

It was four o'clock Sunday afternoon and Kelsey was sobbing on the couch in her apartment. Her knees were pulled up to her chest and she had just sat there, crying, for well over an hour. Kyle was coming back to her place at five-thirty, and it was time for her to pull herself together. She wanted to put the pain behind her. She would keep the affair a secret for the rest of her life. She could count on Bree not to tell a soul and that's the way it had to be. Brady was a fling and she would tuck him away somewhere deep inside of her heart and never look back. *Damn him for lying.*

Kelsey showered, washed and dried her hair, and put on some makeup. She still looked like she had been crying, but it was the best she could do. She felt awful. A few minutes before she was expecting Kyle, she checked her cell phone for messages and there were two.

One was from Bree: *Sorry I missed your call. Can we talk tomorrow? Nic is here.*

And the other was from Brady: *I am so sorry. I love you. Don't do this. I will never give up on us. Please call me.*

Kelsey deleted both of the texts as Kyle was walking in the door. He was carrying a restaurant take-out bag, some flowers, and a bottle of wine. Kelsey was still in her robe, standing in the living room, when he closed the door behind him with his foot.

"Hello there, beautiful," Kyle was smiling and looking good. Healthy. He was definitely getting well. He had dark-washed jeans on with a charcoal gray oxford shirt tucked in and black loafers on his feet, with no socks again. The man hated wearing socks.

"Why are you so dressed up, honey? I've showered and done my makeup but I'm not dressed to go out anywhere." She followed Kyle into the kitchen as he set the table, poured two glasses of wine, and showed her the take-out food, her favorite, sushi. "You are so sweet. And I am starving, but I'm confused as to why you're overdressed if we're staying in tonight?"

"I just felt like getting dressed. I feel really good, Kel. My headaches are under control, and my energy level is back. I just wanna celebrate tonight." Kelsey sat down at the table and crossed her legs which were completely out of her robe. Kyle scooted his chair toward hers and he kissed her lips. "I am so happy you're feeling like yourself again!" she said to him as she put her hands on his clean-shaven face and he smiled at her. "Me too."

Their dinner was delicious and gone, and the wine was going down well as Kelsey filled her third glass. Kyle was not much of a drinker and being on pain medication, he only drank one glass. They moved into the living room once Kelsey helped Kyle clear the table. Kelsey was still holding her wine glass when she curled her legs up close to Kyle on the couch. "Thank you for that wonderful dinner and this amazing wine," Kelsey said feeling a little loopy and Kyle giggled at her because he knew she didn't handle her alcohol well. After a few glasses, she always had a buzz. Kelsey was feeling happy and relieved to be washing away the pain of leaving Brady. She hadn't thought about him since Kyle had arrived and she liked how the two of them existed together. They were simple and they worked, and there was no way she was going to walk away from what they had built and shared in the last couple of years. She realized today how much Kyle had really meant to her. He could have been in harm's way being sedated for that long. At Brady's hand. And because of her. Because Brady loved her. Thinking that there was the slightest chance Kyle could have been in danger made Kelsey want to spend the rest of her life making it up to him. And being good to him.

"Kyle..."

"Hmm?" He was sitting close and looking right into her eyes.

"I am so drunk." He laughed at her again and she joined him. "You are. And it's cracking me up. Hey, are you too drunk to listen to me for a minute or so here?"

"Of course not!" Kelsey let her robe hang open at the chest and it revealed her lacy red bra. She had worn matching panties - a thong - which Kyle also had noticed when she had her legs crossed and robe open at the table.

"I just want to say a few things to you tonight. I want to first thank you for being by my side. It was crazy what happened to me with the car accident and being in a coma for that long. You have been there for me Kelsey, and there is no one in this world, in my world, who I have ever loved and appreciated as much as I do you."

Kelsey felt instantly sober and tears were trembling on her eye lashes. He had no idea. She wasn't *that* person. She used to be, but she had done something she never would have thought she could ever do. She was unfaithful. She had an affair and fell in love with another man. As Kyle sat before her, Kelsey's thoughts became clearer. Clearer than they were earlier today in Brady's office. She knew in her heart now that Brady did what he did because it was just one of those choices he made with his heart. Yes he lied. Just as Kelsey had lied to Kyle. She had made a choice with her heart too, to be with Brady. But now that wasn't meant to be. She felt an overwhelming sense of understanding as she was crying. She had forgiven Brady, and maybe even herself. Those sins would be in the past now. As she listened to Kyle, she forced away her tears and returned his smile.

"So, baby, I know it's been a whirlwind this last month but I'm ready to move forward - with you. With us." Kyle slipped off of the couch, down onto one knee, on the floor. He reached into his pocket and pulled out a little black box. He opened it and Kelsey gasped. Her hand was over her mouth and tears were again pouring out of her eyes. "Oh my God, Kyle…"

The ring was a two-carat diamond surrounded by a circle of emeralds, her birthstone. It was so beautiful. Kelsey was staring at it and then back at Kyle's face with that big smile still plastered on it. He had chosen that ring at the jewelry store just hours earlier. Her reaction to shopping together for a ring wasn't thrilling, so he decided to take matters into his own hands and choose the right one himself. And by witnessing

Kelsey's reaction, he knew he had made a beautiful choice.

"Kelsey Duncan, will you marry me?"

She didn't think twice. She didn't think of anyone but him. But them. She said yes and threw herself into his arms and they both ended up embracing on their knees on the floor. And then Kyle slipped the ring onto her finger and he kissed her. He kissed her softly and sweetly and they shared *their* kind of passion. She knew he was hungry for more. It was time. And Kelsey wanted to give herself to her fiancé.

"I want to take you to bed," was all he said as they walked back to her bedroom holding hands.

His kisses were tender and then hungrier than they had been in a long time. He peeled her robe off and looked at her. He ran his fingers over the lace bra, covering her nipples. He did this to both of her breasts and her nipples responded. Kelsey found herself wanting him, and wanting more, as he stood up alongside of the bed and removed all of his clothing. He was sometimes a selfish lover and she had become used to that. Until Brady. Kyle got back into the bed and he reached behind her to undo the clasp on her red bra. He touched and kissed her breasts as she arched her body and dug her fingers into his back. He slid his fingers between her legs and moved her thong off and then he immediately entered her.

She had wanted more foreplay but he seemed eager. It was okay. She would give it to him. He was ready. She told herself to try to have an orgasm with him inside of her, but she knew it was harder for her to have it happen that way. She would have preferred his fingers or his mouth on her first. His thrusts were fast and almost furious. He was on top of her. That was *their* position and he was pleasing her. It felt good to her. She wanted to feel him hard and fast and deeper inside of her. And then he finished before Kelsey had the chance to. He always did. He rolled off of her and she laid there, still aroused. She hadn't touched him or kissed him in the places where most men would beg for the attention. She wanted to feel as satisfied as he apparently felt after they had just had sex - and she didn't. She pushed those thoughts out of her head and wondered if she should invest in a vibrator.

"God that felt good. It has been way too long, Kel."

"It did feel good baby." *But I'm not done yet.*

"Thank you."

"You're welcome, husband to be. Now get some sleep. You need your rest to keep up your strength because I want you to do that to me every night."

"Oh God..." Kyle responded with an unsure smile and Kelsey thought to herself, *yeah, I know, in my dreams*.

And she could live with that. Kyle is a wonderful man. An honest man. More honest than she - and a man like Brady - had been.

CHAPTER 12

Kelsey's cell phone was ringing as she stepped out of the shower. She grabbed a fresh white towel off the rack on the wall and wrapped it around her as she walked into her bedroom to retrieve her phone on her dresser, still on the charge from the night before. It was Monday morning and Kelsey immediately thought of Kyle. He had already left her apartment an hour ago. It was his first day back to work and Kelsey knew he was ready, but she still worried about him overdoing it.

She noticed it was Bree as she unplugged her phone from the wall socket and answered it. "Hi Bree, everything okay?" The two of them always called each other day or night, early or late, it didn't matter. Since Kelsey had not been able to talk to Bree yesterday – when she ended her relationship with Brady and then later got engaged to Kyle – the two of them were due to catch up. Now.

"I'm good. I hope you are, too. I'm sorry I wasn't able to talk yesterday. That's why I'm calling now. I'm driving in to work and I wanted to see what's going on with you before I get swamped all day."

Kelsey thought about yesterday and all that had happened in one day. When she called Bree she had been unraveling and wanted to tell her what Brady did and why she had ended things with him. Now she had some good news to share. She and Kyle were moving forward, together, and officially planning a future. Getting married.

"There's a lot we need to catch up on and I really don't wanna do it over the phone. Are you free for lunch today?"

"Maybe an early lunch? Something quick? Plan on eleven-thirty, unless you hear from me. And let's just meet at the Café on the Corner, okay with you?"

"Sounds good," Kelsey glanced at the clock. It was seven-thirty. She needed to get moving. She had an interview scheduled for quarter after eight. "I really need to see you, so let's make this work, even if we have to skip lunch to just talk for a half hour."

"You're scaring me now, Kel."

"Oh stop it. I'm fine. See you soon."

Kelsey had wrapped up two interviews by eleven o'clock when she left the office and walked outside and a few blocks down to the Café on the Corner. She wanted to grab a booth away from the line that formed at the counter to order and pick up food. She knew a public place wasn't the best idea but she needed to talk to Bree, today.

It was twenty minutes after eleven when Kelsey was standing at the counter, ordering and paying for turkey sandwiches and iced water with lemon when Bree walked in the door. "Hey, no, I got it. You paid last time sister," Bree was reaching into her new Coach purse hanging on her shoulder.

"Too late. My treat again. Let's go sit over there in the booth. Our food will be ready in a few minutes." They walked across the restaurant so close together, arms touching. The two of them were inseparable. Even with their separate love lives and work lives, they always made time to be together and stay updated on each other.

"So what's going on, Kel? I haven't been able to think of anything but you all morn– what the hell is that?" Bree saw the ring. Kelsey wasn't surprised. The two of them always looked each other over and never failed to detect a new highlight, a manicure, even fuller boobs when it was that time of the month.

"Well this," Kelsey said giving Bree her hand to show her the two-carat diamond ring circled by emeralds, "is the reason I needed to see you today."

"Oh my God! It is amazing and so beautiful! Come here!" They stood up, hugged as close as they could while standing with their upper bodies pulled together over the table. "Tell me everything! I am so happy for you Kelsey, but my gosh your new man didn't waste any time! I want to know how Brady proposed… and I know this is going to make you sad but how did Kyle handle the news of you leaving him?"

Kelsey sighed. Bree's assumption was way off, but understandable considering just a few days ago she was running to Brady, needing Brady, wanting Brady. And that was the last time she and Bree had spoken.

"I need to explain and please try to understand and support me on this, as you have with everything in my life for what seems like forever. This ring isn't from Brady. Kyle and I are engaged." Bree's eyes widened and she grabbed both of Kelsey's arms by the wrist and held them down on the table top.

"But I thought-"

"And you thought right. On Saturday night, I was ready to run to Brady. And I did, after you encouraged me to go to him. He and I spent the night together. We talked about beginning a life together, and we made love like there was no tomorrow." Kelsey pushed the thought of them together, like that, out of her mind. She missed him already. Missed how he made her feel. But she knew she shouldn't. She couldn't do that anymore.

"I'm so confused, Kel..."

"Believe me, I was too, but something happened to make me see things clearly. I went to Brady's office yesterday afternoon. I was feeling incredibly anxious about telling Kyle that it was over. I knew he was going to come to my place for dinner last night and I was going to tell him then. I just needed to be in Brady's arms, to be reassured that I was doing the right thing. I needed *him.* And that's when I almost walked in on a meeting he and a colleague were having. I didn't intend to eavesdrop, outside of the door, but I did. I overheard them talking about the medically induced coma that Brady had put Kyle in. Bree, he purposely drugged Kyle for three weeks. He didn't tell a soul. He didn't tell me. It is because of *me* that Kyle was unconscious for an entire month in the hospital."

One of the restaurant staff members interrupted them with two plates of food. Neither one of them had heard their number called. Their food was ready and they were so engrossed in conversation that they became unaware of their surroundings. They giggled and thanked the middle-aged woman for bringing their food. Food that was probably going to be untouched, uneaten, today. They had a lot to talk about.

"I don't believe what I'm hearing. What are you saying? Brady used his power as a doctor to keep Kyle away from you so he could seduce you?"

"We were already sleeping together and I just think he wanted more time. Kyle started to wake up after Brady and I gave in to our passion and Brady knew I was confused. He knew I was having second thoughts. I didn't want to be a woman who cheated."

"So he drugged him until you fell in love with him? And then what, he just stopped giving him the drug to keep him under?" Kelsey's eyes were filling up with tears. Just the thought of all of it hurt her so badly. Kyle's life was being played with. And her heart had gotten broken in the process.

"I confronted Brady, he admitted that it was true, and he tried his damndest to convince me that medically he didn't do anything wrong. He swore to me that he would have put Kyle into that coma regardless of *us*. He believed that Kyle's brain needed rest in order to heal."

"And do you believe him?"

"I believe that I was lied to, Bree. A man who I thought hung the goddamn moon turned out to be someone I don't even know. Who does that to people? Who lies, who sneaks around like that? I mean, my God, Kyle's life was at stake."

"So you ended it with Brady and now you're going to marry Kyle..." Bree didn't like this. Not one bit. "I don't know if I should be happy for you, or worried about you!" Kelsey laughed at her. My goodness she loved her. She thanked God each and every day for Bree. Friends forever. Sisters by heart.

"I did end it with Brady. The last text he sent me was an hour ago, full of professing his undying love and begging me to rethink my rash decision. I didn't reply. I haven't spoken to him since yesterday afternoon, and eventually I hope those texts stop coming or I will have to change my number."

"I get what you're saying Kel, I do. He lied, but doesn't a part of you understand why he did it? I remember how you told me you both were free falling for each other. If it wasn't love at first sight, I don't know what the hell it was for you two – but it seemed to me that it was real. And magical. That just doesn't come along every day. Can you really walk away from that?"

"I already have, Bree. When I left his office, I was a wreck. I went home and bawled my eyes out." Bree instantly felt awful for not taking Kelsey's call. She and Nicholas had been at odds for weeks and when he showed up at her place, he had a proposition for her, just for Sunday. No talk about his wife, who he was still *only* separated from. No talk about him, and who he was spending more time with. No talking at all. The two of them were in bed, in the middle of possibly the best sex Bree has ever had, when Kelsey's call went to Bree's voicemail. "Later, I had to pull myself together because Kyle was excited about coming over for dinner. He was feeling great and had a surprise for me."

"He proposed to you."

"And without hesitation I said yes. When he was down on one knee in front of me, pledging his love, I was crying. Crying for how Brady had hurt me, and for what I had done to Kyle and our relationship. And in the middle of my tears, I realized what Brady did, he did out of love. Crazy love. The kind of love that sucks you in so fast and so deep where you just can't think straight sometimes. I have forgiven Brady because I understand what it feels like to do something you never dreamed you would do. I guess I need forgiveness, too. I need to forgive myself."

"Before you move on with Kyle?"

"Before we get married. Kyle can never know what I did. It would destroy him."

"And what makes you think settling for a man - who is just okay in your heart - won't destroy you?" Kelsey looked at Bree and the tears were back in her eyes. Bree always said what she was thinking and feeling, even if it was brutal. And then, Kelsey spoke from the very bottom of her heart. "Kyle means everything to me. He is more than *just okay in my heart.* I love him, I need him, and I want to be his wife."

"And what about this chance you have to live, I mean really live, Kel? You can't throw that away! You have to talk to Brady and at least find some closure. I don't think you've done that. You were angry when you saw him last, and rightfully so, but you both deserve a chance to be honest with each other, or at least to say goodbye."

"I already said goodbye to him yesterday when I walked out of his office, and out of his life, for the last time. I can't go back because I don't know if *he* can be honest. I don't know if I really knew that man. I mean think about it Bree…"

"I know. What he did was huge, but I'm not so sure you should be giving up on him…"

"Kyle would never hurt me, or lie to me, like that."

"No, he wouldn't."

"So you understand why I want to marry him?"

"I know you, Kelsey Duncan. You are running to Kyle and with every sprint, every pounce on the pavement, you are also running away - from Brady, from what you did. And from taking a risk that could change your life."

"Stop acting like a shrink and be my sister, Bree!" Bree's words had stung because Kelsey knew she was exactly right. Kelsey was the squeaky one. She was the good girl. The idea of breaking Kyle's heart and moving on with Brady had terrified her. A small part of her was relieved when she found out the truth at the hospital. She had been handed a reason to walk away from Brady - to walk away from one of the two men she loves. The choice had almost been made for her. She was not going to live the rest of her life wondering if Brady was the one. She wouldn't do that to herself. She was not like Bree. Bree was the risk taker, loving men on the wild side, settling for whatever she could get from a man. It may have been one hell of a ride while it lasted with Brady Walker, but Kelsey knew she - the conservative one - would do right by Kyle. *He* was good and honest and true - and that's what she needed in her world. That was enough for her.

"I'm not trying to piss you off. You know me. I am going to be direct with you. This is what you need to hear. Right now. Before you make any more important decisions about your life," Bree looked at Kelsey's engagement ring. Beautiful. Just stunning. But was it worth giving up a lifetime of real happiness with another man?

***

Kelsey was back in the office, writing the stories from her earlier interviews when she received a text from Kyle. She had texted him twice already today, checking on him, and he was letting her know all was just fine. *No worries baby. I feel great. Little headaches aren't going to keep me down.* She replied with a happy face and told him she would see him, at his place, tonight. They were going to eat dinner and then she had planned to go back to her own apartment. She knew Kyle would be exhausted after getting back into his work routine again.

CHAPTER 13

And inevitably, their routine continued. Resumed. Kelsey fell back into what was comfortable. She had quietly and easily slipped back into her life with Kyle. He was almost completely recovered, and she was by his side. She was happy. And also extremely distracted. She couldn't stop thinking about Brady. He texted her every day, multiple times a day, and she had not replied. She would always read his words before she deleted them. Deleted them from her phone, maybe, but not from her mind.

***

It was Wednesday and she had not seen or spoken to Brady since she walked out on him on Sunday. She was back to working full and busy days and fell into a routine of eating dinner and hanging out with Kyle each night at his apartment. He was spending the nights there, confessing that his headaches sometimes kept him awake and he wanted to at least be in his own bed.

Those headaches would have to be addressed today - at Kyle's follow up doctor's appointment at Laneview Hospital. With Brady.

Kyle and Kelsey had almost argued last night when he reminded her of it. She absolutely didn't want to go along with him to the appointment and Kyle didn't understand why. She couldn't come up with an excuse other than she may be working late. In the end, Kyle reminded her that she and Brady were friends, weren't they? And he told her that he needed her there. She was better at asking questions and understanding doctor lingo, Kyle had stated. She understood doctor lingo alright. Especially *this* doctor's. Kelsey had loved listening to Brady talk about his career, or simply talk about nothing at all. She loved hearing the sound of his voice. Deep but gentle. She couldn't describe it but the first time she had heard it, she was so taken by it. He's intelligent and so his language use is interesting, almost captivating. And so was his *body* language. *God she had to forget this man.*

But first she had to see him one more time. She had to get herself through Kyle's doctor's appointment today. Then she could begin to forget him.

***

Kyle met Kelsey in the parking garage at the hospital. She had pulled in and parked first and she purposely waited a few minutes in her jeep. She didn't want to walk into that hospital alone again. She didn't want to risk running into Brady - and being alone with him. Her anger had diminished and she didn't trust herself to not be weak with him again.

She reminded herself to be strong as she and Kyle walked into the hospital, signed in at the nurse's window, and sat down in the waiting room. Five minutes later Kelsey was flipping through a magazine and noticed her palms were perspiring. She couldn't wait to get this over with.

"Kel?" Kyle stood up and looked down at her.

"Yeah?"

"Are you coming? The nurse just called me in."

"Oh yes, of course, I'm right behind you." She recognized the nurse from Kyle's month-long hospital stay and the two of them exchanged hellos and friendly conversation as she took Kyle's blood pressure and checked his weight outside of the patient room door. He had lost fifteen pounds in the month following his accident and already gained back seven. He needed that weight on him. Kelsey had noticed him looking too thin, especially in his face. Kelsey was feeling embarrassed being back at that hospital, for what that nurse and all the others must have thought and said about her while she stayed with Kyle for hours on end for days, for weeks – all that while being involved with his doctor. She had only overheard two nurses one time, talking about her and Brady, and then she didn't care as much as she did now. Now that she wasn't caught up in the whirlwind anymore, she was ashamed of herself.

The nurse said the doctor would be right in and Kelsey took a deep breath as she closed the door behind her.

"You seem tense, what's up?" Kyle noticed Kelsey was quiet and when she was quiet, something was usually bothering her.

"Oh I'm fine. Just tired. Work was crazy busy. How are you? Did you have any headaches today?"

"I feel great, energy wise, but I do keep getting those headaches. I took my last pain pill this morning – and I'm hoping Dr. Walker will refill my prescription today."

"Just make sure you tell him exactly how you're feeling. That's what we're here for." Kelsey was hoping Kyle wouldn't downplay the pain like most men do in front of other men, doctors or not. She could tell when the headaches plagued Kyle. She could see it in his eyes and it worried her. She had been praying for him to be okay.

There was a brief knock at the door and then Brady swung it open. He was wearing his scrubs. *Imagine that.* And Kelsey tried not to go there in her mind. She was staring at him despite the fact that she had told herself *not to*. He was in complete doctor mode as he made his way into the room. He had his game face on, and Kelsey smiled to herself. She knew exactly how he was feeling inside. Awkward.

"So how are you, Kyle? Feeling like yourself again? Back to work yet?" *Back in Kelsey's bed? Been treating her like a real man should? Loving her like she deserves?* Brady looked over at Kelsey and smiled, dimple and all, on those scruffy cheeks. God that smile. And those eyes. Those crystal blue eyes. This time, however, there was pain in his eyes. She didn't have to guess. It was heartbreak. She returned a smile to him and then looked over at Kyle as he answered the doctor's question.

Once Kyle explained his reoccurring headaches and his need for more pain medication, Brady lifted his eyebrows, chewed a couple times on the gum in his mouth, and tugged with both hands at the stethoscope draped across the back of his shoulders and around his neck. "Are the headaches still as bad as they were? Do you notice any difference in the amount of pain?"

"Not really. If I feel one coming on, I take a pain pill."

"Every day?"

"Yes. At least once a day."

"Kyle, I prescribed the painkillers to get you through your days of recovery at home, right after you were released from the hospital. Those were not meant for you to pop like ibuprofen. It's a low dose of Vicodin, and even still, you shouldn't be taking that medication and driving and working and going about your regular day."

"So I guess that means you are not going to give me a script for more then, huh?" Brady sat down on the edge of the counter top in the examining room. "I want you to start taking ibuprofen. Pop an Advil or two when you have a headache. We need to see how you manage the pain with over-the-counter drugs." Kyle nodded his head in agreement, but Kelsey could tell by looking at him that he wasn't in agreement with the doctor. "Also, we are going to put you through a CAT Scan today. I didn't plan on it, but I want to make absolute sure all is well in that head of yours. You experienced a lot of trauma in that car accident and all prior tests have shown that your brain was unscathed. Let's just be safe and run the test, okay?"

"I won't argue with that. I need peace of mind myself, especially since I thought those headaches would be gone by now," Kelsey chimed in and both men looked at her. She hadn't planned on talking. She was just there for moral support, for Kyle. Brady was watching her. He was hearing her, but he was looking at her hair, at her lips, at the way her hands moved when she spoke. And then he saw the ring on her finger. She didn't mean to wave it in his face. She realized at that moment that the stones had caught the light, sparkled like fireworks, and also caught Brady's eye. *He knew.*

"Whoa! What's that on your finger there Kelsey? Do you two have some news to share with me?" Brady was hiding the shock that raced through his body. *She was going to marry that guy. She had already accepted his proposal. My God, she was engaged to another man. That was supposed to be his ring she was wearing.* He tried to catch his breath and keep smiling at them. Both of them. He focused on Kyle as he spoke first.

"Oh yeah man, she said yes. We are getting married." Kyle winked at Kelsey and she smiled at him before looking back over at Brady with the same frozen smile on her face.

"Well congratulations to both of you! I hope you'll be blissfully happy together." Brady shook Kyle's hand and then walked over to Kelsey. He gripped her shoulders with both of his hands and leaned forward and gave her a quick kiss on the cheek. "Best of luck, my friend." Kelsey felt her cheeks flush as she managed to say *thank you* to him while glancing over at Kyle who looked unaffected by Brady's bold gesture. That quick kiss had fazed her though. Her cheeks weren't the only part of her body that was hot.

"Kyle, come with me and I will get you set up with a lab tech for your CAT Scan. I know you two were not planning on being stuck here for very long this afternoon so I will get you in and out of here as quickly as possible. And Kelsey, you can wait right here if you want to." Kelsey had thought she should go back out to the waiting room, to free up the exam room for the next patient, but she agreed to stay. She knew why she was invited to stay.

Kyle and Brady exited the room together and Kelsey watched them both walk away. Side by side. Brady was two inches taller than Kyle. Brady was more muscular. Kyle, despite the weight he had lost and started to regain, was a smaller built man. Kyle was fit and Kelsey had always thought he looked fabulous and sexy. And then she met Brady. That man was toned. That face was scruffy but not too much scruff. Very neatly groomed. Very sexy. And he always smelled of cologne. Kyle was not a cologne man. Kyle's scent was soap. Brady added a little extra touch. Oh God what was she thinking? She was sitting there comparing those two men. She got up from her chair and closed the exam room door. Brady had left it open when they walked away. *Had he done that on purpose? Was he coming back while Kyle went through his test?*

Kelsey was scrolling through her email on her cell phone when the door opened. He didn't knock this time. And he closed the door behind him.

"Hi. Can we talk?" He walked over to her and sat down on the chair right beside her. She was so easily drawn to this man and while that used to completely captivate her, now it scared her. She didn't trust him, or herself around him, anymore.

"Sure, but do tell me this first… Did Kyle really need that CAT Scan or was that just your way of buying some time alone with me again?"

"What do you think? You said so yourself, you need peace of mind. He's having headaches and I can't explain why, so I think it's necessary to run another test."

"I know you're right. I'm just still pissed off about what you did," she may have said the words, but she truly didn't mean them. She was beyond being angry with Brady. She had forgiven him. She wanted to play the angry card with him now though - because if she didn't, she would completely lose herself in him. In them. Again.

"I know you're angry, but I've run out of apologies for not

telling you what I was doing. I want to move past all of it with you," Brady put his hand on top of hers, which was resting on her thigh.

"I've chosen to spend my life with Kyle. We are getting married and you need to respect that," Kelsey removed her hand from underneath his and she stood up. She needed to put some distance between herself and him. She was getting too uncomfortable in that tiny room and she needed this conversation to be over.

"I will respect your choice to be with him - when I know it's what you really want. I cannot spend any more time chasing you, texting you and getting no responses. I don't like feeling desperate. So that's why we're talking now. This is it, and I just want you to listen to me. Listen to me with your heart."

Kelsey leaned against the wall beside the small counter with a sink, and cabinet above it. Her heart was racing, and she was listening.

"I love you. I would do absolutely anything for you. Okay, so, I mean within reason. And I'm saying that because I am a good man. I care about people and I am a doctor because it's been my dream to take care of people. I want to heal them. When I put Kyle into that medically induced coma, I did it for him first. Then, I did it for us. Would I do it again? Most definitely, but I would tell you everything. I know I should have but I was so consumed by you, so caught up in you and in what was happening between us." Kelsey understood perfectly. She too was *so caught up in* him. So much so that she had cheated on Kyle and had justified it. It was wrong and she knew that now. "I also knew you were torn. I have always been able to see how much you love him. But I also know how much you love *me*." Tears were welling up in Kelsey's eyes and she was fighting not to let them free. She couldn't. She needed to walk out of there, strong. She thought about the time in college when she and Bree ran a half marathon. Both of them liked to run long distances and they had enjoyed their first race. She would always remember being a quarter of a mile from the finish line and there were onlookers and supporters cheering for them alongside the street. Someone kept yelling, *finish strong… finish strong…you can do it, finish strong!* And that is what she had to do now. She had to finish this with Brady and walk away strong.

"Please, just think about what you're doing before you *really* do this. If you marry him, you are giving up the person you became when we were together. You were exciting, you were free, and you were seamless. There is so much more to who you are and who you want to be, Kelsey Duncan, and you know that better than anyone. Don't go back to living between those tight seams, making sure each one is knotted individually and securely. Skip one or two, take chances, broaden your horizons, and open yourself up to living Kelsey, I mean really living. Do it for yourself."

Kelsey was openly sobbing. His words had hit home. She had already gone back to being who she was before. She was going through the motions, but she wasn't really feeling the emotion in anything.

Brady stood up and walked over to her. He pulled her close and held her. She cried and her tears were dripping onto the shoulder of the cap sleeve on his shirt. "I want you to fight for what we could have, more than I've ever wanted anything in my life since I wanted my mom back." Tears were in his eyes now and Kelsey pulled herself out of his arms and stood there, face to face, with him - her own face still wet with tears. "I want you to promise me something. Promise me that you will always be true to yourself. Don't just be happy. Be everything you know you can and want to be. Reach far into your heart and seize of all of it. What's in there will sanction you to make it through anything."

Kelsey reached for a tissue on the counter behind her and she was dabbing her face and eyes with it. She had to pull herself together before Kyle came back. "No man has ever seen right through my heart the way that you have," her tears were falling again, "you have empowered me to want to be more. Because of you, I will now dream bigger, reach higher, and love deeper. My life is not going to be with you though. It can't be."

He had lost her. He was going to have to watch her walk away today with another man. He took her face, damp with tears, into both of his hands. "I will always love you," he was choking on his words, still fighting tears, "and I am never going to forget what you and I shared. I don't want you to forget that we still can have that. If you ever change your mind, I will be here."

"No. Brady… stop. You cannot put your life on hold for me, for us, for something that is never going to happen. You just said so yourself, you are not going to chase me anymore. Don't. And don't tell me, don't reassure me that you will be there when I need you. I can't go there. I can't run to you in a weak moment, because believe me there will be weak moments when I will be thinking about you and needing you and wanting you. I know how easy it would be for me to fall back into your arms and erase the rest of the world. But I can't. I won't. Not anymore."

Brady pulled her close and swiftly brought her lips to his. He kissed her and it took her breath away. She kissed him back with everything she had. This was their goodbye. And sooner than either of them wanted to, she pulled away.

"I love you," were the last words Kelsey said to him as she walked away taking steps that felt like her body was in slow motion, and "be true" were the last words she had heard Brady say to her.

Kelsey went into the restroom and splashed water on her face. She pulled herself together and then walked out into the main waiting room. Kyle was already there, waiting for her. He stood up from where he was sitting and walked to meet her, to leave. He told her he had only been waiting a few minutes for her after he had checked the exam room and Brady told him she was in the restroom.

"Everything okay? Did Brady give you the results of your CAT Scan already?" Kyle thought she looked upset, like she had been crying, and he just wanted to get her out of there. He knew being back in the hospital had stirred up the memory of all the worry she had dealt with when he was in a coma and she was alone.

"Everything is good. I'm clear, so I'm just going to have to deal with these headaches and move on with the rest of my life. Our life." He took her hand in his and held it as they walked out of the hospital.

Brady Walker watched them from the far end of the hospital hallway. He swallowed hard, forcing down the lump in his throat, and he silently vowed never to let this painful heartbreak make him a bitter man. He had loved an amazing woman, and lost her. Maybe it was foolish, but he knew he would always hold out hope for her, to one day, find her way back to him.

CHAPTER 14

Two and a half weeks later, Kelsey had completely thrown herself into her work. She scheduled more interviews and wrote more stories for the newspaper than she ever had in the six years of being a reporter. It didn't bother her to work late at night because the more she was working, the less she was thinking about Brady. Her decision to move on with Kyle was the right one, she knew, and it was just a matter of time before it would get easier.

Kelsey was reading over some of her notes from an earlier interview. It was the Wednesday before Thanksgiving and she had wanted to file two more stories before she would be out of the office for four days. She and Kyle were not going back to St. Louis for the holiday as they had the past two years. Her parents were on an Alaskan cruise to celebrate their thirtieth anniversary. They had gotten married on Thanksgiving Day, two years before Kelsey was born. They had not been able to have another baby again after Kelsey. Her mother once told her with obvious pain in her eyes that she had had three miscarriages when Kelsey was a little girl. Finally after Kelsey turned nine years old, they had stopped hoping to conceive again. They adored Kelsey, they had been blessed with her - more than they had truly realized at the time of her birth - and she would have to be enough.

A loud growl coming from her stomach forced Kelsey to realize she needed to stop working and go grab a bite to eat. She would write the other stories after her lunch break.

It was sixty degrees in New York at the end of November so Kelsey decided to take a walk in the park after buying a chicken salad sandwich at a local deli. She unwrapped the white paper from around her sandwich as she strolled along the path in the park, and ate. Orange leaves were crunching under her black ballet flats she had worn with her favorite gray flared dress pants. She wasn't wearing a coat but she had worn a long-sleeved white cowlneck sweater with a short light blue jean jacket over it.

Her sandwich was gone and Kelsey threw away the wrapper in a trash can along the path, and then she sipped a bottle of water. She felt full and uncomfortable in her clothes today. She was due to start her period on Friday and definitely was feeling bloated from it.

She checked the time on her cell phone and decided to walk back to the office and finish writing. She was excited about having some time off of work and she was looking forward to spending the holiday with Kyle. They were going to cook a complete Thanksgiving feast at her apartment. Kelsey smiled to herself and looked down at her diamond. They were planning a spring wedding. After the holidays, she had a wedding to plan. *And some weight to lose, too. Ugh. Time to get back to the gym Kelsey,* she thought feeling disgusted and uncomfortable.

Just as she stepped off the path and onto the street, Kelsey glanced at the runner coming toward her. Dressed fit to kill in black Athleta tights, an orange half-zip pullover, and brand new gray and orange Asics running shoes was Bree.

"Look at you!" Kelsey pulled Bree into a tight hug. The two of them briefly caught up, and then hugged again, wishing each other a Happy Thanksgiving. A couple of weeks ago, Kelsey had invited Bree to join her and Kyle for Thanksgiving, but she had already made plans to go back home to St. Louis - and Nicholas was going with her. His daughter was spending the holiday with her mother, and Nicholas had agreed to meet Bree's parents for the first time. Kelsey thought Nicholas was the real turkey this Thanksgiving but she hadn't said anything to dampen Bree's excitement. Nicholas' wife had served him with divorce papers on the first of November. She had found out about Bree and had given up on saving their marriage, and wanting to be a family with him and their daughter. Savannah was heartbroken not to have her parents together. Bree had told Kelsey she was a difficult child to warm up to. Kelsey warned her not to try to be her mother, and Bree had said she was happy to steer clear of playing the mommy role. She was nowhere near ready for that! And Kelsey had agreed with her. At twenty-eight years old, neither of the two women were ready for that responsibility.

Kelsey had just gotten settled into her apartment, after work, when Kyle called her. "Hey baby, I'm at the grocery store. I think I have everything we will need for our feast tomorrow. Is there anything extra you want to add before I check out and come over?" Kyle was going to stay at her place for the long weekend. Lately they hadn't seen much of each other and they both missed being together. They talked on the phone at least once daily but it was time for a break in their work schedules, and time to be together for a few days and nights. Their relationship needed that. They needed to reconnect.

"Make sure you pick up a few bottles of wine, I'm down to one," Kelsey said opening the refrigerator door to make sure she was right. Kyle knew she loved White Zinfandel and he preferred red wine so he started to make his way over to the liquor department while talking to her on his cell phone. "I'm really excited about us cooking, just for us, tomorrow. I always enjoy your parents on Thanksgiving, of course, and the food is delicious, but this is our first Thanksgiving as an engaged couple." Kelsey could see him smiling as she listened to him and that warmed her heart. "I'm excited too, sweetie. Now grab an extra bottle or two of wine and come see me."

"Be there soon. I love you…" Those words also warmed her heart. He was saying them more often to her since his accident and she welcomed that change in him.

***

Kyle had thought of everything. After making four trips, back and forth, from his vehicle he had all of the grocery bags on the kitchen table, and a brown leather duffel bag sitting on the living room floor that was packed full of clothes for him for the extended weekend. Kelsey helped him put all of the groceries away as she made a take-and-bake pizza in her oven. A little while later, Kyle poured two glasses of wine as Kelsey cut the pepperoni pizza. She also tossed a salad, which she had made while the pizza was baking.

They ate almost all of the pizza and each had three glasses of wine before stepping away from the kitchen table. Kyle was in the middle of telling her a detailed story about an all-night stake out he and Nicholas were on a few nights ago when Kelsey didn't know what came over her. She immediately ran out of the kitchen and down the short hallway to the bathroom. A second later, she was on her knees in front of the toilet, throwing up everything she had just eaten and drank.

Kyle had quickly followed her into the bathroom and he held her hair back. And after the third time of flushing the toilet, Kelsey sat against the wall in the bathroom and tried to take a deep breath. Kyle had given her a cold washcloth to put on her forehead.

"My God that was brutal. I honestly do not know what came over me. I felt fine all day! Maybe I ate too much pizza, or drank too much wine?" Kelsey always ate two or three pieces of pizza, she loved pizza, and tonight she had gone for a third slice. And three glasses of wine was hardly out of the ordinary, in one evening, for her. She had hoped she hadn't caught a virus. Not for the Thanksgiving holiday. Not after everything they had planned to cook and eat tomorrow.

"Just take it easy on the couch for awhile, hopefully it's nothing. I will clean up the kitchen," Kyle walked out of the bathroom and Kelsey stood up to look at herself in the mirror. She looked fine and she had actually felt fine again – strangely fine right after losing her dinner.

The rest of the evening was uneventful. Kelsey had not eaten anything else but she did have a cold glass of water before bed. She had just showered and brushed her teeth for the second time in a few hours. She always brushed her teeth after she threw up. When she walked out of the bathroom, she entered her bedroom wearing only a pair of lacey boyshorts from

Victoria's Secret and no bra, not even her usual bedtime tee. Her breasts were incredibly full and sore, and she didn't want anything on them. Not even the soft material of a t-shirt. She wondered if she would start her period earlier than Friday. She also wondered if throwing up earlier had anything to do with her hormones. Being active and a regular runner, Kelsey barely had periods, just a very light flow, since she reached her twenties. Bree was the same way and she had always joked about *Aunt Flo only keeping her down each month for two days max – and then she could have sex again.* Kelsey wasn't thinking about sex tonight, but she had hoped she and Kyle could be intimate this weekend, at some point, after her period came and went. Kyle was squeamish about blood, so Kelsey never suggested they make love during her period.

As Kelsey sat down on the bed and reached for the Carmex on her nightstand, she was smearing some on her lips when Kyle scooted over to her side of the bed. His hands were touching her breasts. "Jesus baby, those look big and luscious tonight." Kelsey giggled as she slid down under the burgundy-colored top sheet on her bed. "I think I have another day, for sure, before my period comes, but I know – Jesus is right – my boobs are huge, and they are so tender!"

"How tender?" Kyle asked her as he gently took one of her nipples into his mouth and explored it with his tongue while cupping the other full breast with his hand. "Not too tender for that, I suppose…" Kelsey said, giggling again, as Kyle licked the Carmex off her lips. Suddenly she was hoping having sex tonight would make her feel better. She wasn't queasy anymore. That feeling had come and gone so quickly. She just felt like she needed to work her muscles, *down there*.

It had been more than a week since she and Kyle had made love and they were both ready tonight. Their foreplay was unusual, for them. It was endless, and Kelsey was getting more turned on by the second. It was unlike Kyle not to rush sex. Tonight was different. It was good. When she knew he was about to enter her, while he was on top of her, she flipped him onto his back and sat on him. His eyes widened as she reached for him and slipped him up inside of her. She rocked back and forth on him until he was about to climax. She was sure she was about to also, but she couldn't risk it. She wanted more. She moved off of him and got onto her knees, slowing inching her lower body toward his mouth and then straddling over him. He put his mouth on her, *down there*, and with desire he pleasured her. She was holding onto the headboard in front of her, breathing hard, and moaning loudly when she came. Finally she came. With Kyle. He kissed her full on the mouth afterward and began thrusting inside of her, on top of her. She wasn't done with him yet. She pulled him out of her again and got onto her knees with her back to him. He plunged inside of her and couldn't bear it anymore. He came. Like he had never come before.

Still in bed, with their limbs intertwined, Kelsey was satisfied. She had been bolder than she had ever been in bed before – with Kyle. She had been in control. She had shown him what she wanted. *Be true.* Brady's words were ringing in her ears. She was happy, and she was being true.

"Baby, what has gotten into you? My God, that was the best sex we have ever had… Have you been holding out on me?" Kyle smiled at her and she giggled lying next to him.

"Oh that was just a sample of what I have planned for you for the rest of our lives, Kyle Newman," she kissed him and he jokingly rolled his eyes, and said, "I think that one will hold me over for a month." Kelsey laughed and she wondered if there was some truth to that. Kyle was not always in the mood. But tonight he had been - and it had worked out to *her* advantage.

***

Thanksgiving had been wonderful. They had the annual Macy's Thanksgiving Day parade on TV while they baked their turkey and prepared the side dishes. Kyle had made his grandmother's recipe for homemade dressing, and Kelsey prepared a green bean casserole and made gravy for the turkey and the dressing. That would be enough for the two of them. Neither one of them had liked pie, so Kyle had surprised Kelsey with a quart of her favorite vanilla custard from a shop located near Central Park for dessert. When they finished eating their feast, they agreed to save the vanilla custard for later. They were full, and Kelsey was feeling especially bloated.

***

By ten o'clock they had fallen asleep together in Kelsey's bed with the TV on. They wanted to stay awake through the entire "It's a Wonderful Life" movie, but George Bailey was wishing he had never been born as the two of them were sound asleep, holding hands.

The next morning, Kyle was headed to the gym when Kelsey left her apartment to do some Black Friday shopping. As expected, the traffic was crazy already at seven-thirty. While sitting in her Land Rover, in that traffic, Kelsey sent Kyle a text. *Wow. Thank you for last night. I love you. See you this afternoon.*

Kyle read her text and grinned to himself. She is an amazing woman and he was thinking about how blessed he is to have her in his life as he walked into the drugstore to get some more Advil - before going to the gym. He was eating those pills like candy. Those damn headaches were always there.

CHAPTER 15

The holiday weekend was over and Kelsey had a late interview on Monday morning so she was planning to go to the gym first. Kyle had already been at work for two hours, since his start time was six o'clock, and Kelsey was standing inside of her walk-in closet picking out some clothes to wear to the gym.

She had pushed the thought out of her mind all weekend. She hadn't allowed herself to think or to dwell on what had not happened yet. Her period was late. She had never been this late before. Four days. *Come on. She couldn't be. She just couldn't be.*

She had not told Kyle, or Bree, but she had thrown up three more times over the holiday break. Kelsey knew she needed to buy a pregnancy test. She knew her body was feeling different. What she didn't know is... *whose* baby she is carrying.

***

Kelsey skipped the gym and went to the drugstore. *First Response Pregnancy. Rapid Result. Over 99% accurate. Two lines if you're pregnant. One line if you're not pregnant.*

She was sitting on the closed toilet lid in her bathroom. She was back at her apartment. She had read the directions twice. It was time to take the test. This was it. She peed on the stick, and then she waited. She was still holding the stick in her hands when she saw one line appear, and then another. Two lines. *She was pregnant.*

"Oh my God!" Feeling panicked, she had said those words out

loud, alone in her apartment, and then she started to cry. She cried so hard she ended up throwing up her breakfast. She had made herself sick. *What is she going to do now? What if this isn't Kyle's baby? What if Brady is the father of her child?*

She remembered being careless and getting off schedule with her birth control pills while Kyle was in the hospital. She knew there were a few times when she would rush home to shower and change clothes and she would take her pill at a different time each day. Once, she doubled up and took two because she had completely forgotten to take one the day before. She was well aware that she had been careless. But like everything else, she had put it out of her mind. She had lost herself in Brady. She had been so caught up in him that she couldn't think straight. Nothing else mattered. She was well aware that her actions mattered *now*.

Kelsey immediately called Bree's direct line at her office, knowing that she would have her cell phone on vibrate and not be able to take her call if she was wrapped up in work. Bree answered after the second ring.

"This is Breann Jacobs."

"Bree, it's me. I need to see you!"

"Right now? What happened?"

"Please leave work. I'm at my apartment."

"I'll be right there." Bree hung up her phone, cancelling her morning appointments with her secretary as she sprinted out of the building.

Ten minutes later, Kelsey opened her apartment door to a look of sheer panic on Bree's face. She was wearing a black pencil skirt, black pointed-toe heels, and a teal button-down blouse that was snug fitting over her chest all the way down to her waist. The weather had turned colder, overnight, but Bree had left her coat in the car. She never liked to wear a coat while driving. She hated that bulky feeling.

"What is going on?" she asked as she walked in and closed the door quickly behind her. After taking one look at her, Kelsey started bawling. And in the midst of her sobbing she managed to get enough air to say the words, *I'm pregnant.*

Bree's expression said it all. Her eyes were wide and her mouth was open. She covered her hand over her mouth and said, "*Oh my God!*"

They ended up sitting down on the couch after Bree had held Kelsey in her arms for endless minutes as she cried, hard. "This is obviously a shock," Bree said as Kelsey blew her nose into a tissue and began to pull herself together, "but this also is sending panic through you because you know it's Brady's baby, don't you?"

There it was. The question only Bree could ask her because she knew everything that had happened. She was the only person Kelsey could confide in.

"No. I don't know that for sure! Could be though," Kelsey took a deep breath to keep herself from crying again, "I was with both of them the same weekend, two weeks ago." Kelsey was ashamed to say it, but it had happened. It was the weekend she had run to Brady and spent the entire Saturday night with him, in his bed. The next day, she found out about the thiopental drug, left Brady, and ended up getting engaged to Kyle – and also having sex with him.

"Shut the fuck up…" Bree actually giggled, but Kelsey wasn't amused, "You? I never thought you had it in you, kid."

"Stop it. You know what happened that weekend. One minute I was moving on with Brady and the next I found out he lied to me so I left him. Then, I turned around and Kyle was proposing to me and wanting sex so badly after being comatose for a month." Bree was still giggling and Kelsey slapped her on the leg. "A little sympathy here please? You're supposed to be my sister!"

"Sympathy? I envy you sister… all that great sex turns me on just hearing about it," Bree was smiling at her friend and sister. She knew there was a difficult road ahead for her - and she would be there, right by her side, through all of it. No matter what. No matter who fathered her baby.

"Kelsey… you need to be realistic. You were with Brady a lot more than you were with Kyle."

"But, we're talking about just a couple weeks ago when I was obviously ovulating. I just keep thinking that Kyle hadn't ejaculated in well over a month when we got together and just think of all those spermies that shot out at once." Bree laughed so hard she could have peed herself, and Kelsey joined her. When they caught their breaths, Kelsey said with the serious tone back in her voice, "This just has to be Kyle's baby."

CHAPTER 16

Five days had passed and Kelsey had not been able to tell Kyle that she is pregnant. Not yet. Bree called her multiple times a day to see how she's feeling - and to offer her support as only Bree could.

Kelsey had scheduled an appointment with her gynecologist, Dr. Bevan. Kelsey had been seeing her annually since she moved to New York. Dr. Bevan's reputation and practice had grown rapidly in the past six years. She is now the lead gynecologist at Laneview Hospital. Her office is located on the hospital grounds, but not inside of the hospital. Dr. Bevan and her staff did deliver their patient's babies at Laneview Hospital.

Kelsey planned to tell Kyle about the baby this weekend - and she was hoping he would go with her to the appointment on Monday morning. Kelsey wanted to take good care of the baby growing inside of her. She is responsible for a life now and beginning to feel some excitement about this new adventure, and she had told Bree that this baby meant everything to her. *This baby is hers.*

***

It was late on Friday night when Kyle walked into Kelsey's apartment and found her asleep on the couch. He had just come from working overtime on a case. She was wrapped up in a fleece blanket, only wearing boyshorts and a sports bra underneath. Kyle always laughed at her for wearing very little and then complaining of being cold while under a blanket. The only light in the room was coming from the four-foot Christmas tree sitting on a table in the corner. She hadn't heard Kyle come in and he smiled when he saw her sleeping there. He sat down on the couch in front of her and wrapped his arms around her, kissing her softly on the forehead. She stirred, stretched a little and smiled up at him.

"Oh hey, I must have dozed off," Kelsey remembered settling down in the living room and wanting a glass of wine. She loved drinking a glass, or two, in the evenings and especially on the weekends. That habit would have to change now, for the next nine months.

"It's okay. I'm tired, too." *And this damn headache won't go away today.* "I'm just going to grab a bowl of cereal or something in the kitchen and then we can go to bed, if you want to wait for me."

Kelsey sat up straight on the couch. "No wait, I need you to sit back down here with me," she patted the cream-colored, suede couch cushion next to her, "we need to talk." Kyle sat down as she had asked, and Kelsey scooted closer to him and took his hand in hers. "Is everything okay, Kel?" Kyle knew she hadn't been feeling well off and on since Thanksgiving, and he was concerned about her – but she had been working and going to the gym so he had not been too worried. Until now.

"I have a doctor's appointment on Monday and I was wondering if you would like to go along with me."

"Um, yeah, sure if you need me there. Please tell me what's going on." Life was too fragile now. After the accident, Kyle wanted to seize every day. He hadn't wasted a moment asking the woman he loved to marry him and, now, suddenly, he wasn't afraid of losing his life – he was afraid of losing Kelsey.

"I've been feeling pretty yucky lately and that isn't going to change for awhile. I missed my period, Kyle… I'm pregnant," Kelsey never took her eyes off of him. The color didn't drain from his face as she had expected. He didn't even look disappointed that life had just happened. Before they were married. Before they were *ready*.

"You're pregnant? Seriously? A baby? Our baby! Oh my God, Kel, that is so amazing!" He was thrilled and she was shocked.

"Really? I mean, yes, it is amazing… but you're happy about this? We didn't plan–"

"It doesn't matter what we planned on, this is such a huge gift, and I wanna marry your ass now so we can bring our child into this world and be a real family." Kyle's parents divorced when he was ten years old and she knew he had been dreaming about being a part of a real family again, ever since.

There were no holidays celebrated with his family, ever. Only one time had she met his father and his young girlfriend, at the time, over a weekend visit to Pennsylvania where Kyle grew up. The weekend was a disaster. Kyle's father was an alcoholic. His fifty-two-year-old mother has Alzheimer's disease, lives in a nursing home, and Kyle doesn't visit her. Kelsey stopped urging him to after they began seriously dating and he had confessed to her how his mother not recognizing him was just too much for him to handle. He loved his mother as she took the best care of him possible after the divorce. It just wasn't enough. He had always been unhappy. When his older sister, and only sibling, died from a drug overdose at sixteen years old, his mother withdrew herself from the world. Kyle was fourteen years old then and counted the days until he would graduate high school and move away. He took the necessary college courses and joined the police academy. His goal was to become a detective, just as he had. He was grateful for the success he attained in his career and he had worked hard for it. For awhile, it was all he had. And then he met Kelsey.

He wanted so much more for his children than he had growing up, a happy home life was most important.

"You are an amazing man, Kyle Newman. Thank you for not flipping out about the timing, the shock of this. This baby and I are so lucky to have you!" Kelsey was crying, crying for everything she had done to get to this point. Now she would just pray endlessly to be giving him *his* baby in nine months."

The entire weekend was bliss. Kelsey couldn't stop smiling. Kyle had never left her side. He was like a little kid waiting for Christmas. The baby was all he had talked about and made plans for. He even wanted to go shopping for it. Kelsey reminded him that she had not even seen her doctor. Even though the home pregnancy test confirmed she was ninety-nine percent surely pregnant, they still had to take this one day at a time.

Kyle had taken the morning off of work, as did Kelsey, and they were fifteen minutes early for her doctor's appointment. Kelsey was quiet and feeling nervous – and Kyle was the complete opposite. He was chatty and excited. She had never seen him like this before, ever. He was always the quiet one – and totally reserved compared to her.

He didn't have a preference if it was a boy or girl. He wasn't going to be the kind of dad who pushed his kids to play sports. He would be happy, so happy, with an artist, or a dancer, or a writer, whatever she wanted to be.

"Kyle, did you just say *she*?"

"Did I? Well I didn't mean to. I was just saying my kid can be whatever makes him or her happy. I just want this baby to feel loved." He wasn't teary but his face had fallen a bit from expressing excitement. Kelsey took his hand.

"I know. I want all of the same for this baby. We will give her that."

"Hey you just said *her* too!"

"I know I did," and between them they shared a smile - and both secretly wished this baby is a girl.

***

Dr. Bevan was as pleasant and professional as Kelsey always enjoyed her being. A tall, slender, very plain woman who never wore much makeup and always donned flat shoes and solid colors under her white lab coat. She had a sweet smile, a soft voice, and an intuition for women and their bodies that Kelsey believed was genius. Dr. Bevan, who also was a surgeon, strived to fix any and all female problems in every woman she called a patient.

From the date of her last period, Dr. Bevan had calculated and informed Kelsey that she is five weeks pregnant, and the baby will be due on the fifteenth of August. Kelsey looked at a smiling Kyle. He was just beaming as they listened to the doctor speak about prenatal vitamins, the importance of eating healthy and exercising to prevent too much weight gain during the pregnancy. Kelsey was five weeks along. Five weeks ago put her back to the exact weekend when she was with Brady on Saturday - and Kyle on Sunday. This was Kyle's baby. Their baby. They will be married. They will be parents. Together. The Newmans will be a real family. That was Kyle's dream and Kelsey was going to give him that.

And then the doctor asked them if they wanted to hear the baby's heartbeat. She asked Kelsey to lie back on the exam table and lift up her shirt and undo the button and zipper on her jeans. Her jeans that would soon be too snug to wear.

The machine was hand held by Dr. Bevan and when the wand attached to it was placed on her lower abdomen, it echoed the sound of a strong beating heart. *Tha Thump, Tha Thump, Tha Thump, Tha Thump.*

Kyle had tears in his eyes as he got close with his elbows resting on the exam table right next to Kelsey's belly and almost on top of the small gadget that was allowing them to hear the beating heart of the life inside of her. Suddenly this baby was more real to them, both of them, than before. They were bonded, forever, by her. Or him.

CHAPTER 17

Christmas was extra special this year. Kyle and Kelsey were engaged and they had gone home to St. Louis to spend two weeks with Kelsey's parents for both the Christmas and New Year's holidays. A few things had made it a memorable season for them - their engagement, sharing the news of their baby on the way, and their wedding.

Kyle and Kelsey were married in the Cathedral Basilica of Saint Louis on New Year's Day. Bree and Nicholas stood up for them as Kelsey's maid of honor and Kyle's best man. The two of them were also in St. Louis, spending the holidays with Bree's parents. The girls had grown up together in Missouri and, for them, it was good to be home. They had many reasons to celebrate.

Kelsey and Kyle were happy, and just beginning their future together. And Bree and Nicholas were simply enjoying each other. Nicholas had spent the weekend before Christmas with his daughter and Bree was thrilled when he wanted to spend the holidays, at home, with her. He wasn't a perfect man, not even in Bree's eyes, but he was perfect for her. And she didn't want to give him up. Watching her best friend get married had affected Bree. One day she hoped to walk down the aisle, too. God willing, one day soon.

Kelsey wore a sleeveless, white satin long dress with a plunging neckline. She had her hair in an up-do and she looked amazing to her parents, her best friend, and to Kyle. Her seventy-five-year-old maternal grandmother was there and her parents had wanted to invite a few friends. The ceremony was intimate and a small reception was held at her parents' house following the Mass. Kelsey had told everyone she was pregnant, but not even the smallest sign of a growing belly showed in her wedding gown. She didn't have a pooch yet, but she was looking forward to when she would. The only change in her body still was her full boobs and Bree had commented on those to her and they both giggled. Bree had had some work done, silicone implants when she was twenty-one, and Kelsey always teased her about it. Kelsey had no enhancements done to her body and she was blessed with a beautiful figure. Both women were beautiful, inside and out, and felt so blessed to have found each other.

Bree and Kelsey had been talking even more often in the last month as Kelsey was going through so many changes in her life. Getting married. Having a baby. This wasn't a typical woman looking forward to and planning a future. This was Kelsey dealing with the possibility of carrying another man's baby – and carrying that secret.

Kelsey had dreamed about Brady the night before the wedding and she called Bree to talk to her about it the next morning. *Maybe that dream was just your heart's way of saying goodbye to him?* Once again, Bree had known the right words to say, to offer comfort. The dream wasn't anything too vivid. Brady was in the distance, it had looked like he was running outside, and running away from Kelsey. She had watched him until she could no longer see him. She never called out his name in that dream. She just watched him run further and further away. From her.

Bree respected Kelsey's decision to marry Kyle and she initially told her if this baby wasn't Kyle's, everyone had a right to know the truth - Brady included. Kelsey had convinced herself that this baby is Kyle's and after seeing the way he is so wrapped up in this unborn baby, Bree inevitably agreed that maybe, just maybe, this baby would *have to be* Kyle's. If Kelsey wanted to spend the rest of her life with him, and not with Brady, the truth would only complicate everything. So Bree of course would keep her friend's secret. Forever.

***

Six months had passed quickly. Kelsey was looking full-blown pregnant. She had three months to go and she had already started to slow down, especially at work. She had gained twenty pounds, but she carried the baby entirely in the front. Her hips and butt remained unchanged. It was her breasts and her belly that were both huge. She was a happy, pregnant woman looking forward to the birth of her first baby. She had been sick, throwing up, throughout the entire first trimester. Now she just didn't have a lot of energy - especially not to chase down every story at work.

Her editor, a man who was six years older than she, had an eight-month-old baby girl at home and so he understood and sympathized with everything Kelsey was feeling. He had just gone through it all with his wife. His name was Todd and he and his wife had chosen to name their daughter Sydney. They had opted to find out the sex of their baby and plan ahead for *her* arrival. Kelsey and Kyle had both agreed on wanting to wait - and be surprised. Still, they both talked about the baby being a girl.

Kelsey left work early today, she had filed six stories in the last two days and she needed a break. She told her boss, who was editing today's paper before print, and he had been fine with her leaving for the day. Her work was always done on time – and she had always dotted every 'i' and crossed every 't.' She was a thorough reporter and an even more gifted writer. No question was ever left unanswered and she had compassion for the people she interviewed. They sensed how genuine she was and always opened up to her, giving her great quotes for her well-written stories that often tugged at the reader's heart strings. Kelsey loved feature stories. She could handle the hard news, but she didn't particularly like it.

Before going home, she pulled into the parking lot at the grocery store. She was hungry, as she always was during this pregnancy, and she wanted to go home and cook. She was craving tacos and had decided to pick up the ingredients for a Mexican dinner.

It was a warm March day, sixty-nine degrees, and Kelsey was wearing black leggings, black ballet flats, and a tight-fitting peach maternity sweater. She loved showing off her belly. Pregnant women who hid behind big clothes and shapeless dresses looked ridiculous, she had thought. Kelsey had taken off her sunglasses, gotten out of her jeep, and then turned back around to bend down inside of it again to reach for her cell phone on the passenger seat – and that's when, through her windshield, she saw him. Brady Walker was parking his black BMW nose to nose with her black Land Rover.

She froze, said *shit* out loud, and was leaning down further and deeper into her jeep, and for a moment she didn't know what she would do. Get out and start walking quickly into the store? Get back into the jeep and leave? It was too late to do either of those things. He saw her, too.

He had looked up as he parked his car, just making sure he wasn't too close to the vehicle already parked in front of him. He saw that the driver was getting out. He saw the black Land Rover and his heart jumped into his throat. He had seen similar vehicles before, same model, same make, but it was never her. This time it was. Through her windshield, he saw her hair was down, curled today, reaching onto her shoulders. How he missed that face. And her.

Brady stopped thinking and quickly turned off his car, got out, closed the door, and walked over to her, not once taking his eyes off of her. She backed out of her jeep and turned to him. She could feel her face flush. She had kept the door open between them like if it would somehow block her belly and he wouldn't see her in this condition. *Pregnant.*

"Hi… my God… it's been awhile," he looked at her with those eyes. Those very same eyes that she had fallen so quickly in love with - at first sight. He looked at her face and it seemed fuller. And then he saw her. All of her. As his eyes moved down her body, she knew she would have to answer a few questions. One, in particular, *Is this baby mine?*

"Hello Brady… I'm surprised to run into you here."

"Not as surprised as I am… you're pregnant. Wow. You look good. How far along are you?" Brady's heart was pounding. He knew it had been six months since they were together. *This could be his baby. No. She would have told him if she was carrying his child. She would never hide the truth from him like that. After all, it was his lie that she couldn't handle. His lie that forced her out of his life. Forever. It had already felt like forever to him. And it had only been six months.*

"Six months," Kelsey answered, biting her bottom lip. She could do this. She could stand here on this beautiful day and breathe the fresh air in and out until this moment was over.

"Yeah? So life goes on. You're married now?" Yes she was married now. Brady had discovered that during the Christmas holiday when he drummed up an excuse to run an ad for the hospital so he went to the newspaper office, hoping to run into Kelsey. Instead, the secretary at the front desk had told him she was on a trip for the holidays, and getting married on New Year's Day. He had asked about her as the reporter, not as the woman he loved. He tried to hide his disappointment as he walked out of that office just a few days before Christmas.

"Yes. Kyle and I got married over the holidays. We wanted to – before the baby came and before I had to waddle down the aisle," Kelsey laughed and rubbed her belly in a circular motion. Brady thought she looked so beautiful pregnant. She was glowing and still so sexy.

"You look amazing, babe. I'm happy for you, and I wish you and Kyle all the best. You know that."

"Thank you. I mean it, thank you, Brady. This moment could really have been awkward but you're making it easy." *Once again. So easy. Everything with him was always comfortable, and so alluring.*

"You're welcome," he said as he rubbed her arm, "I need to know, Kelsey. I need to know if this baby you're carrying is mine. I think we both know there is a chance. Six months ago we were together, and we never once used any protection. I thought you were on the pill." She allowed him to keep his hand on her arm. He was still rubbing it, softly, as if he was comforting her into telling him the truth – about the baby.

"I was on the pill – but I was careless and I got off track, missing a few days. I know when this baby was conceived. It was the night Kyle and I got engaged. I'm sorry Brady." She was lying, hoping it was true, but lying, nonetheless, to Brady.

And he was crushed inside. *He wanted that connection with her. He wanted her to be the mother of his child. But she wasn't and this baby was another man's. Kelsey would never lie to him about something so important. He was certain of that.* "I see, well okay, there's no need to be sorry. I respect your decision to be with Kyle. You're married and about to start a family. What an incredible time in your life. Seeing you happy like this, makes my day. And to be honest Kelsey, I needed this. I need the awakening of seeing how you've moved on."

Kelsey moved closer to him and they came together in a hug. He held her as close as he could, given her protruding belly in the way, and she inhaled his smell. He was in a pair of old jeans and a YALE t-shirt, and still, he smelled so good. The feel of his scruffy face against her cheek as she pulled out of his embrace sent tingles throughout her body. It was unbelievable how he still made her feel. She hadn't had sex in weeks, or even thought about being turned on. But in the parking lot at the grocery store, one man, from her not so distant past, had made her feel alive again in all the right places.

"You always have the right words, Brady Walker. Now it's my turn to tell you, to be happy. You deserve it. There's a lucky woman out there. Hurry and find her," Kelsey was jealous of her own words. There was a time when she wanted to be that woman and thought she would be. Brady smiled at her, showing that dimple on his left cheek, "I promise to keep my eyes open… but there's only so much room left in my heart. It's your fault, you know, you're hogging space in there." The two of them laughed together and then Brady walked away. *"Take care, babe."*

"I will. You too!" Kelsey waited a few minutes, just sitting in her jeep, with the door wide open. He was inside the store now, and she wanted to give him a head start with his shopping. She didn't want to chance running into him again. After another few minutes had passed, she couldn't do it. She couldn't go in. Her craving for tacos would have to wait. She closed her door, turned the key in the ignition, and drove away.

CHAPTER 18

Two weeks before her due date, Kelsey had insisted she and Kyle take a walk in Central Park. It was a sunny Sunday afternoon, eighty-five degrees and not too hot, for June, to be outside. They walked slowly together and talked about how soon the baby would be here.

"I don't know about you Kel, but I think we need to have her name ready to go for when she pops out," Kyle's excitement was contagious and Kelsey smiled at him. They had not been able to agree on a name for a girl. They had one boy's name that would work, but neither of them thought they would need it in two weeks. They were both still so set on having a baby girl. "I told you, I don't really like Tammy. Sounds like the name of an old girlfriend of yours or something. I know I've heard it from you before. Maybe you mistakenly called me *Tam* in bed one night and I was turned off forever?" Kelsey was laughing at Kyle, shaking his head at her. "First of all, I never had a girlfriend named Tammy - and second, you never get turned off in bed," he was speaking more about the pre-pregnant Kelsey than the uncomfortable woman with the large belly and bloated boobs that he married six months ago. She laughed at him and blushed a little as they came upon a bench, and sat down to rest. Kelsey had lifted her feet onto Kyle's lap. She was terribly uncomfortable all sprawled out on the hard bench.

"I think we should name her after she arrives. I just want to see her first," Kelsey was serious. She had liked Abigail, Angie, Megan, and Jennifer. Any one of those names would work - and Kyle had liked all of them - but she wanted to see their baby girl first. Or if it was a boy, they would be shocked and then they would name him Miles. The two of them had agreed on the name Miles because when they first met, they were each running separately on the very same trail they were walking on today. Kyle had seen her first and he watched her finish her run, sit down on the ground off to the side, and open a bottle of water she had carried with her. She was sweaty and just a hot mess, he remembered her saying afterward when they were talking, but to him – she looked beautiful. Kyle had stopped running when she did, and he had purposely stayed behind her. He didn't want to pass her and never see her again. He wanted to keep her pace, and meet her. He didn't have a pick-up line. He had just smiled, said *hi*, plopped down on the ground beside her, and asked her how many miles she had ran. *Miles*. Maybe this baby would be a boy and they would be able to use that special name. For him.

"There's somewhere I wanna take you today," Kyle said helping her up off of the bench.

"Where? I just need to go home now and lay on the couch."

"Oh I'll take you home, but first there is something I want you to see."

***

They drove out of the city, away from the hustle and bustle of it all, and Kyle eventually brought them to a gated subdivision in Greenville, New York. From his open car window, he punched in a code at the closed wrought-iron gate which opened and allowed them in.

"Where are you taking me? I really don't feel up to visiting one of your work friends and their family today," Kelsey had never been to a subdivision like this one. It was beautiful, and both ritzy and homey. She was looking at the immaculate lawns and gigantic all-brick homes. One after another. Big yards, flowers, perfect landscaping, fences, and swimming pools. She suddenly wanted to see inside one of those dream homes. Just to see what it was like to spread out your things, room to room, instead of cramming everything she owned into a two-bedroom apartment. Even her bicycle was stored in the spare bedroom of her apartment. And the space she used to have free, her husband had filled when he moved in. Kelsey's thoughts were interrupted when Kyle pulled onto a driveway of a home at the end of a cul-de-sac. It had a four-foot black wrought-iron fence all around the backyard. It was a two-story, tricolor white and gray and black brick - and it was breathtaking. A house, someone's home, had taken Kelsey's breath away.

"Okay let's go in," Kyle helped Kelsey out of the car and before she could ask who lived there he was already ahead of her and digging into the front pocket of his jeans for a single key. He unlocked the front door as Kelsey caught up to him - and he held that door open for her as she stepped up one step and peeked inside.

"Welcome home."

"What...?" Kelsey looked at Kyle's face. Beaming. Again. Tears immediately sprang into her eyes and it wasn't because she was twice as emotional now from hormones - it was because she had just walked into their home. "You bought this for us?"

"I did... don't you love it?"

"Oh yes I do love it!" Kelsey walked into the living room, stepping carefully onto the oak wood floor. It smelled new and looked so clean and she was hesitant to be wearing her Asics tennis shoes on it. "I love you so much, Kyle. And our baby." He held her and kissed her, standing in the middle of their new home. The Newmans would live there. She could not wait to see the rest of the house and when she asked him to show it to her, every room, she took one step and suddenly she was standing in water. A pool of water at her feet on the immaculately polished wood floor.

"My water broke!" Kelsey was looking at her wide-eyed husband when he swooped her up into his arms with a loud grunt and got her out of *their house* and into their car. They had to get to the hospital. *Laneview Hospital.*

Before she allowed him to leave the driveway, she made him go back inside with a roll of paper towels from the trunk of their car to soak up the mess on the floor. This was her house now – and she didn't want a warped wood floor when she moved in with her family. Kyle had laughed at her and hurried to clean up the puddle before she had that baby on the driveway in a quiet subdivision.

Kyle had driven to the hospital as cautious as ever. A few times Kelsey could have screamed at him to *speed the hell up, she was having a baby for chrissake,* but she knew he was just keeping his family safe. They had gotten to Laneview Hospital within twenty-five minutes and the pain from the contractions was beginning to escalate. Kelsey had paged Dr. Bevan from her cell phone in the car and she was ready and waiting after the staff in the emergency room had put Kelsey into a wheelchair at the entrance and quickly rushed her to the maternity ward. Dr.

Bevan examined her and told her she had already dilated to a six and it was too late for an epidural. The pain she was feeling now was nothing compared to what she was about to experience. Kelsey was ready though. With Kyle by her side, coaching her through it, and holding her clammy hand in his, she would bring this baby into the world. *Their* world.

And exactly one half hour and one last excruciating push later, Kelsey's baby was born. Seven pounds, thirteen ounces, twenty inches long.

It's a girl! Dr. Bevan asked Kyle if he wanted to cut the umbilical cord and, through his tears, he did. Kelsey was crying, too, as she stared at the beautiful life, so warm in her arms. Wrapped in a soft pink blanket, this baby girl settled down from crying in her mommy's arms… and she opened her eyes. My God. Those eyes. *Those bright crystal blue eyes.*

Kelsey now knew what it felt like to wear her heart outside of her body. She loved and would do absolutely anything to protect her baby girl. And she knew that Kyle would, too. He was holding her now and softly kissing her cheek and her forehead.

"She's beautiful Kel, so beautiful. We both knew our baby was a girl!"

"Yes we did. I'm thinking it's time to name her…"

"Of course! Now that you've seen her, what's it going to be?"

"She's a Bailey."

"Bailey? Yes, I like that, but that name hasn't come up before."

That name had, in fact, come up before. Kelsey would never forget the first time she had heard the name, Bailey. She was *his* mother. Brady's mother. The mother who had meant the world to him – before he lost her. Cancer had taken his mother from him and shattered his little heart. He still loved his mother as much to this very day, as a man.

When he told Kelsey what her name had been, she felt something. She not only loved the sound of the name, but she had felt compelled to use it, one day. And especially now.

Part Two

15 years later

CHAPTER 19

At the age of fifteen, Bailey Newman is one of those girls - blessed with the complete package. She is smart, athletic, kind, compassionate and beautiful. She has her mother's dark hair, creamy skin tone, and tall and toned figure. Kyle and Kelsey have raised a wonderful, good girl and they are both over the moon with pride.

When Bailey was nine years old, her little brother Miles was born. And from the first moment she saw him, Bailey has mothered him. She is his big sister, his protector, and always will be. That little boy is a carbon copy of Kyle. He has his father's sandy blonde hair and round, sweet face. He even has the exact same walk as Kyle. Kyle, Kelsey and Bailey adore that little boy - and he knows it.

The Newmans are a happy family, living in Greenville, New York, in a beautiful home. Kyle's career as a detective for the NYPD has led him to a few promotions in the last several years and he is now a forensic investigator - creating sketches of crime scenes, collecting evidence, and formulating a hypothesis about the crime. Kelsey had accepted the editor's position at the newspaper when Bailey was five years old. Her former editor and friend had been promoted to publisher and had convinced Kelsey to make the change and become the editor. That job required her to report and write less, but after having a child, and later two, she appreciated the desk job and more stable hours. She often edited her staff's stories and formatted the newspaper on her laptop from home.

She loved being a career woman and didn't want to give that up after she became a mom. She could juggle both her job and motherhood, but she never could have done it without Kyle being an incredibly involved father. When he is not working, he is with his children. Bailey adores him and is very much a daddy's girl, and Miles sees his daddy as his best friend in the world. He wants to be just like him now - and when he grows up.

Kelsey's life is complete. Their years together have not been without struggles and pain. She was not sailing through life unscathed. In the last eleven years, both of her parents had died. She lost her father first to a heart attack when Bailey was four and half years old, and then her mother died last year of lymphoma. Both of her parents had only been in their sixties. It was heartbreaking. Life was too short, Kelsey knew that all too well now - and she thanked God each day for what she has.

***

Kyle was calling for her at the bottom of the stairs in the living room. She was squeezing into her skinny jeans after putting on a navy blue NYPD t-shirt - one that belonged to her dad but she liked to wear it. She made one last check in the full-length mirror hanging on the back of her bedroom door before grabbing her Ugg boots, leaving her bedroom, and descending the stairs.

"Sorry dad, I couldn't decide what to wear."

"So you just raided my closet again, I see," Kyle was smiling at her. He loved that girl. *His* girl. She had been wearing his POLICE tees for a few months now. Kelsey had complained about it because she had bought a lot of school clothes for Bailey which continued to remain unworn in her closet. Bailey had thought the tees were cool - and when you're fifteen, in your first year of high school, you have to be cool. Another reason why she had liked her dad's tees was because they were his, the police investigator that she was so proud of and loved so much. Everyone at school, all of her friends, knew her dad was in law enforcement. The guys thought it was exciting and dangerous, and the girls thought of him as the good guy who catches the bad guys. Bailey was never embarrassed to have her parents around. Her friends secretly envied her for that. She was a teenager, she was supposed to rebel and hate her parents. Or at least pretend to. Bailey was different. She was the girl everyone wanted to be at Bond High School in Greenville, New York.

Kyle drove Miles to his grade school first. Bailey was sitting in the front seat of her dad's 4 Runner jeep and Miles was sitting buckled up in the middle of the backseat, so he could see both his dad and his sister. He was always talking about something - or nothing at all, like most six year olds. Kyle and Bailey were laughing at him, glancing at each other off and on as their jeep moved through the morning traffic.

He loved bringing the kids to school every morning. His work hours were more flexible than Kelsey's and she relished the idea of being able to pick up the kids after school - after being done working for the day. With the exception of a few deadlines, which forced her to bring work home in the evenings, Kelsey always dedicated her time to her kids. She and Kyle never missed a sporting event or music program or drop-offs and pick-ups at friends' houses. They didn't just make a great team, they were a family in every sense of the word.

Kyle pulled into the circle drive in front of the grade school, shifted his jeep into park, unbuckled his seatbelt, and got out of the car to open Miles' door and say goodbye for the day. Miles scooted across the backseat and slid out of the car. His feet landed on the concrete and both of his shoes were untied. He had his backpack slung over his right shoulder and his left hand wrapped around the handle of his lunchbox. "Whoa buddy, hold on. We need to tie those shoes before you trip and fall," Kyle squatted down on the ground in front of his son to tie his shoes. He was smiling up at him as he double knotted the laces on both of his NIKES and picked him up for a hug. Cars were lining up behind them and some were driving ahead. They were in the drop-off lane where cars were not to park for more than a few minutes, just long enough for the students to get out and walk up to the school.

Kyle was holding things up, but today he didn't care. He wanted this moment with his son. He held him close and kissed the top of his head as he placed him back onto his feet, on the ground. "I love you Miles, don't ever forget that."

Bailey was watching her dad and her brother with a warm smile on her face. She heard those words often from her father. *Don't ever forget that.* When she was a child, those were just words followed by her father's *I love yous.* As she got older, she realized her father needed to say that because he went to work each day in what could sometimes be a dangerous profession. Law enforcement officers were killed in the line of duty. She just never really thought about it. Her dad is her hero and he would always come back at the end of the day.

"I love you too, daddy," Miles said before running up the sidewalk leading to the school. Then, he stopped and turned around, and Kyle immediately rolled his window down before driving off. "Don't ever forget that!" The little boy yelled those words as loud as he could and Kyle laughed out loud and gave him a smile and a big wave, with his whole arm out of the window, before pulling away.

The next stop was Bond High School, but Bailey had other plans for the day. "Dad, I want you to drive me to mom's work. I didn't want to say anything about it in front of Miles but I don't want to go to school today, I want to put my time in for an assignment that we have coming up due in two weeks. We are supposed to spend a day with a parent at work. I've already talked to mom about doing this sometime soon but now I want to go today." Kyle knew about the assignment and remembered the conversation he and Kelsey recently shared one night after the kids were in bed. His feelings had been a little hurt that Bailey had not been interested in his line of work. Not that he wanted her to be a police officer, it was too dangerous, but he had thought she perceived it as cool - considering her interest in wearing his POLICE t-shirts. Kelsey had reassured him it was best if she hung out at the newspaper office or tagged along for a story interview. Their fifteen-year-old daughter didn't need to be present at any crime scenes. They both agreed because Kyle often saw the end result of some crazy crimes.

"Does your mom know about this?"

"No but she will be fine with it, please dad?" Kyle glanced over at his daughter and smiled as he made the turn onto the exit ramp. He was bringing her downtown New York City to her mom's office. His attempt to call Kelsey with a warning failed when he heard her voicemail, so he told his daughter she was on her own if her mother was upset.

Bailey started to get out of the car after Kyle temporarily parked in front of the newspaper building. She turned back to her dad as he made a fist and wanted her to bump her hand with his and give him what the kids were now calling *knuckles*. "Have a good day, baby girl. May this assignment be what you had hoped it would be, and may your mom be okay with me dropping you off here." Bailey laughed at him and returned his knuckles right before she threw her arms around his neck and gave him a squeeze. She also kissed him quick on the cheek as he beamed. "I love you, Bailey…" Kyle said to her and then she helped him finish his sentence, "Don't ever forget that!" They laughed together as Bailey got out of the car and shut the door.

Kelsey was walking away from the fax machine when the elevator doors opened and Bailey stepped right in her path. "Bailey? What are you doing here?" Kelsey was startled, fearing something had happened. She had absolutely no idea how her teenage daughter, without a driver's license, had made it to downtown New York City when she should be in school. Bailey was almost as tall as her mother, but Kelsey had towered her today standing next to her in two-inch heels with a gray and black tweed skirt.

"On the way to school I asked dad to bring me here so I can complete my assignment for school, you know spend the day at work with a parent. I wanna be here with you today."

"Geez Bay, we could have planned ahead for this a little bit better. I suppose your dad called the school to let them know what you're up to?"

"Yes and he tried to call you too, but–"

"I was probably in the middle of a phone interview. This isn't going to be the most exciting day for you to hang out here, Bailey. I'm writing one story, editing my staff's stories, and then laying out the paper - which you've already seen me do a thousand times at home." By now, the two of them had turned the corner and went into Kelsey's private office. Bailey threw her backpack on an empty chair alongside the wall and then plopped down in her mom's cushioned swivel chair behind her desk.

"It's okay mom, you don't have to entertain me. I will just hang out and write some notes for my report later," Bailey could not have been more uninterested in what her mother does for a living. And Kelsey knew that.

"So now you're wishing you would have followed your dad to a bloody crime scene?" Kelsey sat down on the edge of her desk in front of Bailey. She knew the sight of blood would not bother her daughter. She remembered when Miles was four years old and fell off the top step of the ladder leading up to the steepest slide at the park. He had hit his chin on the old steel steps during the fall and busted it open. Bailey had gotten to him first and had already taken off her jacket and wadded up the sleeve to apply pressure on the open wound where blood was gushing out of her brother's chin. When Kelsey heard her son screaming and approached the back of the slide, she and another mother whom she had been talking to at the time were panicked and amazed at the very same time. Her thirteen-year-old daughter was in complete control of the emergency situation. The bleeding was temporarily taken care of and she also had managed to calm Miles.

"I know dad wants to spare me from seeing what he sees almost every day so I didn't bother to go there." Kelsey was eye level with her daughter. Her beautiful daughter who was growing into a woman. Kelsey could see so much of herself in her daughter. Everyone commented on how much the two of them looked alike. Kelsey had blue eyes as well, but not the same blue that Bailey had. Bailey had those bright crystal blue eyes that made people wonder if she wore colored contacts.

From the day she was born, Kyle thought his daughter couldn't be any prettier and he always said as much to Kelsey. A conversation about their daughter's eyes had never come up. Kelsey only smiled when other people made comments about her daughter's captivating blue eyes. The only person she had ever talked to about it was Bree.

It was the day after Kyle and Kelsey had brought their baby home from the hospital. They were still living in Kelsey's downtown apartment then, with plans to move into their new home in Greenville. Kyle had gone to the store to buy some formula after Kelsey's milk hadn't come in soon enough for her to nurse the baby. Bree was sitting on the couch, holding the baby. She had been sleeping all the while Bree was cooing over her best friend's baby girl. A short time later, still in Bree's arms, the baby stretched and opened her eyes. Her eyes caught Bree's attention immediately. She had been in the middle of a sentence talking about the smell of a baby and how she too was getting the fever, to have her own. She had stopped talking and stared down at the baby, and then over at Kelsey who was seated next to her. Kelsey was silent, waiting for the words she already knew Bree wouldn't hesitate to say.

"I've only seen these eyes once in my life, Kel. She has *his* eyes."

Bree was thinking *no need for any fucking DNA tests now,* when Kelsey spoke, in no uncertain terms."Yes. I know. I didn't want to know, but God yes I know. I do not ever want to have this conversation with you again, Bree. She is Kyle's baby. *He* is *her* father - and he always will be."

"Whatever you want for her is what she will have, Kel. You are her mother and I know, with Kyle, the two of you are going to make wonderful parents. The three of you are a family now. What happened with Brady was a whirlwind and it was almost as if it happened out of your control and I don't even think you can call it a mistake now," Bree looked down at the precious blue-eyed baby girl in her arms.

"No. How can I? I have her because of what happened, because of the choices I made - and I know my choices from here on will be the best ones for her. I'm bursting at the seams with love for her and I would do absolutely anything for her."

"I know," Bree pulled her friend into a hug with the sweet baby girl in the middle of them. And that was the last time either of them discussed those bright crystal blue eyes and the secret they revealed.

Kelsey was brought out of her thoughts of that memory when she heard Bailey's words. "Besides, I would rather get into the medical field."

"What did you just say?" Kelsey asked her daughter to repeat what she had already heard, word for word.

"I want to be a doctor, mom"

You cannot force your child, growing into adulthood, to pursue any career. They have to want to do it. They have to feel their heart and soul in it, all by themselves. It can't be about money, or lack thereof, it has to be about passion and drive and pure interest. And despite the fact that Kelsey wanted to feel surprised at this very moment, she wasn't. She had seen this one coming, especially after Miles was born. The amount of care and compassion inside of her little girl was amazing so why shouldn't she follow her heart and become a doctor? She wanted to help people. Just like, all those years ago, Brady Walker had told her he did.

"I think that's wonderful honey," Kelsey stood up and hugged her daughter. "Do you have any idea how proud you make your dad and me?"

***

Bailey's dad… Miles' daddy… Kelsey's husband… was leaving the police station at four o'clock. He wanted to make it to Bailey's high school volleyball game at four-thirty. He had spoken to his wife on the phone at lunchtime and she had told him they were having a productive day together at the newspaper. They had planned to pick up Miles at school and all meet up with each other in the high school gymnasium, for the game. Kyle reached into the front pocket of his jeans to retrieve a travel-sized bottle of ibuprofen. He had kept that in his pocket for years, never knowing when a headache may come on. The last few days were the worst. Again. Those headaches, since the accident, would strangely come and go. They would be worse and then not so bad. Never bad enough to see a doctor. Until today, Kyle was thinking about making an appointment - just to be sure everything was fine. He has a family to take care of so he needed to take care of himself.

Kyle thought back to his earlier conversation with Kelsey as he started up his 4 Runner and drove out of the parking lot. *"So you're not mad that I dropped off Bailey this morning with you instead of at school?"*

"No I'm not mad, it's an assignment for school, but I know she couldn't care less about the newspaper business." Kelsey hadn't told him about Bailey's interest in the medical field. She would let his daughter tell him for herself. And she wanted to be there. She wanted to see the pride on his face.

Kyle told her he wanted to take the family out for pizza after the volleyball game. And before they hung up from talking to each other, Kyle told her he loved her – as he always did. Kelsey said it back – and then she giggled when she heard him say, *"Don't ever forget that,"* as he ended the call between them.

Smiling while he drove down the road, Kyle looked, acted, and felt like a lucky man. He had a beautiful wife of fifteen years who loves him as much as he loves her, and they shared two extraordinary children. He would have worn that smile all the way to his destination a half hour away if it hadn't been for the pain behind his eyes. The sun was too bright and he didn't have his sunglasses with him. He squinted as he drove up to a stop light that had just turned red. He shifted his jeep into park and put his head in his hands. He massaged his temples, rubbed his eyes, and willed the pain away. The light was still red as he looked up from his hands. He was sweating. The moisture was pooling inside the palms of his hands and dripping off of his forehead and around his hairline. The pain was intense and worsening.

He thought of his wife again, and his kids… and then there was a thunderclap within his head. Only Kyle had heard it, echo inside of his head, between his ears. The pressure was momentarily unbearable. And then he was gone.

The traffic light turned green. Impatient city drivers started honking their horns around him. And Kyle Newman was slumped over the steering wheel.

CHAPTER 20

Bailey set off the first serve to start the volleyball game at Bond High School when Kelsey checked her iPhone for messages and took note of the time. Kyle was never late, and if he was running behind he had always called her. Miles was out of her sight, probably playing under the bleachers somewhere in the gymnasium with his friends, or sipping a soda she didn't want him to drink before dinner. Kelsey was half listening to the conversation among the other mothers around her when her cell phone vibrated on her leg. She couldn't have heard a ring in the loud gym during the game so she had purposely put her phone on vibrate and set it down on her lap. She needed to hear from Kyle. She was seriously starting to worry.

The call that was coming through was from Laneview Hospital and Kelsey had that specific number logged under Dr. Bevan, her gynecologist - and friend she had come to know as Dana. Kelsey answered the call.

"Is this Kelsey Newman?" Dr. Bevan couldn't hear anything other than the loud gymnasium crowd.

"Yes it is. Dana is that you?" Kelsey could barely hear on the phone as the referee blew the whistle and the fans were cheering and hollering. "Did I miss an appointment or something?" Kelsey asked placing a few fingers over the ear that she didn't have her phone pressed hard against, trying to hear better.

"No. There's been an emergency. I'm at the hospital and I need you to come here. Come to Laneview Hospital, Kelsey," Dr. Bevan wasn't sure if Kelsey had heard her so she had repeated herself.

"What kind of emergency?" Kelsey raised her voice into the phone, and the other mothers around her stopped talking and from where they were all sitting they immediately scooted over, moved down, and around her on the bleachers. If there was anything at that moment that she knew she could count on, it was the support of those women. They all had children the same ages and they all had shared the pain of each other's hardships through the years as well as the joys of the good times.

"Kyle has been in an accident. Please. Just get here. Come to the hospital. I am here waiting for you," Dr. Bevan hung up the phone in her office and she had tears in her eyes.

Kyle has been in an accident. Suddenly, it was all those years ago, and Kelsey was on the phone with Nicholas Bridges and in a state of sheer panic over the possibility of losing the man she loved.

Kelsey had said, "I'm on my way," and ended the call. She stood up, grabbed her purse, and looked back at the three women sitting on the bleachers. "There's been an accident, I don't know what happened. I just know it's Kyle and I have to get to him. Please take my kids home from here." Kelsey was instantly reassured by all of her girlfriends that she should not worry about her kids. They would take care of them. *Just go to Kyle. Be careful. Let us know.*

Kelsey didn't remember driving to the hospital, a half an hour away. She just kept thinking and even said out loud to herself a few times, *Here we fucking go again.* She cursed, she prayed, and she drove as fast as she could back to the city. Back to the hospital.

Kelsey ran through after the emergency doors opened automatically for her. *Jesus how many times do I have to do this in my lifetime? Running through these ER doors filled with panic and worry and fear – not knowing what to expect on the other side. Not knowing if I can handle what lies ahead.*

Dr. Bevan was right there waiting. She put her arms around Kelsey's shoulders and walked her quickly to the waiting room. *That same fucking waiting room.* Kelsey didn't even take notice if there were other people in there. She had just listened when Dana had said, *come with me.*

Kelsey sat down with the doctor who had delivered her two babies. The doctor she had lunch or dinner with a few times a year. The doctor she trusted. The doctor who knew something about Kyle. She could not have treated him today, in this hospital, because she is a gynecologist. She knew something though. She was here to give Kelsey some news. Maybe some bad news. *God forbid.* And to offer support.

"Kyle was in his car–" Dr. Bevan started to explain.

"Oh my God, another car accident? How bad is he?" *Please not another dreadful coma.*

"He was parked at a traffic light. There was no damage to the car. No one hit him, and he didn't hit anyone. He was slumped over the steering wheel when the man in the car behind him found him." Kelsey was choking on sobs as Dr. Bevan kept talking, "The tests show he suffered from a brain aneurysm. I'm so sorry. He's gone, honey."

"No! No, God, No! Gone? As in he died? My husband died? No, I won't believe it. No!" Kelsey was beside herself. She fell to her knees onto the floor in front of their chairs and Dr. Beven slid down onto her own knees, to hold her. Two nurses came from behind the ER desk and Dr. Bevan shook her head and waved for them to back away. She held her patient who had become her dear friend over the years. She cried with her as she knew the pain she was bearing and the pain that she would now carry for the rest of her life.

Dr. Bevan managed to bring Kelsey to her feet almost ten minutes later. She had pulled herself together enough to speak again. "I want to see him." And that is why Dr. Bevan wanted to be the one to call Kelsey and be there for her at the hospital. When the emergency personnel brought Kyle Newman to Laneview Hospital and Dana Bevan had heard the tragic news - she took charge. She read the scan results with the emergency medical doctor on staff and together they had discovered the brain aneurysm. She wanted to do this for her friend. She wanted to be by her side when she heard the news, and when she identified her husband - in the hospital morgue.

Dr. Bevan walked Kelsey as far as to the door, and that is when she asked to be alone. With Kyle.

She fell apart at the first sight of him. She had every right to lose it. Being in control would have to come later. She had two children to be strong for. She had to hold it together for them. They needed her now. She was all they had. This, however, was her moment. Her moment to lose control. She sobbed, she screamed. There he was, just lying there on top of a cold table with a sterile white sheet over his lifeless body. It took her a few seconds to convince herself that he wasn't just sleeping. It took the moment of putting her hands on his face to feel that there was no warmth, no life there. She kissed him. She held him. All the while, she choked on her sobs. It eventually took Dr. Bevan to interrupt her and to help her down off of that cold slab of a table which Kyle's body was lying on. Kelsey had lifted herself up onto that surface and just laid there with her husband, her body curled around his, one last time.

Dr. Bevan drove Kelsey home in Kelsey's car, and she had a cab driver follow them to bring her back to the hospital. She wanted to make sure Kelsey made it home safely - and she knew she was in no condition to drive.

She had not answered any of the phone calls or texts but as she got out of the passenger seat of her own car on her driveway and Dr. Bevan left in the taxi, she saw light in her home and she knew she now had to break the news to her children and her friends inside. Kelsey hadn't made it up the driveway to the house yet when Bailey came barreling out of the front door, letting it slam behind her.

"Mom! What happened?" She was still wearing her orange and black volleyball uniform from the game, but her hair was no longer tied back and it hung down to her shoulders. She had hoped one of the other mothers had fed her children some dinner, because in a few minutes no one was going to feel like eating. Kelsey knew the feeling all too well. She wondered if that sick feeling deep inside of her stomach would ever subside.

When her neighbor and friend, Tasha peeked out of the front door to check on Bailey, Kelsey waved at her and asked for a moment alone with her daughter.

"Mom, you're scaring me. What happened to dad? Is he okay?" Kelsey took her daughter's face into her hands and with tears spilling over in her eyes, she told her that her father had died.

The rest of what Kelsey was saying sounded all jumbled together to Bailey as she cried and screamed and when Kelsey attempted to hold her - she pulled away and ran to the curb at the end of their driveway, leaned over it, and heaved. Kelsey held back her hair for her as she cried for the pain Bailey was in. Her father was gone.

When Bailey had finally stopped, she turned to her mother and in the dark night with only the street lights allowing them to see each other's faces, Bailey saw a pain in her mother's eyes that she had never seen before.

"Mom…how are we going to tell Miles? He worships dad…and I don't think he will fully understand that he's gone."

Kelsey wanted to cry and keep crying and never stop. The idea of breaking her son's little heart with the news of how his father is never coming back to him, to their family, was unbearable.

"We will help him understand this and somehow we all will get through this," Kelsey said the words, but she didn't believe it. *It was bullshit.* It felt like the end of the world - her world, their world as a family - and she didn't know if she would survive this loss. She would try though, with every ounce of strength left inside of her, to get her children through the pain. They were all she had left now. All that mattered.

CHAPTER 21

Kyle's funeral was two days later. Kelsey fought to hold her own as she promised herself she would - for her children. And Bailey stood next to her, overwhelmed with pain and sadness. She would tuck her arm into her mother's, bow her head, and cry. All of her friends came to offer their support and their sympathy. Seeing them, each and every one of them, made Bailey cry harder. She knew how much her friends loved and admired her dad. It was not half as much, however, as she did. Seeing him laid out in a casket was awful. Just awful.

Kelsey had chosen jeans and a long-sleeved plaid shirt for Kyle to wear. She had spent hours sitting in their walk-in closet in their master bedroom sorting through his clothes and knowing he never was comfortable in a suit and tie, she chose a casual look for him. That was Kyle. He may have met the eye as a simple, ordinary man - but to those who knew and loved him, he was extraordinary. She had held each piece of his clothing close to her, inhaling the scent of every one, and savoring what was left of him that was real.

Miles held tight to Kelsey's hand throughout the entire funeral. He never left her side. Kelsey stood strong in the middle of her two children and wiped away the tears as quickly as they sprung to her eyes when all of the people they knew and loved cried, hugged, and offered to help in any way possible.

Kelsey had tried her best to explain death to Miles. He knew his grandparents had died and gone to heaven, but he didn't want to think of his daddy way up there, far beyond the clouds -

without him and his sister and his mommy. He just told himself to pray very hard, to God, to Jesus, and even to Jesus' mother Mary - and soon his daddy would be back.

At one point near the end of the Kyle's funeral wake, Miles left his mother's side and walked directly up to Kyle's casket. He didn't touch him, but he was close enough to. He hadn't wanted to look or stand right in front of his daddy - looking like that and lying there like that - but when he finally did Kelsey noticed two big tears dripping off of her little boy's cheeks. She immediately picked him up and held him as tight as she possibly could, and then she broke down and cried with him. At that moment all of her strength had drained from her body. There was just something very wrong with a forty-three-year-old man, a husband, a father, lying dead in a casket. Bailey turned away from the scene of the two of them, overcome with sadness. She wanted to scream. She wanted to yell. Maybe there is a God, maybe there is a place called heaven. If so, she hoped with all of her heart that - if he had to be - her dad was there now. Safe and happy. But there was one thing Bailey knew for certain, there was no hell after death. Hell was right here on earth where she, her mother, and her little brother were living it. Her dad was dead.

CHAPTER 22

Kyle died on the nineteenth of May. It was now three months later and summertime. Kelsey was learning how to function as a single parent. She continued to work full-time and juggle everything at home as well.

Sometimes she was too busy to think and dwell and cry, but it was obvious that she was grieving. At work, her writing wasn't quite the same and she knew it. She no longer had the passion and the drive so she kept with editing her staff's stories and piecing together the newspaper issues.

At home, her kids kept her busy. Their school schedules and extracurricular activities had left Kelsey with not enough hours in each day. She was grateful the schools in Greenville had adopted the year-around policy a few years ago. She knew that if this summer her kids had been home, like so many other kids in America, their grief would have consumed them.

Bailey could tell that grief had consumed her mother. She was busy and she kept her kids busy, always making sure she wore a smile on her face for them - but she was not the same mom because she was not the same person. She was no longer a wife to a husband she dearly loved. She no longer was complete. Kelsey had lost ten pounds in the last few months, she had no appetite no matter what she tried to eat. At forty-two years old, she was a beautiful, youthful-looking woman who now bore pain and heartache and that had shown in her eyes and on her face. Kyle's death had changed her and Kelsey wondered if she ever would feel whole again. She wanted to feel better, she wanted the emptiness inside of her to subside and so she took the advice of Dr. Bevan and began to see a psychiatrist. Her kids did not know, but Kelsey considered sending both Bailey and Miles to talk to someone if she herself saw results from her own therapy. Time would tell.

She had two hours before she had to pick up her kids from school, she had already left work early and was on her way to see Dr. Judy Winthrop, her shrink at Laneview Hospital. This would be her third session with Dr. Judy, as she preferred to be called, and Kelsey wasn't looking forward to talking and crying. Dr. Judy was like Barbara Walters – she always found a way to dig deep inside and bring on the tears. She had told Kelsey that she needed to cry more. She had been bottling up too much emotion. It was unhealthy, and she reassured Kelsey that crying didn't mean she was weak, it only meant she had been strong for far too long.

When Kelsey was waiting in the lounge outside of Dr. Judy's office, she found herself staring at the lettering on the wall which spelled out for her exactly where she was, *Laneview Hospital: Where We Get To The Heart Of The Matter.* It was the hospital's motto and had been for more than fifty years as that New York hospital was known for having the best heart doctors in the country. It wasn't just a hospital for heart patients and Kelsey was reading a catchy phrase that was supposed to make patients feel like no matter what they are being treated for at Laneview Hospital, the doctors and staff will get to the root of any issue. And of course – they care.

Laneview Hospital has played an immeasurable role in Kelsey's life since she moved to New York from St. Louis twenty-one years ago. A lot had happened there, for Kelsey. *Kyle's coma.*

Meeting Brady Walker, falling in love with him, and then letting him go. Her children were born there. Her husband was pronounced dead there. Kelsey felt lightheaded. Her husband was dead. And she was lost without him.

Dr. Judy interrupted Kelsey's thoughts which had suddenly consumed her with sadness. Again. "Kelsey, I'm ready for you." Dr. Judy defined classy. She dressed to the nines every day, for work or for play. She was in her early sixties, built stocky, and she wore her cropped jet black hair spiked all over her head. Her facial features were striking and always accented with makeup. Despite twenty-five or thirty extra pounds, Kelsey thought this woman in front of her - this doctor who was supposed to help heal her mind and her heart - was picture perfect.

"So how are you doing this week, honey?" Dr. Judy had a vanilla-scented candle burning on the table in front of the couch where Kelsey had sat down and her doctor took a seat beside her. She didn't have a pen in her hand or a file on her lap. She just sat down beside her, as she had every session with Kelsey, and wanted to talk. There was a hand-held tape recorder, the old-fashioned kind with a mini-sized cassette tape, on the table near the candle which Dr. Judy had already begun recording on.

"The same, really. I go through the motions at work, doing what I have to do. I no longer love my job. And I go home with a phony smile and bubbly attitude to get my kids through another day or another night. They seem to be doing well. They talk about their dad all of the time." Tears sprung to Kelsey's eyes with her next thought and Dr. Judy waited for her to continue. If she wanted to.

"I heard my kids talking last night in my son's bedroom. Bailey was trying to console Miles. He was crying about wanting to play basketball with his friends and not wanting to do his homework. The crying intensified so I went to his bedroom door and before I walked in to help him, Bailey started talking to him so I waited, and listened. She managed to calm him down by talking about their dad. She reminded Miles that their dad was a lot of fun, how he never passed up a chance to play basketball or play Lego's or watch a movie with them. But, she told him, he also was a very smart man who went to school and became even smarter so he could get a good job one day. Bailey told Miles that is what he should do. He should finish his homework because his dad would want him to. And he should always try very hard in school so he can grow up to be a smart man like Kyle was." Kelsey was fighting her tears as she continued talking and Dr. Judy listened. "And then she told her little brother that she loved him. And–" Kelsey choked on a sob and grabbed a tissue from the table, "then Miles replied, 'I love you, too. Don't ever forget that.'" Kelsey cried harder and Dr. Judy knew, from a previous session with Kelsey, that Kyle had a history of regularly saying those words to his wife and kids.

"It's going to get easier," Dr. Judy said softly after a few minutes had passed. "What you need to focus on is not how sad that moment was for you to watch your children missing their father, but rather the big picture here is your daughter is guiding your son and encouraging your son to become the kind of man that Kyle was. And your son, only six years old and such a little boy still, is reminding his sister and you of how deeply his father loved. That little boy is keeping Kyle very much alive in your house and in your lives. I think Bailey sees that, at least it sounds that way from what you have told me.

Now you need to see that and you need to embrace that."

Kelsey stood up and paced around the room. She stopped when she was standing near the door and she wanted to turn the knob and walk out. She wanted to keep Kyle's memory alive. She just didn't know how. Her children found it so easy to talk about him and to laugh about happier times - but she only felt sadness. Every time.

Kelsey had actually cracked the door slightly open but then changed her mind, turned around and asked, "How do I do that? Everyone says it's going to get easier, well in fact it has gotten harder. He's not here for sporting events, family time, and the big and small accomplishments in our kids' lives. He's not here for anything anymore."

Dr. Judy ignored the fact that Kelsey had almost walked out. The door was still cracked but she left it that way when she stood up and walked over to Kelsey. Kelsey was more than three or four inches taller than her, but this woman's strength was not in her size. She looked up at Kelsey and gently spoke. "In order to get through this, in order to deal with all of that, you need to allow yourself to grieve. You need to cry when you're not here in this office, when you're not in the shower, when you're not in bed alone muffling the sounds in your pillow. You need to feel and be real in front of those people who love you. It is okay to do that."

Kelsey couldn't do that - and she wouldn't do that to her kids. She believed she needed to be a pillar of strength for them. But that belief was slowly killing her. "So much easier said than done!" Kelsey raised her voice. "I don't want to fall apart and watch my kids react to that. I don't want to let go and not be able to find my way back. I would drown in my own goddamn tears!" Kelsey was yelling now and Dr. Judy allowed her to. Kelsey was finally feeling some emotion and her doctor had hoped she was reaching the point of being angry, an important stage of grief. "It's his fault for dying! How bad were those fucking headaches? He didn't tell me. He didn't even tell me if he thought he needed to see a doctor! I hate him for dying! I hate him for leaving my children without a father and leaving me without him. I need him! I need him so much it hurts! I don't want to do this without him! I just don't want to live anymore..." Kelsey's words trailed off and she herself couldn't believe she had said them. She just stood there with her face in her hands and cried. Dr. Judy reached out for her, pulled her close, and held her. Their session was over for today.

When Kelsey walked out of Dr. Judy's office, she put her hand on the doorknob and just pulled the door open from where she had left it earlier when she thought she wanted to escape. At that moment she saw the waiting area in the lounge was not empty. Sitting in two chairs along the wall were Nicholas Bridges and his eighteen-year-old daughter, Savannah. My how time flies, Kelsey thought to herself, as she managed to look at Nicholas, knowing her own face was red and blotchy from crying, and then she said *Hello*.

Savannah was dressed in all black clothing and had her fingernails painted black as well. Her hair was long, stringy and badly bleached blonde and her eyes had dark circles under them. Nicholas had his hands full with his daughter. She had experimented with drugs off and on since she started high school and it was just six months ago when Kyle had a serious discussion with Nicholas about finally getting his daughter some professional help. Kyle had been adamant about it. He told Nicholas he lost a sister to drug addiction and he knew the dangers, the serious life-threatening dangers that stemmed from drug abuse. Nicholas had taken Kyle's advice and even allowed Kyle to tell Savannah some horrific stories from his sister's life - and how her life had ended. All because of drugs.

Kelsey was relieved to see Savannah there, trying to get some help from Dr. Judy. She realized too that Nicholas knew why she was there, seeing a psychiatrist, and he most likely had heard her outburst a few minutes ago through the open door.

Nicholas walked over to Kelsey and awkwardly hugged her. "How are you holding up?" he asked as Kelsey quickly separated herself from him. There was no love between Kelsey and Nicholas. There never has been. Kelsey was there when he left his wife and three-year-old child. Kelsey was also there when he married her best friend. Bailey was two years old when Bree discovered she was pregnant. She had gotten pregnant on purpose in hopes of trapping Nicholas into marriage and a life together. They were married by the time their son, Max was born. Max, now thirteen years old, is a good kid and Bree deserves all of the credit for doing an amazing job raising her son in a difficult marriage. Savannah was now living with their family - because her mother had kicked her out, sick and tired of the drug use.

"I've been better," and that was all Kelsey said with a forced smile as she walked out of the waiting area and into the main hallway of the south wing of the hospital.

Kelsey drove directly home after her appointment. She still had forty-five minutes before she had to pick up her kids. She parked her car on the driveway because she knew she would be leaving again soon. When she walked in the front door of her home, she kicked off her shoes in the living room and went to pour herself a glass of wine. She normally waited until the kids were asleep to drink, she and Kyle had always shared a glass or two of wine late at night, but today called for an afternoon drink. She felt emotionally drained as she sat down on the couch and took her first sip. A moment later, the doorbell rang. Kelsey had no idea who would be stopping by but she has gotten used to her wonderful, caring friends and neighbors checking on her the past few months.

When Kelsey opened the door, she was completely surprised to find Nicholas Bridges standing there. Same as always, clean shaven face and bald head. Jeans that fit him like he was still twenty-five years old and a tight t-shirt molding his every ab. The man thought he was all that, and that unnerved Kelsey to no end. Kyle had been a handsome, fit man – but he never acted like he thought he was God's gift to mankind. Even Brady Walker had it going on, but he too never carried any arrogance.

"Oh, hi, I thought you were in therapy?"

"It didn't last long today. Savannah stormed out after the first few minutes. Some sessions are better than others, I guess." Kelsey knew how she felt, but didn't say anything to Nicholas.

"Look, can I come in for a minute? I need to talk to you." Kelsey stepped back to allow him to enter her home and he felt a wave of sadness seep through him. He hadn't been there since Kyle was alive, since their weekend of golfing and drinking beer and just being guys. Three weeks prior to Kyle's death, Nicholas had picked up Kyle at his house and, as always, Kyle wanted him to come inside for a few minutes to see his family. Kyle encouraged peace between Kelsey and Nicholas, and he had wanted them to be friends but it never happened. Maybe it could have happened if it hadn't been for Bree. Kelsey was fiercely protective of her friend and sister – and she hated the hold that Nicholas had over Bree. Recently, Bree had told her how she suspected Nicholas of having an affair. Another one. He always came crawling back, saying all the right words, and Bree caved. Each and every time.

Kelsey offered him a glass of wine as she sat back down on the couch but he declined as he sat down in the armchair adjacent to her. "I have to pick up my kids in less than a half hour," she told him, hoping he hadn't planned to stay long. There was a great amount of discomfort and awkwardness between them in the room. Kelsey felt it, at least, as she drank some more wine.

"I'm here because I know you're hurting, I heard what you said to Dr. Winthrop today." Kelsey thought she should feel embarrassed but she wasn't. She was a widow. Kyle's widow. And she had every right, in therapy, to cry and to scream and to feel like her life is over now.

"I am grieving, Nicholas – and there isn't anything anyone can do to help me heal. My shrink is very good and she is trying but I don't know if I can be fixed."

"I keep telling Savannah she has to want the help in order for it to work."

"In her case, you're right. In mine, of course I want to heal and be whole again but that is just not going to happen. Only one person could make this emptiness go away – and he died on me," Kelsey finished the wine in her glass and set it down on the coffee table in front of her.

"You weren't the only one who loved and lost him. I miss him, too. More than anyone will ever know." Kelsey was touched by his words, but she didn't show any emotion to allow him to see that. "You have to move on with your life because that is what Kyle would want for you, and for the kids."

"My kids are doing very well, considering…"

"When I say move on I don't mean find another guy to play husband and dad around here. I mean you have to take what Kyle gave you, all those fifteen plus years and wear it proudly and gain strength from his love and his goodness. He loved you and those kids more than you will ever know – and I mean that." Kelsey wiped away the tears on her cheeks. She was not going to cry in front of Nicholas, but now she couldn't help herself. "He was such a good man, wasn't he?"

"The best I've ever met," he answered.

"Thank you, Nicholas," Kelsey said standing up and giving him a cue to leave. She had to leave soon. Nicholas stood up and when her back was to him, he spoke as they walked toward the door.

"He knew..."

Kelsey turned around to face him walking behind her, and asked, "Knew what?"

"About you – and that doctor – while he was in a coma after the car accident."

Kelsey felt her face flush and a moment later all of the color drained from it. Her eyes widened and she never looked away from Nicholas. She could not believe the words she had just heard from him. She shockingly was about to revisit her past. The past she had buried, and the secret she still carried. She didn't know what to say, and Nicholas didn't hesitate to speak first.

"He knew about the doctor because I told him."

"Did Bree tell you?" Kelsey spat the words at him and couldn't fathom that as the truth. Bree would never betray her. Ever.

"No. I swear to God. No. I've never brought this up to her either. I know how tight the two of you are. You're so damn close, the two of you should be married. Who loves each other like that? Crazy lucky people, I guess." Kelsey had never heard Nicholas, or anyone, talk about her bond with Bree like that. She was proud of that bond and she would do absolutely anything to protect Bree.

"I saw you myself, with him, more than one time at the hospital. You two didn't bother to hide it. And I was the one who repeatedly sat with Kyle at his bedside on those nights. I would stop in and find him alone so I stayed," Nicholas wanted to say *while you were out screwing another man* but he didn't. He knew how fragile she was right now.

"So you told Kyle I had an affair?" Kelsey felt a lump form in her throat as she said those words aloud and tried to imagine the moment Kyle heard those exact words about her. *He knew. God no, he knew.*

"I owed it to my friend to tell him the truth. I told him after he told me he had proposed to you. I wanted him to know the truth before he married you."

Kelsey was thinking back, trying to piece together when and where and how Kyle may have acted toward her that day or that night – or from that moment forward. He had known she cheated on him before he knew *they* were having a baby. And he said nothing? And he stayed with her? He married her! Kelsey felt like everything Nicholas was saying to her was fabricated. He was lying to her. He had to be.

"Kyle did what he wanted with that truth. He wanted you. And *his* child. He chose to ignore there was a possibility the baby you were carrying was not his. He wanted a family with you."

"Get out of my house, you bastard!" Kelsey would not listen to this. This was not what she needed now. She didn't want to carry this guilt in her heart. She needed to believe that Kyle loved and respected her all the days of his life. Nicholas didn't budge. He kept standing, facing her, and he wanted her to face the truth.

"I'm not leaving until you hear me out. I know you've never liked me." He wanted to say she judged him for leaving his first wife and carrying on with Bree. He wanted to say what she did was so much worse. But he wouldn't say that to her, especially now, because she was hurting so badly. He was there because he wanted her to heal. And he had hoped by telling her everything, she would find the peace that she needed to carry on. "I'm here to help you. Not hurt you."

"Oh my God, are you serious? This is not helping me. Believe me, I don't think I could feel any worse than I do at this moment."

"Stop talking, just stop, and listen to me. I am here to help you see that you had all of those wonderful years with Kyle. And those years were more goddamn real than you may have realized. A lot of men would say he was a loser for staying - for not confronting you and seeking the truth about everything - I say he is a brave man. Bravest I ever met. He knew what he wanted and he kept it close, protected it, and held on to it every day of his life. You and those kids were his family. You were everything to him. He would want you to be happy, to keep living. I know you are taking good care of your children, Kelsey. Now it's time for you to take good care of yourself. For Kyle. Do it for him."

Nicholas walked out of her house without uttering another word. He came to say what he knew she needed to hear. He had never planned to tell her the truth. It was a secret he thought he would take to his grave, like Kyle had. But after seeing her and hearing her in the psychiatrist's office today, he knew he had to try to help her. And telling her was the only way he knew how. Now, he hoped she would take his advice - and do more with the rest of her life than simply survive in sadness.

Kelsey put on her shoes, grabbed her purse, cell phone, and car keys off of the table by the door in the living room and she left to go pick up her kids. She needed time to think and to process all that Nicholas had confessed, but first she had to keep herself together and get through the evening focusing on her kids.

Bailey announced her plans to Kelsey as soon as she got into the car. She was going to the football game tonight and had already arranged for a ride. A mother of one of her girlfriends was going to be the taxi driver for five freshman girls because she had volunteered to work the concession stand during the game. Kelsey had told her she could go and was pleased that she had a responsible adult driving her. Kelsey wasn't ready to allow Bailey to get into any car with her teenage friends with brand new licenses to drive. Bailey understood and she was so excited about the first football game of the season that she never noticed her mom's silence in the car.

As they drove to the grade school to pick up Miles, Kelsey was thinking about how she would keep him busy tonight. Bailey was always a huge help entertaining her brother, and Kyle had always played everything from basketball on the driveway to Lego's with Miles. She had hoped he would want to watch a movie, maybe eat some popcorn, and then fall asleep early. Kelsey needed some time alone, to think.

The three of them ordered pepperoni pizza before Bailey's ride arrived to take her to the football game. Later, Kelsey found Miles dribbling his basketball outside, alone on the driveway. He was a natural athlete and basketball was his favorite sport. Kyle had loved to tell his guy friends what a basketball star his son was going to be one day. *He already was the best player on his kindergarten team last school year*, he would say with a proud smile. Kelsey stood back and watched her son dribble the ball and go for a layup, which he swooshed into the net. He was his father's son. She was looking at a miniature Kyle right now and for the first time since Kyle had died, she felt so grateful to have a piece of her husband left to her in this world. Kyle was still very much alive inside their little boy. And one day he would be a man, a handsome, caring and wonderful man. Like his daddy.

"How about a game of pig?" Kelsey interjected as she jogged over to her son. And the two of them had a sweet time together playing basketball on the driveway for the next hour. She didn't intend to, but Kelsey had worn Miles out. After his bath he didn't even get through the movie they had started before he fell asleep on the couch with his hand in the popcorn bowl.

After Kelsey carried her son up to his room and tucked him into bed, she went back downstairs into the kitchen and poured herself a glass of wine. She sat down on the couch and turned off the TV. Bailey wouldn't be home for another hour and she just wanted the quiet time she knew she needed since Nicholas Bridges had dropped in this afternoon with the news that had rocked her to her core. She sat there wondering how it could be true. Why had he suppressed his anger, his rage, and his disappointment? Had he truly loved her *that* much and wanted her in his life *that* much? Of course she knew he loved her. This, however, was unimaginable.

Losing him hurt so much more right now. Knowing she had hurt him and never had the chance to say she was *so sorry* was causing her unbearable pain. She finished her wine and sat alone in the dark living room. She had a lamp on near the front door. She had always left that lamp on when someone was out of the house for the evening. When Kyle worked late, he would walk in and set his keys and his police badge down on that sofa table against the wall after he had closed and locked the door behind him. He would then turn off that lamp and head up the stairs. Kelsey can remember the numerous times she heard the door close and that lamp click off and she knew he was home, safe.

He had always kept her safe, his family safe. And now she was struggling with the fact that she hadn't honored their commitment and their love before they were married. And he had known about it. Her secret. Her affair with Brady Walker. He had known *all these years*.

She wanted to talk to him. She wanted the chance to explain. It was nine-thirty and Bailey was due home in forty-five minutes. Kelsey wished it was that time now. She needed to go somewhere. Tonight. Bailey could watch Miles, or at least be present in the house while he slept. While Kelsey went to the cemetery.

***

When Bailey walked in the door, Kelsey had a few more lights on so she wouldn't startle her in the dark room. "Hi Mom, the game was awesome! We won and the fan vibe was so amazing throughout the entire game. Everyone was so wound up!" Kelsey was smiling at her. Oh those carefree days of being in high school. As Bailey kicked off her flip flops in the living room, Kelsey asked her to stay with Miles for a little while.

"Tonight? Right now? Where are you going?"

"I need to, um, talk to your dad."

Bailey's eyes widened. "Mom are you okay?" Bailey glanced at the coffee table in front of the couch and saw the empty wine glass. "How much have you had to drink?" Kelsey giggled at her daughter. "Oh my gosh, just one glass honey, and yes I am fine. I just really need to feel close to your dad tonight. I need to go to him."

"Please don't. You're the one who told us that dad isn't at that cemetery. He's in heaven, he's in our hearts, he's with us all of the time. Remember?" Bailey had tears in her eyes and Kelsey pulled her close.

"And that's exactly right. Now do me a favor and take a shower, watch some TV, and I will be back soon. Okay?" Kelsey had already slipped into her black Sperry shoes. She was wearing a black t-shirt and short khaki shorts on this night in late August. Bailey told her to *be careful* and to *come back soon* before she closed and locked the door after her mother walked out of it.

Kelsey drove through town and ten minutes later she was on the outskirts of Greenville at the Catholic cemetery. She had only been there once since the day they had buried Kyle. She and her kids went to see Kyle's headstone one Saturday morning after they had found out it was ready and in place. It had been a difficult visit. Bailey cried and didn't want to stay, while Miles kept sitting on top of the black marbled-stone engraved with his father's full name, birthdate, deathdate, and the words – *unforgettable husband and father*. Kelsey hadn't been able to hold it together that day and she swore they wouldn't return to Kyle's gravesite anytime soon.

And yet here she was. She had parked her car as close as she could and then walked a little ways down the rocky path that led to the newer tombstones. The cemetery wasn't very well lit so she brought a flashlight with her that she had taken out of her glove compartment in the car before walking up.

Kelsey stared at the tombstone, the lettering spelling out his name had made it so official. He was *dead*. She felt sick to her stomach standing there and again like last time, she wanted to leave. But not before she said what she came to say. To him.

"Hi baby…this just doesn't seem right. It sure as hell doesn't seem real. This void inside of me, inside of my heart, feels so raw. I miss you. I love you…and I still need you." Kelsey choked on a sob but managed to contain herself again.

"Kyle you know why I'm here. I'm here to say I'm sorry…" she was crying now, "I'm so sorry I hurt you. I thought it was best to keep my secret. I didn't want to cause you that kind of pain. You didn't deserve it. And now I found out that you knew? You knew all along what I did…" Kelsey was tasting her tears now as they were flowing uncontrollably out of her eyes, down her cheeks and onto her lips.

"Why? Why didn't you confront me? Why didn't you leave me? I deserved to be on the receiving end of your anger! I don't understand how you could love me that much and continue to trust me? Dammit Kyle I am so confused right now! I'm feeling like I didn't deserve you!" Kelsey was screaming out the words to him. She was all alone in the dark cemetery as she fell to her knees in front of the headstone and her flashlight fell out of her hands and rolled onto the dirt.

"Am I supposed to assume that you forgave me because you never confronted me and you stayed with me - and with Bailey? I need to know that I have your forgiveness. Please, Kyle, please, I need to know that or I can't go on with my life. I just can't…" Kelsey put her face in her hands and cried harder. On her knees she could feel the damp ground, still fresh soil where not all of the new grass had grown in yet. When she lifted her head from her hands, the wind picked up and she could feel autumn in the air on her face, on her arms, on her legs. She inhaled deeply and as she started to stand up, she could smell white Dial soap. She was instantly startled. Kyle had never worn cologne. He hated *those fancy smells,* he would say, but he had always smelled of Dial soap. Kelsey used to tell him any time of day he smelled like he was fresh out of the shower. She had loved to hug him and stick her face and her nose into his neck, behind his ear. It was white Dial soap that she smelled right now. It was Kyle's scent. He was there with her.

She stood up quickly and glanced all around her. Side to side. In front of her. Behind her. That scent, that refreshing scent - of him - was becoming stronger. He was there. But she couldn't see him. The hair on her skin was standing up, but it wasn't from fear. She wasn't scared.

She felt a sense of peace come over her as her body instantly felt warm. She was being embraced. By Kyle. She could feel his arms around her. She could feel her face in his neck and her nose behind his ear. God if only her eyes could see him right now. Just one more time. But that wasn't going to happen. She had gotten her gift from him, from heaven. She felt him holding her one last time. She had smelled him one last time in this life. And above all else, she now felt forgiven.

It was over before she wanted it to be. The wind picked up again and he was gone. And so was the scent of him. She hadn't imagined it. He was there. He had been there with her, holding her in his arms. And then leaving her with the will to live again. She had experienced an epiphany. She wanted to live again and she would live every day for the rest of her life to the fullest because Kyle gave her that. She now knew that he had loved and forgiven her at all costs. And that price was high. Sky high. Kyle was an incredible human being. And now it was time she be the kind of person he was. She would start by forgiving herself.

CHAPTER 23

Four months had passed since everything had changed for the better, for Kelsey. Her kids could see it and feel it in their house. Their mom was back. She was happy, or as happy as she could be without Kyle. She still felt the emptiness, daily, but she had a healthier handle on it now.

The holidays were going to be especially difficult for all three of them. With Kelsey's parents both gone and now Kyle, they didn't have any family to celebrate with. Bree had invited them to spend Christmas with her, Nicholas, Max and Savannah – but they had opted not to.

Kelsey knew Christmas in their house in the suburbs would never be the same again. Kyle had always decorated the outside of the house with white lights, greenery, wreaths, and did just as much or even more inside of the house. He had insisted each bedroom have a Christmas tree, as well as the living room – every year.

Since it was the first Christmas without him, Kelsey wanted to change things and make new traditions for her and her kids. So she planned a trip and the three of them went on a week-long cruise to the Bahamas. They returned on New Year's Eve, all of them tan, relaxed and feeling refreshed. The sun and the water had done each of them so much good. The food on the ship was delicious and available around the clock. Kelsey was starting to regain her appetite again and she had gained five pounds on that one-week vacation. She looked better than she had in months, and she felt it too. She had spent hours lying in the sun reading, people watching, and just thinking about her life.

When they returned home on the afternoon of New Year's Eve, the kids immediately wanted to catch up with their friends. Bailey was on her phone, planning to attend an all-girls party for the evening at a friend's house in their subdivision. And Miles was already across the street playing basketball on the driveway with Tasha's son, Spence. The two of them were in the same class and shared a love of basketball. The weather was sunny but a cold forty degrees so Kelsey had made him wear layers but he refused to wear gloves, *because mom, how would I be able to handle the ball?*

Kelsey was unpacking all of their suitcases in the laundry room when she heard her cell phone buzz on the kitchen counter. She stepped over the laundry on the floor near the washer and walked into the kitchen to retrieve her phone. It was a text from Bree, asking if she was home yet, hoping she enjoyed the trip over the Christmas holiday, and to call her. Kelsey went back into the laundry room with her phone on her ear. She didn't know how she ever would have survived these last several months without Bree. Bree was her rock. She didn't have the easiest life being married to Nicholas - dealing with *his* philandering, and *his* daughter's problems. The only thing that kept Bree from feeling defeated was her son. Max is her world. He, at thirteen years old, knew that his dad could be a better father and a better husband.

"Hi Kel, I'm glad you're back."

"It is good to be home, but I'm telling you that trip was heaven - uh well, not quite. If it had been heaven, Kyle would have been there," Kelsey giggled. She was comfortable making comments like that now, but Bree's heart ached for her. "We are making this our annual tradition. The kids love the idea. Maybe next year you all could come with us?" What Kelsey really meant to say was she and Max were welcome.

"That sounds so nice. Christmas, here, was a good one for us. Savannah ended up choosing to spend a few days with her mom - so it was just Nic, Max, and I for a change." Kelsey knew how hard Bree had tried to be a good stepmom to Savannah, but the girl had just never let her in - and never gave her a break. At least she was clean now, not having used drugs for almost a year. That alone, made life less stressful in their household.

"I'm happy for you, Bree. So is she back yet? Do you have plans for tonight?" Before they called themselves wives, Bree had always insisted she and Kelsey have serious plans together on New Year's Eve. Bree had loved to party, but that changed for her when Max was born. She didn't want to be one of those mothers who always hired a babysitter so she could drink and party. Her son needed her so she chose to be with him while Nicholas continued his wild ways. Tonight he had wanted to check out a new bar in the city and he wanted her to go along with him - but Bree had asked him to stay at home, order some take-out or cook a nice dinner, and spend some time with her and Max. Savannah had a sleepover planned with a girlfriend, whose parents they trusted, and she had already left for that. Bree had propositioned her husband, they were due for some hot sex after Max was asleep and Nicholas had told her to pencil him in for later because he was going to the grand opening of that new bar, with or without her. And Bree cried when she told Kelsey.

"Damn that son of a bitch. I'm so sorry, honey. Why don't you and Max pack up and come over for the night? Bailey will be out until twelve-thirty, but Miles and I will be here to ring in the New Year. Come on, it will be fun to spend all night together again. Bree didn't know how her teenage son would feel about hanging out with a six year old all night, but she assumed he would bring along his new iPhone to keep him busy, or maybe get caught up in a Playstation game with Miles and actually have fun.

"I think that sounds like too good of an offer to refuse. Thanks Kel. You always know what I need." Kelsey knew that worked both ways. Bree had been there day and night for her when Kyle died. She let her talk, cry, and sometimes they just shared silence. They were friends through it all - and always would be.

***

The holidays were over and everyone made it through. School resumed on the second of January, which is also when Kelsey returned to the newspaper. She felt good all through the work day and had already made plans for Tasha to pick up her kids after school and then drop them off at home. She was going to be late because she had an appointment with Dr. Judy. Dr. Judy had also accepted her children as patients in recent months. Sometimes all three of them shared a session with the therapist - and other times they each needed to talk, privately. Kelsey eventually told her children she was seeing a psychiatrist and when she suggested help for them, they were reluctant and nervous. Therapy had helped all of them though - and Kelsey wanted Dr. Judy to be a part of their lives indefinitely.

After Nicholas' confession and the occurrence in the cemetery, Kelsey realized she hadn't dealt with the fact that she carried and burdened herself with a huge secret all throughout her marriage. She never realized that she needed to truly forgive herself. Knowing that Kyle had known and had freely chosen to forgive her allowed Kelsey to finally grant herself that forgiveness.

During a session following Kelsey's awakening, Dr. Judy had pressed hard for what was really going through Kelsey's mind and heart. Initially she didn't want to, but Kelsey ended up telling Dr. Judy what had happened. She told her about the affair she had - but she refrained from mentioning that the man had been a doctor in that very same hospital - and about the child who was, without any DNA proof, a result of that affair. She also told her how she had never told Kyle, and just recently learned that he had known.

Dr. Judy never encouraged Kelsey to come clean about her past. She knew that man was no longer a part of her life, no longer living in New York City. She didn't think it was right to tell her patient to reveal a secret that could change her teenage daughter's life, and not necessarily for the better. That young girl had worshipped the man who raised her and who, in her eyes, would always be her father. Kelsey believed there was no reason to tell Bailey the truth. Brady was gone from her life and wouldn't be back in it, ever. Kyle was their life, he was a phenomenal husband and father - and that is how they would always remember him. He could not be replaced in their hearts. She did admit to Dr. Judy that she is lonely. Her children keep her busy and she purposely jumped back into writing at the newspaper for something more to occupy her mind. But to her doctor, she had said *I miss my husband. Talking to him. Holding him. I'm lonely.* She had felt embarrassed, saying those words out loud, but she was only forty-two years old and still a very sensual woman. She looked sexy and she felt sexy. She just wasn't doing anything about that these days. At least she was feeling alive again. For so many months, she hadn't felt anything but pain and sorrow. She obviously wasn't ready to date. She had her kids to think about, and time she needed to spend with them. And it had only been seven months since Kyle died. She didn't know if she would ever be ready. And she wasn't looking for just sex. She was feeling lonely and needy, and Dr. Judy had suggested she give it time.

Kelsey was thinking about Kyle as she left her session. There was something Dr. Judy said, which triggered her thoughts, and she hadn't really allowed herself to go there before. She had tried to think about *when* Kyle found out the truth, exactly *when* it could have been. Had he acted differently toward her? Had he seemed angry or distant? He knew the truth after she had accepted his marriage proposal. Kelsey wasn't ready to drive home yet. Her thoughts were racing and she just wanted some fresh air. She got onto the elevator, alone, and on a whim decided to take it all the way up. To the rooftop.

It had been years. More than fifteen years. Maybe it was even closed off. Kelsey watched the elevator door open and she was staring at the outdoors from on top of the hospital roof. She stepped off and walked out into the air. It was cold so she zipped up her coat and wrapped her scarf around her. She was dressed up for work, wearing ivory low-rise dress pants and a black cashmere sweater underneath her long black winter-lined trench coat. Her heels hit the cold ground one after the other as she walked over to the ledge on the rooftop.

She thought of all the times she had been up there, with Brady. She couldn't believe that was her. Living so carefree, pretty much to a fault. Seamless she used to say. And while it had felt damn good then, it wasn't right. And she knew that now.

Kyle was the man for her, and right after they had gotten engaged he proved that to her. Without a doubt. Kelsey stopped to rethink her last thought. *Right after they had gotten engaged.* It was then that Kyle had changed. She hadn't realized it then. She never realized it. Until now. She had been so caught up in planning a wedding and being pregnant that she never once stopped and thought about how Kyle had become somewhat of a new man. He had gone from a tad bit boring and routine to adventurous and full of surprises for her. She had thought, back then, that she was seeing the excitement of a first-time father but it was more than that. He had stepped outside of the box for her, outside of his comfort zone. He had become *almost like* the kind of man she had seen and fallen in love with, in Brady. He was still Kyle, kind and caring and laid back. But he also had showered her with attention and made a point to tell her every day, multiple times a day, that he loved her. *Don't ever forget that*. That's when he started to say those words. All of the time.

Kelsey, all alone, on the rooftop, had a shocked look on her face. She could see her breath in the cold as she closed her mouth and shook her head. She had never thought about any of this before. Kyle became a changed man in order to keep her and to keep their family together. Kyle had become everything to her. As she stood there she began thinking about the selfish lover he had been during the two years they had dated. It was just who he was, and it had disappointed her time and again. She was thinking now though how after Bailey was born, they had an amazing sex life. Kyle was attentive and more focused on pleasing *her* every time. Kelsey felt her body warm up underneath her coat and her clothes. They had become the best of lovers, too. They had it all. Together they, too, were seamless. Their love and their happiness as a couple, and as a family, was perfect.

***

Kelsey texted Bailey, telling her she was running a little late but would be home within the hour and she would bring dinner. Miles had asked his sister to text back for Mexican food. Kelsey smiled, replied okay, and asked them to look at the Mexican restaurant menu in the kitchen drawer and text her with their food order soon. She was smiling to herself as she tucked her phone into her coat pocket just as the elevator doors opened. Someone else had also needed some fresh air and that was fine because Kelsey was just leaving.

She walked toward the open elevator and saw a man step off. He turned back to hold the sliding door for her, but as he did there was something so familiar about him and he saw it in her as well at the very same time. This man was wearing a coat over top of his - scrubs.

"Brady?" She managed to say his name without stuttering from the shock she was feeling all throughout her body. And he let go of holding the elevator door behind him.

"You've got to be kidding me! Kelsey… how in the world are you?" She couldn't believe he was there. One of her colleague reporters at the newspaper had written the story more than ten years ago. The prominent doctor at Laneview Hospital had been offered and accepted a chief of staff position in Washington, D.C. at a well-known hospital where even the President of the United States and his family members were treated. Brady had moved out of New York City. That was the reason why Kelsey had felt so at ease about seeing other doctors at Laneview, giving birth there, and now seeing a psychiatrist there. She knew her fear of the chance of running into Brady Walker was unfounded. And now here he was, right in front of her.

"I, um, I'm fine. I had no idea you were back…" She hadn't stepped any closer to him. She just wanted to get on that elevator, but now he was standing in her way. He looked almost exactly the same to her. His body was still incredibly fit at forty-five years old. He did have a few laugh lines and crow's feet around his eyes - just as Kelsey had noticed in her own mirror over the years. His dark hair was scattered with a little gray and his beard, that scruff, was gone. He looked so much like himself, yet different.

And Brady had been thinking the same about Kelsey. She was still slim and fit, barely five pounds heavier than he remembered her and maybe a smidgen wider through the hips. She had looked amazing to him. Still the same Kelsey he often dreamed about, at night and in his daydreams. She had grown into a complete woman as a wife and a mother. But when he looked at her, really looked at her, he could see pain in her eyes. He didn't know if he had just brought that on right now, by being there, forcing her to remember and to feel – or if she had suffered in the years since he had seen her last.

"I am back. I guess you could say I've made a career out of being a chief of staff in high demand. My former mentor just retired from here as the chief of staff and the hospital board offered me the job, at his recommendation. So here I am. I've moved back to NYC after a decade in DC," he smiled at Kelsey and she noticed the dimple on his left cheek, and my goodness those blue eyes were sparkling. She hadn't seen him in so many years, but she had seen those eyes – every day.

"Wow, well congratulations and welcome back," Kelsey wanted to leave it at that and end their conversation. She didn't want the attention to be turned to her now. She didn't want to talk about her life – and what she had just been through.

"Thank you. So how are you? And how's Kyle – and your child? I believe the last time I saw you, you were preggers in the parking lot at the grocery store."

"That child, a girl, is fifteen now," Kelsey offered and Brady managed to utter, *unbelievable!*

"I also have a son, he's six. His name is Miles," Kelsey smiled at the thought of her sweet boy. He and his sister were the light of her life. They were all she had now. It had taken several years for Kyle and her to conceive Miles. Bailey was nine years old when he was born, they had tried to get pregnant for more than seven years. Kelsey prayed hard to be able to conceive Kyle's baby. She never suggested that he be tested for infertility because she was scared that the truth about Bailey would be forced out.

"Oh how fun. A teenage daughter and a little boy," Brady smiled, wishing he could keep her there, talking and catching up. Just seeing her again had brought back so much for him. And he wondered if she was feeling even a flicker of that. "So how's Kyle?" Those were the words, that was the question, she was dreading for him to ask her. She didn't want to go there. Not now. Not with him. She had to get home to her children. She was bringing dinner. She needed to leave. Now.

"I really should go, Brady. My kids are home from school and waiting for me. It's so nice to see you again."

"Okay, sure. I don't mean to keep you from your family. I just got a little caught up in catching up with you." Kelsey had wondered about him, too. Was he married? She couldn't see a ring because he had his hands stuffed into his coat pockets to warm them in the cold. How many children did he have?

"I understand. I want to ask you a million questions too," Kelsey was being honest, and suddenly she thought a few more minutes with him wouldn't set her back too far in her quest to get home within the hour.

"Ask away, I'm an open book."

"Are you married?" It was easier to ask him the questions.

"No I'm not married." Kelsey thought she saw a familiar sadness in his eyes. A sadness she had also seen in the mirror in her own eyes. "I was engaged eight years ago to a woman I believe came into my life to show me that I could love again – after I'd lost you." Kelsey was listening raptly as Brady continued. "Her name was Joanie. She was a nurse at Washington University Hospital. A petite little blonde with a short cropped haircut who filled my heart with so much joy."

"What kept you from marrying her?" Kelsey interrupted.

"She died of breast cancer three months before we were supposed to be married. I didn't want to believe that she wasn't going to make it. I pushed her to live. I told her everything was going to be okay. But I was wrong. I failed her. I'm a doctor and I couldn't save the one woman I needed to move on with my life." Kelsey felt a wave of sadness overcome her. He had lost yet another woman he loved to cancer. He also admitted that he hadn't been able to move on. He had implied that he was not over her. It had been more than fifteen years and he was still holding on to what they had shared.

"Cancer is out of our hands, even big-shot doctors like you cannot save everyone from that dreadful disease. Brady I know how painful it is to lose someone you love to cancer, to watch them succumb to that pain. I lost my mother to lymphoma. I was there with her throughout her battle and at the very end. We can't save the people we love sometimes – no matter how badly we want to keep them here with us." Now, Kelsey was talking about Kyle as her eyes became teary.

"I'm sorry babe. I can see you've felt that same pain," Brady had called her *babe* and she had felt an instant electricity shoot through her body. She thought how he didn't know the half of it. She had felt more pain, losing Kyle seven months ago, than she ever imagined she'd endure. "It's been eight years since my fiancé died, and I'm still not sure I'm past the pain. We didn't see a reason to rush. We met right when I moved to Wash U and we were both content just being together. I wish I would've married her Kelsey, I wish I could have spared her the pain and suffering she went through. I now know what my dad went through when he lost my mom, his wife, the love of his life. To this day I have no idea where that son of a bitch lives, or if he's still living, but I can finally understand what he felt when my mom withered away in front of his eyes from that fucking disease that ate up her pancreas," Brady was angry, still angry about losing his mother - and now it was as if that anger had intensified dealing with losing Joanie, the woman he wanted to make his wife but they ran out of time together.

Kelsey was openly crying in front of him, for his pain, for her pain, and for how life was sometimes just plain cruel to those left behind. "I wish you could have married her, Brady. I wanted you to be happy." Brady wanted to walk over to her, and hold her, but he remained standing where he was - away from her and still in front of the closed elevator.

"After Joanie, I couldn't think about finding a woman I wanted to marry. I loved her differently than I loved you, Kelsey. She taught me a few things, she opened my eyes. I have realized why you loved Kyle - and why you chose him. I always wondered if, despite everything, you chose him because you loved him more than you loved me. But it was just different, wasn't it?" Just as *different* as his love for Joanie.

"Yes it was," and that was all Kelsey had managed to respond. She wanted to cry again. She missed Kyle so much. And now Brady was back. She was confused and cold and needed to go home.

"Just appreciate every day that you have with him and your kids. Life is too short not to–"

"Brady stop. I know all about life being too short. I was robbed of my years with my husband as were my children with their father. Kyle…died last May," Kelsey choked on a sob and turned away to allow herself to cry, once again. Brady felt as if the wind had been knocked out of him. He took a deep breath and walked over to her and turned her toward him and she fell into his arms. He was holding her again. He wanted to comfort her, to take away her pain. He had no idea she was a widow. When Kelsey stopped crying, she quickly pulled away from him and stepped back, far enough away again. "He had a brain aneurysm. It could have been from his head injury all those years ago. There was no warning, at least I don't think there was. He still had headaches, off and on, he just didn't complain much. I never saw enough to make him go to the doctor. It could have been one of those things, there all along, or just appeared and took his life in an instant." Brady was listening and wondering how and where it had happened, but he didn't ask her. He could see her pain was still so raw.

"I'm so sorry. There's a sadness in the wind sometimes and it seems as if you and I both have had our share of being blown over by it in this lifetime." Kelsey smiled at his words, and nodded her head yes. "I have to go, Brady. My kids are waiting."

"Of course, you go, and I will see you again. I hope." Brady hadn't asked why she was at the hospital, but he knew she would be back. He now knew his move back to New York City and back to Laneview Hospital had been for a reason. He had renewed hope in his heart after seeing her again. And she had felt it too, but she wasn't ready to admit that - to herself or especially to him.

CHAPTER 24

For two weeks, Kelsey had avoided Laneview Hospital. She canceled two visits with Dr. Judy, making excuses that work was hectic. She also wanted to cancel the scheduled monthly session for her children, but last night Bailey had mentioned how refreshed she feels after talking to Dr. Judy and how she had looked forward to the next session. That session was today.

Kelsey was nervous again, for the first time in many years, about going back to Laneview Hospital. Especially with her children in tow. The last thing she needed was Brady seeing Bailey. She feared that her whole world would come crashing in around her if that happened. She could only imagine Brady's wrath if he were to take one look at her and figured it out – and Bailey's pain and disappointment would destroy her. Kelsey was never a person to keep secrets, not from her parents when she was growing up, not from her friends – especially Bree – and not from Kyle. Not until Brady Walker waltzed in and changed her life. Changed *her*.

She had no choice. She couldn't hide from Laneview Hospital. She and her children both saw doctors there and she was not going to change their lives because Dr. Walker was back on staff. She is a grown woman, a parent now, and she would act like one and stop fretting about it. Starting today.

Kelsey was a bundle of nerves despite her mind over matter theory. No matter how many times she told herself that everything would be fine, she still felt pangs of panic inside. Bailey was in her session with Dr. Judy while Kelsey and Miles sat together in the therapist's waiting room on the fourth floor. Miles was flipping through a Sports Illustrated magazine in search of any basketball pictures and Kelsey sat there with sweaty palms, counting the minutes until Bailey would be finished and Miles could go into his session. They would be there for an hour. They hadn't seen Brady on their way into the hospital on the main floor, or in transit up to the fourth floor. She had expected to, but hoped not to, as she and the kids made their way through the hospital. Her kids were chatty and playful with each other so neither of them noticed Kelsey glancing around her as they walked, turned corners, and headed down corridors. Kelsey sighed and sat back in her chair as Miles stood up and put his magazine on the shelf with the others.

"I have to pee." Miles and Kelsey were the only two people in the waiting area so he spoke outright to her and she sat up straight in response. "Now? Can't you wait? The bathroom is all the way down the hallway and you're up next with Dr. Judy."

"I know I'm next and that is why I need to pee first. It takes too long with Dr. Judy and I know I won't be able to hold it," Miles looked confused. He didn't understand his mom's strange reaction. "I'll be right back," he said acting like a big boy who always went into public restrooms alone. He wasn't that grown up yet - and Kelsey never let him walk alone anywhere in public. This had gotten harder for her since they lost Kyle. Kyle used to go with Miles into the men's restroom. Now she was forced to walk him to the door and wait outside while she sent him in alone. There were weirdos and perverts out there and it flipped her out to think about it. "You're not going alone. I will walk you down there," Kelsey got up from her chair and left the waiting room with her son.

They walked down the hallway, made a right turn and found the bathrooms on the left. Miles went ahead and Kelsey stood against the opposite wall and waited. The hallway was empty except for one nurse who had passed her and smiled, and a housekeeper pushing a cart at the far end.

The restroom door opened up and Miles walked out. Kelsey smiled at him, "Okay, all better now? Let's head back. It's almost time for your session." Miles wasn't thrilled about talking to a therapist, but he had heard his sister mention how much it helped her and so maybe he could be helped too, he had thought. He wasn't sure what exactly he needed help with. He missed his dad and wanted him back, every day, and no one could take those feelings away or make everything all better.

Just as they rounded the corner to walk back, Kelsey collided with a man coming from the opposite direction. He stopped himself with his hands on her shoulders and she had pushed her hands up against his chest, also to come to a halt. Miles stood there, looking up, watching them.

"Oh! I am so sorry. I need to watch where I'm going… Kelsey!" As they separated from their collision, Kelsey blushed and nodded her head. "Yep it's me, my goodness you scared me!"

Brady laughed and put his hands up in the air as if to beg for forgiveness. "Please, excuse me."

"Of course, no harm done, I'm still standing," she looked down at her son, knowing he was okay and out of the way at the time, and she put her hand on his back. "This is my son, Miles. Miles this is Dr. Brady Walker."

Miles held a hand out to Brady, just like a little man, just like he had seen his father do time and again. "It's very nice to meet you Miles," Brady said taking the little boy's hand into his own and gently shaking it. My goodness, Brady had thought to himself, that little guy was a miniature version of Kyle Newman. He had sandy-blonde hair, the same round face, and even stood there like him. His legs, in jeans, though much smaller, were the same too. "I should tell you that I am an old friend of your mom's. I also knew your dad. He was a wonderful man."

Kelsey smiled at Brady and back down at Miles. That was a very kind thing to say to a little boy who had recently lost his daddy, and it warmed her heart when Miles responded, "Thank you, I know he was, and I'm very proud to be his son." Brady was impressed with the manners and the compassion he was witnessing from Kelsey's son. She had raised him well already. He couldn't wait to meet her daughter, also.

"Well we should go. We have an appointment to get to," Kelsey said leading the way for Miles, and Brady stepped back for both of them. "Of course," he said offering Miles knuckles to which he responded and then looking directly at Kelsey, "Always nice to bump into you!" She giggled as they rounded the corner, safely this time, and then she sighed with relief. Bailey was still in Dr. Judy's office - and out of sight.

***

On the way home from the hospital, the kids talked Kelsey into getting take-out food for dinner. They knew it never took too much convincing for her to buy them dinner. Kelsey didn't like to cook, especially after working all day, and in their family Kyle had been the cook. He had loved being in the kitchen. He was creative with recipes and he always said, *There's nothing to cooking a good meal, all you gotta do is follow the directions.*

They all agreed on sub sandwiches for something quick and healthy. They brought three six-inch subs home to eat in their own kitchen. Kelsey had not allowed her kids to drink soda, except for maybe one a day on the weekends, so she poured herself and Bailey tall glasses of iced water and a cup of milk for Miles. And when she sat down at the table with her kids, Miles spoke about meeting his mom's friend today.

"Bailey, you missed it. I met a doctor who is a friend of mom's – and he knew dad, too." Kelsey looked at Miles and then over at Bailey. Now might be the time to talk a little bit about the past.

"While you were in session with Dr. Judy, Miles had to go to the bathroom and when I walked him down the hallway we ran into the doctor who treated your dad years ago when he was in that awful car accident." Miles interrupted and laughed when he told his sister that they really did *run into* each other. After Kelsey explained the mishap to Bailey and laughed it off, Bailey wanted to talk some more about the past.

"So that was when dad was in a coma for like an entire month?"

"Yes, he was in a coma for a month. His brain needed time to heal, and it did."

"I don't know mom, maybe that is why he had the aneurysm? Maybe that stemmed from the head injury he had back then?"

"Maybe, but we will never know for sure, honey."

"So his doctor still works at Laneview? How come you've never mentioned him before, I mean if he's a friend of yours?"

"Well, he actually left Laneview about ten years ago and took a top job at a Washington, D.C. hospital. Now he's back because they wanted to fill that same position at our hospital and this is his home, he wanted to come back," Kelsey felt comfortable talking about him in front of her children. She hadn't before and she never did in front of Kyle. She hadn't wanted him to see something on her face or hear something in her voice. She had thought of Brady. Often. Throughout the years. She never dwelled on *what might have been,* but she did hold a special place in her heart for him and having Bailey, a part of him, had made her secretly feel as if she really hadn't totally lost him.

"So you two became friends while dad was in a coma?"

"Yes, we got to know each other because we spent a lot of time together. I was trying to be at your father's bedside as much as possible and of course Brady was his doctor and around all of the time too," Kelsey was choosing her words carefully.

"I'd like to meet him, too. Maybe next month when we see Dr. Judy?" The kids only had monthly sessions with Dr. Judy. That seemed to be enough for them. Kelsey, however, was still talking to her weekly because she felt like she needed more time and more help. Having missed the past two weeks of therapy, Kelsey knew she needed to get back into that routine. Especially now that her former lover was back in town.

"Maybe sometime," Kelsey suggested as she took a bite of her turkey sandwich, chewed, and then swallowed hard.

***

Kelsey couldn't sleep that night. She was restless, thinking about Brady bumping into her. His hands gripped firmly on her shoulders for a split second. Her hands pushing off of his tight chest just as quickly. The dangerous fact that her daughter, *their* daughter, was right down the hallway. She pushed that thought out of her mind. This was going to be okay. Just fine. Seeing Brady occasionally at the hospital was nothing to worry about. She had already explained to her kids that he is an old friend. An old friend with a body that she couldn't get out of her mind. Again. "Lord have mercy…" Kelsey said aloud and alone in her dark bedroom as she rolled over and forced her eyes shut. Hoping to sleep - instead of thinking so much. About him.

CHAPTER 25

"So work has been busy, or is there some other reason you have been canceling our sessions lately?" There it was. The direct, and not entirely surprising, question from Dr. Judy. Kelsey loved that woman. She was such a beauty, that face of hers, and she in so many ways was very motherly. Kelsey could use a mother right about now in her life. She missed her own, who had been gone from this world for two years already.

"I wasn't avoiding you, I was trying to keep myself out of this hospital in fear of running into the man I had an affair with, my daughter's biological father," and so Kelsey told her everything. She admitted that Dr. Brady Walker had been the physician on staff who treated Kyle years ago - and who had captivated her, body and soul. Dr. Judy didn't know of Brady and had not heard his name until he was recently hired as Laneview's new chief of staff. She reminded Kelsey that even if she knew him, personally or professionally, everything they talked about in their sessions was confidential.

After listening to Kelsey tell her the entire story, Dr. Judy had only one question for her. "Are you trying to avoid him because you still have feelings for him?"

"I will always have feelings for him. I don't want to rekindle what we had, if that is what you're asking. My life is different now. I'm not that woman anymore. I'm just terrified of the truth coming out."

"I know you're afraid of hurting your daughter, above all else.

But let's back up a moment. Why do you think you are not *that* woman anymore? Who was that woman and why is she gone?" Dr. Judy was pressing her and Kelsey allowed her to go there.

"Early on in my relationship with Kyle, I felt like I needed more. I found more when I was with Brady. I found myself feeling like I was living, really living, almost in someone else's body, through someone else's eyes, someone else's heart. I felt more free and sexier than I had ever felt in my life – when I was with him. But that wasn't real. That was me being young and acting out a fantasy. It was alluring and dangerous and I could have lost Kyle if I had chosen to continue making the wrong choices."

"And you came to that realization all by yourself? After Kyle's medical crisis, you left your lover and went back to him. Just like that?" Kelsey was not going to reveal the fact that Brady had drugged Kyle, prolonging his coma. She was not going to admit that he had forced her hand when she uncovered the truth. Brady's actions had forced her to leave him.

"Getting pregnant grounded me. Everything was suddenly put into perspective, my baby growing inside of me opened my eyes to reality," Kelsey explained, truthfully, "I needed to get back to being that responsible person who didn't make crazy choices. I didn't want to be someone who lived with regrets."

"Do you have any regrets, Kelsey?"

"I've lived with guilt, probably more suppressed guilt, but not regret. I have never regretted loving Brady because of the daughter he gave me. And I never, honestly, regretted keeping the truth from Kyle. I thought I was protecting him. I also knew that I had chosen him, finally, with my whole heart. I had planned on spending my life committed to him because I loved him and I wanted him. And I know he felt the same way about me, and our family. We were happy together."

Yet when she saw Brady again, twice now, something inside of her had stirred. She once quickly and passionately had gotten so caught up in that man. And she knew, so effortlessly, she could lose herself with him again. That is why she needed to keep as much distance as possible between them.

Kelsey once again finished another session with Dr. Judy and felt like she needed a release. Talking about her feelings took a toll on her sometimes. Bailey was staying at the high school after school for volleyball practice, and Miles had basketball practice at his grade school. It was Tasha's night to pick up the kids, her kids and Kelsey's kids, from their practices. It was something the two friends and neighbors had started doing after Kyle died. Tasha, who owned a home decorating business, worked from an office inside of her house and she had offered to help Kelsey anytime with transporting the kids. Kelsey often returned the favor when she was out of work on time, or didn't have a therapy session. So today Kelsey wanted to go for a run. It was late January in New York and still too cold to run outside so she opted to go to the gym. She had her workout clothes packed in a gym bag in the car, so she was going to take advantage of her free time to sweat and hopefully clear her mind.

Kelsey changed her clothes in the locker room at the gym. It felt good to her to be in shorts and a t-shirt again. The last time she wore summer clothes was on their cruise over the holidays. Kelsey was fit for a woman in her early forties and she never felt uneasy slipping into a pair of shorts, no matter what season it was.

She was about an hour ahead of the after-work crowd in the gym so she had planned to get her run finished before more people filed in. She had her iPhone strapped to her arm and she put in her earbuds and stepped onto the treadmill. She found herself selecting the latest music from the country music group, The Band Perry. Kyle loved country music, and over the years he had hooked Kelsey as well. She felt close to him, when she thought of things like that now, or did things he used to enjoy.

Forty minutes later, Kelsey had slowed the treadmill and walked a bit before bringing the machine to a stop. She had worked up a good sweat and definitely had a clearer head. As she was walking back to the locker room, she was planning to just throw on some yoga pants and a jacket, which were also in her bag she had packed, so she could avoid having to take a shower in public. She preferred to do that in the privacy of her own home. She now had plenty of time to drive home and be there before her kids. The after-work crowd was starting to file through the doors and start up the machines as Kelsey reached the entrance to the locker room. And that's when he stopped her.

"You're done and out of here already?" It was Brady. He was wearing workout shorts and a sleeveless t-shirt. He was, still, an obvious gym rat.

"Oh, hi, yes I'm done with my run and headed to grab some clothes and go home." Her face was rosy from the run but it felt hotter at that moment, seeing him.

"That's always a good feeling…to be done working your butt off and knowing it's time to go home," Brady smiled but he wished he had more to go home to. No wife. No kids. Just a lonely apartment. Being back in New York, just knowing she was so close by again, made him miss her in his life more. He knew that seeing her, running into her now and then, was making it worse for him. He didn't want to spend any more time, or waste any more time, trying to get over her. He wanted to be with her.

"It is a good feeling, but honestly Brady it's hard for me to go home sometimes. I love my kids and I need to be with them, but I miss my husband and the family we used to be - together," Kelsey surprised herself with her own words. She never did hold back with Brady. That was one of the things he had loved about her. If she was thinking it, she said it. If she was feeling it, she expressed it.

"I understand, I really do. Joanie and I had lived together the last year of her life. I know what it's like to want to go home, but to hate it when the emptiness sets in once you get there. I'm sorry you're missing Kyle. I can say that it will get easier, with time, and I can also say that you are one lucky woman to have those children to go home to. I have a lot of regrets, and not having any children is top on that list."

Kelsey felt a pang in her heart. He did have a child, a daughter, who she had deprived him from knowing and raising as his own. "Thanks for getting me, Brady. It's nice to know I'm not alone in my sadness sometimes."

"No, you're not alone. Please know that I am here for you. If you want…we could grab a bite to eat or a drink sometime? I mean, when you're kids are busy for awhile." There, he had said it. He had wanted to say it since he saw her again on the rooftop for the first time in so many years. And Kelsey was thinking that this is not where she wanted to go with him. She couldn't travel down that road again, not without taking a huge risk. *Could she?*

"I don't know, Brady. Given our history…"

"That's all the more reason to, don't you think? We could call it old friends catching up, and sparing each other a little loneliness for a few hours."

"Maybe sometime."

"Okay, I'll take your maybe. It's better than a no," Brady was smiling at her, dimple and all, and Kelsey smiled back at him and giggled at how he hadn't really changed at all. Still so boyish. Still so convincing. Lord have mercy, she had to go before she fell into that quicksand with him again.

"Have a good evening, Brady Walker." She flashed him one last smile and headed through the locker room door which had just opened when another woman walked out. She caught the door, looked back at Brady one more time as he said to her, "You too, babe."

She saw herself in the mirror as soon as she entered the locker room. She looked again because she didn't know if she should feel startled. She was back. That woman who felt like the seams of her life had been let out a bit, just a bit this time, was staring back at her in the mirror on the wall. There was something alive in her eyes again. She knew she should be telling herself to walk away, run if she had to, but she couldn't. Because she didn't want to.

***

When Kelsey left the gym, she didn't look around. She didn't want to risk seeing him. She just walked directly out of the door and to her car in the parking lot. Her phone had buzzed in the pocket of her jacket and she checked it once she got into the car. It was a text. *Taking a chance. New phone, I'm sure. Same old number, I hope.*

She sighed, smiled, and felt warm tingles inside. *Same old number. And same old feelings.* She closed out of that text, put her phone in the cup holder between the front seats, and drove away.

***

She was feeling especially weak and lonely after the kids were asleep. She poured herself a glass of wine and carried it up the stairs to her bedroom. She missed those nights with Kyle, staying up late sharing a glass or two of wine, and just talking about their day or the kids. And many times those nights would end with the two of them making love before going to sleep in each other's arms. God she missed him. And now she was missing that feeling of being close to someone, being touched, and feeling affection. From a man.

She knew that responding to Brady's text would be a mistake. She had to think of Bailey and how this would affect her. She was a well-rounded young girl who didn't need any more disappointment in her life. Losing her father was almost too much for her, but she - like Kelsey - had bounced back and carried on amid the heartbreak and the sadness.

Halfway through drinking her glass of wine, Kelsey picked up her phone and reread his text. *Taking a chance. New phone, I'm sure. Same old number, I hope.* If she responded, she knew it would be because of a moment of weakness. She also knew if she would turn off her phone and go to bed, she would feel so much better in the morning if she had chosen to having left well enough alone.

The next morning Kelsey was busy getting herself and her kids out the door when she thought of how vulnerable she had felt the night before. She was proud of herself for not giving in and reaching out to him. The old Kelsey would have done that. She was a mother now. Her children were her life. She didn't have time for romance, or so she tried to convince herself.

Work was extremely busy all day long so she didn't have a chance to think about anything else. When they all returned home at the end of the day, Kelsey prepared spaghetti with meat sauce and a lettuce salad for dinner while her kids were both doing their homework. When the three of them sat down at the kitchen table to eat, Kelsey wanted to hear about their day - and Bailey couldn't wait to speak first.

"You are never going to guess who I met at school today!" She was beaming and Kelsey smiled at her daughter, thinking she was about to hear she had met the captain of the football team or some hot boy, older than her in high school. The thought of Bailey dating had made Kelsey tense but she knew it was going to happen sooner than later. "Well it was career day for the sophomores, and I was one of six students who signed up for having an interest in the medical field, remember?" Kelsey nodded her head as she thought of Dr. Brady Walker, while Miles slurped up two spaghetti noodles at one time and splashed sauce on his nose. "And I met the chief of staff from Laneview Hospital!"

Kelsey choked on the water she had started to sip from her glass. When she finished coughing, trying to hide her wide eyes behind her glass, she asked, "Brady?"

"Yes! Your friend and dad's doctor, Brady Walker!" Kelsey could not believe what she had heard. She had spent the last month trying to keep that chance meeting from happening each and every time they entered the hospital and here her daughter goes to school and ends up meeting him, and not just talking to him, but spending time with him.

"Oh my goodness, wow, what a small world. So how did that all go?" Kelsey had no idea what had occurred today. Did Brady know the truth now? Had he taken one look at her and been instantly shell-shocked?

"Well he was so nice, and very smart, and he said he liked my name. He seemed surprised at first when he saw that my last name was Newman, and he made the connection to you and dad. He had an alphabetized list of our last names with our first initials so when he figured out that I was your daughter, he asked me what my first name is and he couldn't get over it for a minute. Not so common to be a Bailey nowadays, I guess." Bailey giggled and Kelsey thought to herself, *yeah not so common to find out your former lover named her baby girl after your deceased mother.*

"So the cool part is there were six of us signed up to work with Dr. Walker and four of them ended up switching over to business at the last minute. So that left me and Emily - but poor Emily started her period today and had an awful migraine so she went home." Kelsey had gotten up from the table to bring Miles' plate up to the stove for more spaghetti that he had asked for and she looked back at him, listening to his sister speak. She had thought to herself many times how Miles will make an understanding husband one day, given all the girl issues he has heard about growing up with a teenage sister.

"So, wait, are you telling me you were with Brady, one on one, all day today?"

"Yes, for the workshop, and it was so awesome to be the only one listening and asking questions." Bailey obviously loved attention.

Kelsey sat back down at the table and wanted to sigh and say *oh Lord have mercy.* She pushed her plate forward, she was definitely not wanting to eat anything more for dinner. She was a nervous wreck thinking about what had taken place today. "So what's next with this career workshop, I know you told me you would be working closely with the professionals for the rest of the school year…"

"That's right, we will meet at school once a week for the next few months. Then, each professional will choose one person from their group to do an internship at their workplace. And I already know it is going to be me since no one else in my sophomore class wants to get into the medical field. Emily just chose it at school so she could be with me for this project, she just wants to work at the mall someday and maybe not even go to college if her parents don't freak about it."

Kelsey chuckled, shook her head, and got back to the subject at hand. Brady. Miles had asked to leave the table and go outside to play basketball. It was already dark so Kelsey turned the outside house lights on for him while he bundled up in his coat and hat. "Only for a little while, come in if you get too cold," Kelsey called after him while Bailey helped her clear the dishes off of the table and put them into the dishwasher.

"I'm really excited about this opportunity to work with a real doctor. After today mom, I am more certain than ever that I want to be a doctor. Dr. Walker even helped me narrow down my specific interests. I think I want to be a pediatrician. You know how much I love babies and kids." Kelsey was so proud of her daughter, setting lofty goals for herself and just believing in attaining a dream. And, at that moment, she was extremely grateful for Brady's guidance. She was still scared out of her mind about what he was thinking right now, but after seeing her daughter's face and hearing the excitement in her voice, she wanted with all of her heart for this to be a good thing for the two of them.

***

The next morning, Kelsey returned home after dropping off her kids at school. She had planned to be out of the office for the day. She had taken part in an early morning phone interview before the kids were awake and later she planned to write that story on her laptop. Otherwise, she wanted the day for herself. She was going to go for a run outside in the cold but sunny thirty-eight degree weather, and then she had a few errands including grocery shopping on her to-do list.

***

After her four-mile run, Kelsey took a hot shower, blow-dried her hair, and then slipped on her favorite thick pink terrycloth robe. She was only wearing a pair of lacy boyshorts underneath, not ready to get dressed yet, when the doorbell rang. She thought for a moment about not answering it but she knew her car was parked on the driveway and she also thought one of her neighbors might need something. They had all been there for her, so she wouldn't ever hesitate to return the favors. Kelsey descended the stairs, tightening her robe around her body - and then she unlocked and opened her front door. She had to have looked every bit shocked as she felt when she saw Brady standing on her front porch.

"What in the world? Brady..." She wanted to ask how he knew where she lived but Googling someone's name and finding an address wasn't so difficult to do on the Internet.

"I apologize for hunting you down like this, I know I must look desperate, but I called your office and they told me you weren't in today. I was hoping to catch you here, to talk. I know you're busy with your kids after school and at night so here I am, I took a chance to see if you were at home." Brady had gotten her address off of Bailey's contact information sheet which she had filled out for the career program.

"No, you're fine, please come in." Kelsey stepped back and he walked into her house. She felt awkward being half-dressed and she felt uneasy with the urgency of his visit. She wondered if it was judgment day, on earth, for her.

Brady stopped and waited for Kelsey in her living room. He didn't want to just sit down, until she invited him to. She pulled her robe tighter around her again. She wondered if she should excuse herself to go put on some more clothes but she felt silly thinking about saying those words to him, a man who had once upon a time seen her naked.

"Would you like some hot tea or something? I just got back from a run before I showered and I was going to fix myself some." Brady said yes and followed her into the kitchen, and then they both sat down at the table to wait for the water to boil in the teapot on the stove.

"I know this may seem crazy, but you and I have been through crazy before, so I'm just going to tell you what's on my mind. We used to be able to talk about anything, so please just listen, I need to say this to you." Kelsey nodded her head and waited for him to continue. "We have bumped into each other more than a few times in the last month since I moved back. I love seeing you, talking to you, and I can't get you off my mind. I'm hoping that you feel the same way… I'm hoping our quick chats every once in awhile leave you looking forward to the next time and wanting more, too. I can be patient, and I was planning to be. Until yesterday. I met someone and she left me with the feeling of wanting to be more to you than just a memory."

"You met my daughter…I heard all about it," Kelsey forced herself to stay completely calm. Maybe he was there in her house, for them, and not to ask questions or make accusations toward her about Bailey.

"She is a beautiful girl, a carbon copy of you, and so incredibly mature for her age. I am thrilled that she truly wants to become a doctor someday. She will be an amazing one." Brady was taken by Bailey. He knew she had reminded him of Kelsey, but there was something more. He wished he could have known her as a child. There was something about her that was captivating. Her level of compassion was incredible. She was indeed an old soul and Brady was honored to be her career mentor at school. He thought of it as fate bringing them together, maybe bringing him back to her mother.

"Thank you for saying all of that. I am very blessed to have my daughter. She has been something else since day one. Kyle used to say that she has the whole package - kind, smart, pretty, social, and an athlete. She's my girl and I'm so proud of her." By now Kelsey had made them each a cup of tea and Brady had taken off his coat and hung it on the back of the chair he was sitting on. He was dressed casually in jeans, tennis shoes, and a blue crewneck sweatshirt. She assumed he was not on duty at the hospital today, or at least not this morning. The last thing she was thinking about now was work. She would write her story and run her errands later. Right now she needed to give Brady this time to talk about what he was feeling. Kelsey truly believed he had felt a connection with her daughter, his daughter, and it both scared her and fascinated her.

"So do you think I'm a complete nutcase showing up here at your home and spilling my heart like this?" Brady leaned back in his chair and smiled at her. She was still getting used to that clean shaven face of his. The attraction she had felt toward him was most definitely still there, alive, inside of her.

Kelsey giggled. "No of course not. I'm just not sure what to say or do, right now," she was being honest. She wasn't sure what was right or wrong. She had kept the truth from him about their daughter and now he wanted to be a part of *their* lives. *How would she continue lying to them both now?*

"You have been awfully quiet…"

"That's because you told me to shut up and listen!"They both laughed and it felt so good to be together, like this, again. Kelsey had already gotten past the fact that he was in her home that she shared with her children - and used to share with her husband - and she also no longer cared that she was sitting there with him in a robe with very little clothing on underneath.

"I want you to give me an answer. Talk to me, babe," Brady reached for her hand across the table from him. He held it and she allowed him to. He slid his fingers in between hers. She was responding to his touch. Again. And with their fingers still intertwined, she spoke.

"My husband was my life. He has not even been gone a year yet. I don't know if I am ready for you, for us, for this, again." Kelsey pulled her hand out of his and she put her face into her hands for a moment, realizing then that she also wasn't wearing any makeup. "I just don't know, Brady." She was looking at him again and he moved his chair around the table leg between them, and closer to her.

"I get that. I know what it's like to need time. I also know that there isn't a template for grieving and there shouldn't be a time frame placed on it. Just because we say it's been so many weeks or so many months or so many years doesn't take away the pain and the sorrow of it all. Does time heal? No, time just allows us to get used to the fact. Maybe time makes it easier to be less sad with each passing day. I don't know. All I know is you and I have a history, a real love between us, so if we need to find that again, if we want to find that again – then I say damn it let's seize it while we can." Brady's words had touched her. What he said had made perfect sense to her. He always knew how to say the right words.

The tears in Kelsey's eyes had told Brady what he needed to know at that moment. He had reached her, and she hadn't pushed him away. There was no running this time. All those years ago, there was another man she chose to love and honor. Now, during their chance meetings in the past month, it was always her kids she had to put first. Her kids she had to get home to. Right now, at this very moment, neither one of them had any place they needed to be. It was just the two of them with only each other on their minds. Brady leaned toward her and put his hand on her cheek, his palm moved downward to her chin, and he pulled her toward him as his lips met hers. She didn't resist and he didn't hold back. And moments later they were lost in each other and breathless. Again.

When they stopped, Kelsey looked down and noticed that her robe had come open a little more than she had realized. Part of her breasts were visible. She reached up and covered herself, tightening the robe around her once again. Brady was staring at her. "Don't cover up on my account…" Kelsey blushed, laughed nervously, as she never took her eyes off of him. She was so lonely. It had been so long since she had been made love to. God she wanted him to touch her.

"We can't do this here, not in my home that I shared with my husband."

"I understand, and I respect that. I do. So does this mean you and I–"

"Have a chance again?" she interrupted him and he came toward her in an instant so swift that she lost her head again. She lost herself in him. His lips on hers, their hands on each other. Her robe was opening up again and he was kissing her neck. Before she allowed him to go any further, she pulled away. "We can't. Not yet."

Brady smiled at her and backed away. He stood up, took his coat off the chair and slipped it on. "If you are asking me to behave, I had better go." He was still smiling at her as she crossed her legs under the table and put her robe back together. He started to leave her home through the door in the kitchen that led out to the driveway, and then he looked back at her.

"Kelsey?"

"Yes you can call me. Same old number." His face lit up and she giggled again. She was so into this feeling again. With him. Between them. God help her, if the truth would eventually have to come out.

"I was going to ask you something else…"

"Okay, ask me."

"Why did you name her Bailey?" He had wanted to ask the

moment he found out. Yesterday. He wanted to run straight to her and ask her if there had been a reason behind her choice to name her daughter after *his* mother. He knew it couldn't be true. He knew Kelsey as an honest woman. He knew she would have told him if the baby was his. From the very bottom of his heart though, he wanted it to be true. He had wanted that young girl's blue eyes to be those that he and his mother both shared.

Kelsey was caught off guard. This is what she had feared about letting him into her life again. She wanted to crumble in his arms and beg for his forgiveness and his understanding, but she couldn't. She wouldn't. This was her daughter's life. She had already decided, when her baby girl was born, what was best for her.

"Because once, when you told me what your mother's name was, I was taken by it. It's a beautiful name and I wanted it for my beautiful girl."

Brady smiled at her and he felt his eyes sting with tears. "Thank you, babe. It means a lot to me to know you never forgot those meaningful things, like that, that we once talked about."

"Of course I remember. You mean a lot to me, Brady."

"I love you." There. He said it. Already. He was not going to hide how he felt. "I feel like I always have. And I know I always will."

Those were powerful words, and Kelsey believed him and felt all of that, too. Before she could say anything, he walked out of the door and closed it.

Always have. Always will, she said aloud to herself, all alone, in her kitchen.

CHAPTER 26

Kelsey spent the next half hour in a daze. All she could think of was how he felt, how he had tasted, and how risky this was going to be for her, and for her daughter.

She was upstairs in her bedroom, had just slipped into a pair of skinny jeans and was buttoning up her long-sleeved white oxford blouse when her cell phone rang. She had left it on the table in the hallway so she walked out there to pick it up on the third ring, noticing it was Bree.

"Hello sweet thing, what's going on with you today?" Kelsey asked with a smile on her face that quickly faded when she heard Bree's panicked voice. "Oh God Kel, please, I need you. Come to Laneview. It's Max, they're telling me his injuries are not good-"

"I'm on my way! Tell me what happened!" Kelsey flipped off her bedroom light switch and saw Bailey's Ugg boots lying in the doorway of her bedroom. They were wearing the same size right now so she slipped barefoot into those, pulled them up, and made her way down the stairs to retrieve her purse and keys on the table by the front door. She was in her car seconds later, backing out of the driveway, when Bree told her what happened.

"He was in a jeep this morning going to school, Savannah was driving. I had no idea Kel, but Nicholas gave her permission to drive him to school when he left for work." Bree was sobbing and Kelsey was confused. "Oh dear God, since when does

Savannah have a jeep?"

"Since last weekend, her mother's new husband bought it for her. Please Bree just hurry up and get here! I need you."

"I'm in the car now and I'm hanging up so I can totally concentrate on the road and get to you as soon as I possibly can, or sooner." Kelsey prayed the entire half hour drive back to the city, back to Laneview Hospital. She remembered, again, the last time she rushed to that blasted hospital. Kyle had died. *Please God, please let Max be alright. Bree needs that boy. He's everything to her. Please…*

***

Kelsey arrived in the emergency room and was directed to a private waiting room on the first floor, where family and friends waited for loved ones in surgery. She obviously now knew that Max was in surgery. She walked swiftly down the hallway and rounded the corner to find Bree sitting on one side of the waiting room, and Nicholas standing in front of the window, and staring out of it, on the opposite side of the room.

"Bree!" Kelsey ran to her and she stood up and fell into her arms - and sobbed. Nicholas turned to them and then walked out into the hallway. He knew they needed to talk and he didn't want to hear the story again. It was bad enough that he was living it. And is to blame for it.

Savannah's mother had gotten remarried last weekend. Her new husband had, like everyone else, found it incredibly difficult to reach his stepdaughter. He's a wealthy man so he bought her a jeep, hoping to buy her love, or maybe just get her out of the house more often so he could be with his new wife without the complications of a teenager in the house and in his life.

When Savannah had driven the brand-new jeep home to her father's house at the end of the weekend, Bree had flipped out. Savannah was not a responsible person, or a careful driver. She had gotten her license when she was a sophomore and had two accidents within the first six months, finally totaling her car in the second accident, and both Nicholas and her mother had refused to buy her another vehicle. It had been two years since that girl had driven a car alone. She had driven Nicholas or her mother around numerous times, but that was it. Either her friends picked her up or she stayed at home. She had never asked for another car, she was too wrapped up in where she would get her next high. Her drug use was over now, and had been for quite some time, but Savannah continued to have issues and Bree had totally given up on her. She had told Nicholas it was time for her to move out. Her destructive, wild ways were not something she wanted her son, a brand new teenager, around any longer. Nicholas and Bree had an awful fight about his daughter and he had been sleeping on the couch since they exchanged harsh words on Sunday night. It was now Tuesday morning, and Savannah's actions had resulted in Max fighting for his life in the operating room at Laneview Hospital.

Kelsey was holding onto Bree as she helped her sit back down on the chair against the wall. "I left for work. Nic was supposed to take Max to school. Then I got a call that Savannah and Max were in an accident on their way to school. Nic gave her permission to drive my son to school in her brand new jeep with reckless driving and inexperience running through her veins." Bree took a deep breath to keep herself from crying as she told Kelsey what had happened. "He was not wearing his seatbelt, the jeep flipped, and he was thrown out of it." Bree started to cry and Kelsey felt overwhelmed with panic. How would her best friend's young son survive being thrown out of a moving vehicle, flipping end over end? "He has internal injuries. Dr. Walker is trying to save him now."

"Brady?"

"Yes, of all doctors. When you told me he was back, I wondered if that man would be any good for you - but if he can save my son's life I will be forever grateful to him." Kelsey squeezed Bree's hand tightly and hoped that Brady would walk into the waiting room, soon, with good news. Bree continued to speak, telling Kelsey that her son had a lot of internal injuries and her stepdaughter had walked away from the accident, unscathed. She had been at the hospital to be examined by a doctor but when she was through, Bree couldn't look at her. Savannah never said a word to her as she, Bree, and her father all sat in the same room and waited. When Bree had walked out to find a nurse to see what was happening with her son, she overheard Nicholas and his daughter talking about the accident. He asked her why his son had not been wearing a seatbelt and Savannah replied, "You know how he is, a spoiled brat, he didn't have it on or want to put it on, so I didn't make him. I didn't want to listen to him whine about it..." Nicholas didn't have a chance to yell at her, or shake her, or have any response at all, because Bree flew into the room and ended up right in Savannah's face, screaming, "If my son dies, it's your fault, you little bitch!"

Nicholas had physically removed Bree from standing in front of his daughter, so full of rage. He then called Savannah's mother and she picked her up and took her home with her. He knew Savannah being there was making the situation so much worse, if that was possible. Nicholas had known how bad things looked for his son, and it was killing him to know he was the one who allowed this to happen. He was in a hurry to get to work and he had given his daughter permission to drive his son to school. He hoped and prayed, to a God he had rarely turned to in his life, for his son to survive.

Forty-five minutes had passed, and there still had been no word about Max. Kelsey had gotten Bree a cup of coffee and a bottle of water, both of which she refused to drink. The panic in Bree's eyes was all too familiar for Kelsey. She would never wish those feelings on anyone, sitting in a hospital waiting for the news of life or death. She was thinking about Kyle now and had silently prayed to him. *Hey you, up there, if you can take a break from whatever it is you're doing right now and put in a good word with God…tell him to save Max, ask him to save my dearest friend in the whole world the pain and sorrow of losing her son. I love you Kyle Newman, and I love our kids and we're making it, we're doing okay without you since you gave us no other choice but to carry on… but I'm telling you I can't do this anymore. I can't face more death and dying. I just can't.*

Kelsey and Bree were sharing silence, sitting very close together in their chairs with their arms and legs touching, when Brady walked in. He immediately looked directly at Kelsey and what she saw in his eyes sent panic through her as she and Bree both stood up and met him in the middle of the room.

There were tears in his eyes as he reached for Bree's hand and Kelsey didn't hear much else after that. Nicholas was standing in the doorway and he had fallen to his knees with his face in his hands. A big, strong, invincible, and arrogant man coming apart at the seams. Kelsey held Bree as tightly as she could and Brady enveloped them both in his arms. He hadn't been able to save that boy, that thirteen-year-old boy who had massive internal injuries. He knew taking him to surgery with too many inoperable injuries had not made complete sense. He had to try though. He had to attempt to stop some of the bleeding, sew up those major organs – by God, work a miracle, if he could. But, he couldn't. That young boy had died. Max Bridges, the light of Bree's life, was dead.

CHAPTER 27

The following six weeks were a blur. A child's funeral. A mother's grief. A marriage unsalvageable. Kelsey had done everything she could for Bree. It was her turn to be there for her grieving friend. She talked to her, she held her, she cried with her. Though Kelsey could not fathom what it was like to grieve for a child, she did know grief, all too well, and she did know how it felt to let it take her down so far that she never thought she'd get back up again. But, she had, and she would make absolutely sure that her dearest friend in the world would also survive.

Bree left Nicholas Bridges the day after their son's funeral. Their divorce was already final now, six weeks later. Burying Max had taken away any chance in Bree's mind, and in her heart, of ever wanting Nicholas Bridges in her life, or anywhere near her, again. She hated herself for not leaving him sooner, years sooner. He didn't love her, he didn't try to be a good husband to her, or any kind of a father to Max. It was always her and Max. Mother and son. *They* were in this thing called life together, and now he was gone.

When Bree moved out of her New York City apartment and left Nicholas and Savannah behind, Kelsey had insisted that she move into her home, with her and her kids – who also were suffering from losing Max because he had always been like a cousin to them. Kelsey wanted to take care of Bree for as long as it took for her to begin to mend. Bree had moved into the furnished downstairs area in the Newman house, where there was both a spare bedroom and a bathroom.

Kelsey's parents had stayed downstairs as guests many times, but in recent years no one had used that extra space. Bree had taken a leave of absence from her job, and Kelsey had taken as much time off as possible to be with her. Some days were better than others. Living with Kelsey's kids had definitely helped to keep Bree busy. She needed to feel useful, she needed to be depended on the same way Max had needed her. Kelsey's kids were helping Bree to heal.

So much had happened since Bree lost her son. Bailey continued to thrive in the career program at school, and she and Brady had grown very close. He was stopping by the house now to visit all of them, checking on Bree, dropping off old medical books from college for Bailey to read, and even playing basketball on the driveway with Miles. The two of them had become instant buddies. Kelsey saw their friendship forming the first few hours they had spent together one Sunday afternoon. No one had played basketball like that with her son since Kyle. He had a man in his life again, teaching him things his mom couldn't. Her life was coming together again while she tried tirelessly to keep Bree's from falling apart. Bree was going to be okay, and she told her that while the two of them were drinking wine, late, after the kids were asleep.

"You know you have to stop taking such good care of me, or I may never leave," Bree said, laughing, and Kelsey scooted closer to her on the couch. There was never an issue of personal space between them. The closer they could get to each other, the better. "I don't want you to ever leave," Kelsey said and meant those words.

"Oh stop it! You need to move me out so you can move that hot doctor in..." Bree has seen the way the two of them look at each other, interact with each other, and just exist in the same room together. No one knew that there was anything going on between them, especially not Kelsey's children. And truthfully, there really wasn't anything going on.

"Really? Just move him in, huh? I don't think so sister. He hasn't kissed me in well over a month. We're never alone together to talk or well you know..." Kelsey smiled and Bree knew she wanted that man back in her life, and in her bed. Kelsey was so happy watching him get to know her children and spend time with all of them, even with Bree. Especially with Bree. Brady was so supportive of her loss and had tried to help ease her pain. They were all acting like a family, watching movies, sharing pizza, and playing outside in the winter's first snowfall last month, in February. It was all good. But Kelsey still worried about the truth coming out. And of course Bree could always read her mind.

"So he really has no idea that Bailey is-?"

"Shh... no. No idea. The connection the two of them share is unbelievable though. A part of me wants them both to know...but I can't risk the damage it will do."

"I hear you, and it is your choice to make. I just have one question... can the man not see that she has his exact same eyes? Jesus Kel, it's so fucking obvious."

"It's only obvious if you know, and we know, so please let's stop talking about this."

"Sure. I would rather talk about you and Brady taking some

time for yourselves this weekend. I want to watch the kids. I miss my son so much it pains me every second of every day, but being with you and your kids here in this house has been so good for me. I won't stay forever, I promise, but I need to stay for awhile longer. So let me take the reins and stay with them this weekend."

"Of course you can stay. I want you to stay, my kids want you here, too." Kelsey loved Bree more than ever right at this moment. Her strength was inspiring. And she was so relieved to hear Bree imply that she would survive. And that she wanted to survive. "I can't make plans with Brady. What would I tell my kids?"

"Maybe it's time that you do tell them something. Something like, you know the man who has slowing been winning all of our hearts the past month? Well, I want a piece of him, too." Bree and Kelsey laughed out loud together.

Kelsey thought about what Bree had suggested and she wondered if Brady would accept her offer to at least have dinner. It didn't have to be an entire weekend away. Kelsey couldn't justify that to her kids. Not yet. She did like the idea of spending some time alone with Brady, and having him pay attention to her and only her. Now she wondered how to tell her kids she and Brady were going on a date.

While Bree was in the living room, talking on the phone with her boss about returning to work, Kelsey pulled both of her kids back into the kitchen after dinner to talk – about Brady.

"What's going on, mom? You have that serious look on your face again," Bailey was extremely observant and very perceptive - especially when it came to the people she loved.

"Well I do need to talk to you both about something and it is serious, but it's a good thing. At least I think it is a good thing…" They were all three sitting down at the table now and Kelsey was trying to find the perfect way to tell them, or ask them if her dating Brady would be okay.

"I want to talk to you both about Brady."

"We love Brady, mom!" Miles interjected and Kelsey was touched. Bailey was smiling and shaking her head in agreement.

"It makes me very happy to hear you say that and to know you both adore him. I happen to think he is wonderful, too. He also feels the same way about me. So, if it's okay with the both of you, I would like to go on a date with Brady this Saturday night," Kelsey felt so awkward talking to them about this and she feared what their reactions would be.

"So you like him?" Bailey asked.

"Are you two going to kiss and be all gross?" Miles asked, clearly feeling disgusted at the mere thought of two adults getting *that* close.

"I do like him. As you both know, he and I were friends a long time ago - and it just feels right to have him be a part of our lives lately. Bailey, it warms my heart how much you are learning from him and how the two of you have connected over medicine. Miles, you have a basketball buddy again, a man to talk to and look up to."

"He's not dad," Bailey said, sounding a bit unnerved.

"Oh my gosh, no, he's not dad - and he isn't trying to be. He is just here when we need him and want him around and it's just a nice feeling."

"I'm okay with you two going out on a date, mom. Now can I go outside and shoot some hoops before it gets dark and you make me come back inside?" Kelsey smiled at her son, kissed him on top of his head, and told him to go.

Kelsey felt like it wasn't going to be quite as easy with Bailey. "So honey, are you okay with this? Please be honest with me. I want to know how you're feeling."

"I'm feeling like I should have seen this coming. I don't mean that in a bad way. I just mean that the two of you always seem so comfortable together. I like seeing you happy again, mom. And you know how much I like spending time with Brady. I don't think I'm ready to think of him as a dad in this house, but I'm fine with you seeing him, and seeing where your relationship goes."

Kelsey felt like crying. She hadn't expected such mature words from her daughter. Not about this. She was touched and obviously deeply moved by her approval. "You, my baby girl, are wise beyond your years and I couldn't love you any more than I do right at this moment." Kelsey hugged her daughter and Bree was wiping away tears, standing in the doorway of the kitchen. Life was coming together again for her dear friend, and one day she knew it would again for her, too. The pain of losing Max would always be there, she knew that, but Kelsey had taught her to take this tragedy one day at a time. And right now she was happy for Kelsey and her children. Brady Walker had become a part of all of their lives and no one was objecting.

Kelsey called Brady after everyone had gone to bed. It was their ritual to talk at nighttime, even when he was on duty at the hospital, but he didn't work the night shift as often as he had all those years ago when they first met. They loved talking to each other, privately, late at night. They would rehash something that had happened with the kids when they were together, or they would talk about the two of them - and express the mutual feelings they shared for each other.

"So how did it go?" Brady asked when Kelsey's call came through. He had been nervous all evening about what her kids might say regarding the prospect of them dating. He was thrilled when Kelsey had asked him out for this Saturday night. She was ready, and he had been waiting forever for that moment. He loved being with her and her children - and even got a kick out of Bree being in the mix now. They all felt like a close-knit group. Not a family, not quite, and not yet. Brady had high hopes for that to happen when everyone was ready.

"It went amazingly well. Miles expressed his love for you and asked if we are going to be all gross and kiss," Kelsey laughed, "and Bailey is very happy for us, as we see where our relationship goes, and those were her exact words."

"Well I hope I know how this love story will go, but right now I am just focused on how our first date again will be. You leave all of the planning to me, okay? Just be ready for me to pick you up at five-thirty on Saturday night, lady." Kelsey giggled. "Are you going to get all bossy on me Dr. Walker, now that we're officially dating?

"Of course not. Just shut up and listen to me when I say that I love you and I cannot wait to plan an evening you will never forget."

"Ohhh...well put it that way and I'll be very obedient." The two of them laughed together and talked for two hours before saying goodnight.

Saturday night couldn't come soon enough for either of them.

***

"So what are you wearing? Did he say where he's taking you?" Bree was sitting on the end of Kelsey's bed with her legs crisscrossed while Kelsey stood inside of her walk-in closet wearing only her matching black bra and panties. She had her hair and makeup already done and now she was being indecisive about what to wear.

"He wouldn't tell me where we are going and when I asked him what I should wear he said, whatever I felt like wearing would be perfect," Kelsey was beaming like she was a young girl again, about to go on her first date with a boy she really, really liked.

"Well then that just means whatever you do decide to wear is coming off," Bree laughed out loud and Kelsey joined her, adding somewhat under her breath, *"I hope so"* as the two of them laughed harder.

"I will say one thing sister, you sure do look good in your undies at forty-three years old!" Bree and Kelsey had always complimented each other on their bodies. Both women continued to take exceptional care of themselves and looked amazing for women over forty.

"Oh please now *you're* trying to get me into bed," Kelsey teased her.

"Damn right I am. It's been too long for this chic!" They were still laughing when Miles came into her bedroom. "What time will Brady be here, mom?" He walked right into her closet while she was sorting through her clothes. "Very soon and that is why I have to get dressed right now." Miles giggled at his mom, in her underwear. "Good, because I need to show him my three-point shot. Do you think he will have time to watch me before he takes you out on a date?"

"I know he will have time to watch you, sweetie," Kelsey pinched his cheeks together and kissed him on the lips. Then she pulled a little black dress off of a hanger and slipped into it. Bree got off of the bed and zipped her up and gave her approval. "You can't go wrong with a little black dress. You look amazing, sister." Kelsey thanked her as she slipped into her stilettos and took one last look in the mirror as the doorbell rang and Miles announced he would get the door as he barreled down the stairs.

Kelsey was ready and looking out the window in her kitchen at the two of them on the driveway. "It melts your heart, doesn't it?" Bree asked her as Bailey walked into the room to say goodbye to her mom.

"Yes it does. I love how both of my kids like him in our lives," Kelsey said, looking at Bailey and she hugged her quick before grabbing her long off-white coat from the chair and slipping it on.

"Have fun tonight mom, and don't worry about us… Bree is taking us out for dinner and a movie.

"Thank you," Kelsey said looking at Bailey and then over at Bree as the boys came inside the kitchen door.

"Your boy is one star shooter," Brady said tousling the hair on Miles' head and winking at Kelsey. "You look beautiful, by the way." Bailey was watching them both and then Brady glanced over at her. "How are you tonight, Bay?"

"I'm good. Can I ask you a quick question though? The book you gave me last week is in the living room and I was reading it this morning and–"

"I will follow you in there, so you can show me." Brady put his arm around Bailey's shoulders and the two of them walked out of the room, followed by Miles who wanted to turn on the TV.

Bree walked over to Kelsey and hugged her tight. "The two of you desperately need this time alone."

"Oh I know…I'm looking forward to it," Kelsey sighed and Bree asked her if she was nervous.

"I am, can you tell? It's been so long…and I don't know… am I betraying Kyle? Again? I feel a little bit like I am."

"Hey, stop," Bree took Kelsey's hands in hers, "Kyle loved you, but he's gone honey, and it is time to move on. The special part here is you have this chance to move on and it's not like you and Brady are brand new to each other - you've shared a rare love for a long time, and it's time to grab ahold of it while you can," Bree was speaking straight from her heart and from all the experience both she and Kelsey have had with loving and losing someone in their lives.

"You're so right and I love you so much. Thank you. For everything!" Kelsey pulled her close and the two of them hugged again as Brady walked into the room.

"Can I pull my date away from you for a few hours?" Brady laughed and Bree and Kelsey separated from each other as Bree gave Brady a squeeze on his shoulder, and told him to enjoy the evening with her sister.

***

Brady and Kelsey buckled up and backed out of her driveway in his car. "I can't believe this is really happening, you and I are alone," he said as he squeezed her knee which was bare because she was wearing her short little black dress. She put her hand on top of his and intertwined her fingers with his.

"Me either. Now tell me where we're going, hot stuff." Brady did look dapper in his black pants and powder blue long-sleeved dress shirt under a black sport coat.

"We are going back to the city." And that is all he would reveal about their evening until he drove her to his apartment. He had found another apartment near Central Park when he moved back to New York and Kelsey had yet to see it.

"And we're back at your place, why? Did you forget something?"

"You'll see…" he said unlocking and opening the door of his apartment for her. And when she walked in she gasped and put her hand over her mouth. His living room was candlelit and in the middle was a small round table, decorated with a white table cloth and set for dinner. There was a man, dressed like a waiter, coming from the kitchen as they walked in. "Everything you asked for is ready, Dr. Walker." Brady thanked him, paid him in cash, and he left the apartment.

Kelsey had walked over to the table and noticed a wine bottle chilling and two plates covered with metal lids. She lifted one of the lids and saw Italian food. Pasta. It was from the restaurant where the two of them had shared their first carry-out dinner, many years ago. Kelsey always enjoyed the food from that restaurant, and still did, and she was so touched that Brady had remembered. "You are something else," she said with tears in her eyes, and Brady walked toward her.

"No, you are," he said, taking her in his arms and kissing her for the first time tonight. The two of them stood there, with their coats on still, lost in each other. When they did pull apart, Brady was grinning mischievously at her. "You know, it's been seven weeks since I have been able to do that to you."

"Seven weeks since our first kiss, the second time around in our relationship, huh? That's impressive, given the fact that the first time you ever kissed me, we ended up making love five minutes later." Kelsey was flirting with him and he poured her a glass of wine, and then one for himself. "If you make me think about doing that to you right now, our dinner will get cold…"

They took off their coats and sat down to enjoy the exact same meal they had shared sixteen years ago. They talked endlessly about her children, and about Bree and how she is really trying not to let losing Max consume her. Throughout dinner, Brady reveled in talking about Miles and a move he made on the basketball court at his last game which Brady attended and cheered him on. And then he brought up Bailey. He could not believe how smart she is, and he had expressed how he is thoroughly enjoying being her mentor. Kelsey kept smiling and thinking how lucky she is to have found this man, again, and this time he didn't just want her. He also wanted her children. He already adored them.

"Why are you looking at me like that?" Brady asked emptying the rest of the bottle of wine between their two glasses.

"I am so blessed to have you back in my life. And now my children are, too. You are making us feel like a family again, a revised family nonetheless, but it's such a comforting feeling for me." Brady stood up from the table and took Kelsey's hand to help her up. In her heels she was standing almost up to his full height.

"I have never stopped loving you, and now after getting to know your children and spending so much quality time with them - I know I can never walk away from any of you, ever. I need all of you. I want all of you in my life - forever." Kelsey was crying as Brady bent down and ended up on one knee in front of her. He reached into his pocket and pulled out a little black box. She couldn't believe this was happening, but it was. He opened it and revealed a four-carat princess-cut diamond ring. "Say you will marry me, babe…"

"Oh my God, Brady, what are you doing? Can we do this? Can we really do this?" He slipped the ring onto her finger, and replied, "We just did it. Now say yes…be my wife."

"Yes, oh yes, I will marry you!" Kelsey kissed him hard on the mouth and he responded. Afterward, he told her, once again, what she needed to hear. "I want you to wear this ring when you are ready. I do not expect you to go home tonight and tell your kids that we are getting married after our first date. In their minds, we are just beginning. You and I both know this is far from the beginning of what we have shared but this is a new beginning. So take that ring with you and keep it safe and when you're ready, wear it and we will tell your kids that we are getting married because we all want to spend the rest of our lives together."

For the second time this evening, Brady had Kelsey crying. Happy tears. She reached for him and pulled him close, whispering *thank you* to the man she loved. The man she had loved for a very long time.

They made their way over to the couch and savored each beginning moment of being together, again. He kissed her, he touched her, and she was feeling half out of her mind when he carried her - in her bra and panties, and still wearing her stilettos - into his bedroom. He was wearing only his black dress pants and had kicked off his shoes and pulled off his socks after he put her down on the bed that again had all-white linens. He then moved his body over top of hers as she reached for his belt buckle and undid it. Finding each other again was effortless. It was as if, body and soul, they were custom made for each other, still.

CHAPTER 28

Kelsey was unbelievably happen again. She spent the rest of the weekend walking around with a silly smile on her face. Bree was laughing at her, when the kids weren't around, and asked her if Brady had a brother. Kelsey confided in Bree about their engagement and showed her the ring. Bree was truly happy for both of them but she agreed it would be too much, too soon for the kids to digest.

Bree told Kelsey that she too had a secret. She wanted to begin again with her life, and after some thought she was certain she wanted to have another baby, before it was too late.

"Don't you need a man for that sister?" Kelsey had asked her, feeling like she was jumping in way too soon after her son's death.

"All I need is a sperm bank. I've already made an appointment to set things up. I want this, I want to be a mother again more than anything. I don't need a husband or a man to complete me anymore. I was wrong when I clung to Nic like he was all I ever wanted and needed. I was wrong to trap him, but I don't regret it because I had thirteen years with my boy."

Kelsey supported Bree because she loves her. And so she encouraged her to get all of the information to have a lawyer look over first. Kelsey's neighbor, and Tasha's husband, is a lawyer so Kelsey offered to get his help and Bree agreed. Bree has the money to raise a child alone and she certainly has enough love to give.

***

Kelsey was sitting at the kitchen table with her laptop. She had a few more stories to edit before dinner would be ready. Miles was playing a game on his PlayStation upstairs in his bedroom, Bailey was due home from school within the hour and Brady was going to drive her. When it was career day, the two of them always came home together and Brady stayed for dinner. It was Bree's first day back to work and she had told Kelsey not to plan on her for dinner. She would be working late for a few nights just to get caught up again with her advertising clients.

Kelsey heard a car door and walked into the living room to see if someone was outside. Brady's car was on the driveway and Bailey was getting out of the driver's seat as he walked around the car and met her. She was not as tall as him, but almost as tall as Kelsey already. They were talking and Kelsey was reading their body language. Bailey looked so captivated by him. Kelsey was staring and processing what she was seeing. A moment later she had read her daughter lips, *I love you*, and she watched her daughter practically jump into Brady's arms. He lifted her up off of the ground and hugged her with a priceless expression on his face, holding her for a long time. Kelsey knew that was the first time her daughter had told Brady she loves him. She had tears welling up uncontrollably in her eyes as she knew there was a real and true love there, between those two. She has been so grateful for Brady's influence on Bailey. The most recent difference he made in her life was getting her comfortable behind the wheel. Bailey had turned sixteen, earned her driver's license, but she didn't want a car of her own and she was adamant about not driving. The accident with Savannah, resulting in Max's death, had scared her – and she refused to put herself or anyone else in any kind of danger by driving a car. Brady had talked to her and convinced her to face that fear and work through it. By driving. Kelsey walked away from the window and went back into the kitchen to check the chicken that was baking in the oven. Her heart was heavy. This had been weighing on her mind for awhile, and even more so since Brady had proposed to her and promised to love all of them, forever.

She wondered if it was time to tell them the truth. She needed to know it was the right thing to do, and that reassurance just wasn't happening. It would be a risk for her, she knew, but maybe this wasn't about her anymore. This was about giving those two people in her world, whom she loved so much, a real chance to be father and daughter. She didn't know if she could deny them that, any longer.

Kelsey knew she was about to cause confusion and heartache. It would take time for both Bailey and Brady to process the truth - and embrace it. She knew Bailey would eventually forgive her. Their bond was unbreakable. They could get through anything. She wasn't so sure about Brady. She wanted to trust that he wouldn't leave her, but lying to him about his baby, his daughter, might be too much for him to handle. The two of them had never again talked about the lie that drove Kelsey out of Brady's life and back into Kyle's many years ago. Brady, however, believed Kelsey was the most honest person he had ever met. He had said as much to her, time and again.

***

After dinner, the kids went upstairs to do their homework and

Brady helped Kelsey clean up the kitchen. He knew the kids were both busy upstairs, so he pulled her close for a kiss. The two of them stood in front of the kitchen sink kissing and moving their hands up and down each other's bodies.

"Brady…" Kelsey managed to mumble his name in between kisses with him.

"Hmmm?" He was concentrating on nuzzling her neck and attempting to bring his mouth lower, to her chest, when she stopped him. "We can't! Not here. My kids could walk in any second."

"Oh I know you're right, but I can't take this. I want you babe, right now."

"Well then you two had better hightail it downstairs and use my bedroom while I make sure your kids are busy." Bree was standing in the kitchen, holding her briefcase and cell phone, looking for a place to set everything down but the table was still full of dinner plates and dishes.

Kelsey blushed, "Oh my God, Bree, I didn't hear you come in!" Brady and Kelsey pulled away from each other as Bree laughed at them. "Obviously you both were totally distracted." She pulled out a chair and put her briefcase down when Brady walked over to her. "So were you serious a minute ago, Bree?"

"Brady!" Kelsey was embarrassed and Bree found it too funny, given the fact that they have always told each other all of the intimate details of their sex lives.

Bree sat down to eat some of their dinner leftovers and she told Brady and Kelsey about how rough her first day back to work was for her. "There are two kinds of people in my world right now, those who want to talk about Max, and those who think if they ignore the fact that my son died then I won't burst into tears or even think about my loss. Wrong. Mention my son and I'll feel like you are keeping his memory alive. For me, that is such a gift. Just please don't act like I've been on a fucking vacation for almost two months."

Kelsey sat beside her and gave Bree's hand a squeeze. "I know honey, believe me, I know. It will get better. Today was new for you and for everyone at work. Talk about Max with them if you want to, if not I'm here anytime to talk about that sweet boy who graced all of our lives for thirteen years. I miss him terribly, too." Bree gave in, put her fork down on her plate, and cried. Kelsey's words had touched her, but the emotions that she had been fighting inside all day long had finally boiled over. Kelsey held her, as they both sat close in their chairs, and Brady walked over to rub Bree's back.

"I need a baby now," Bree said wiping away her tears, "I need this in order to move on."

Brady gave Kelsey a look with his eyes wide. She had told him about Bree's plans to get pregnant through artificial insemination, via a sperm back. And he thought it was a crazy idea and too soon after losing Max. He had told Kelsey that Bree's life was not over. She is a beautiful woman who will definitely still meet someone and have a family one day. Kelsey, however, reminded him that she is in her early forties and getting pregnant might not happen now, and especially if she waits too long. Bree had certainly talked Kelsey into this idea. If Bree wanted it that badly, Kelsey would support her no matter what.

After the kids were showered and headed back upstairs to bed, Bree excused herself from the living room to go downstairs to do the same. She was tired from a full, and emotional, day back at work and she had wanted to give Kelsey and Brady some private time alone.

They were kissing on the couch again when Brady asked her to take him upstairs, to her bedroom. Kelsey froze. They could not be together, like that, in her bed, the bed she had shared with Kyle, in their home. She thought they would save their love making for at his place, for now. She didn't want her children to hear them or, worse, walk in on them. It just didn't feel right. "I can't bring you upstairs, not with my kids in the house."

"And not in Kyle's bed?" There was a tone in his voice that Kelsey didn't like.

"It's not Kyle's bed anymore. It's my bed, but please respect the fact that it was our bed when we were married."

"I do, babe, I'm sorry. I just want to be with you again."

"So what do you suggest we do? Get naked in the laundry room?" Kelsey was joking but Brady was up for the challenge. After a little while longer of kissing and touching and probably doing too much on the couch in her living room, Kelsey and Brady peeled themselves away from each other and said goodnight at the front door before he left to go back to his apartment.

Kelsey closed and locked the door, and when she turned around to turn off the light and head upstairs, she saw Bree open the door leading up from the basement steps. She had taken a shower, brushed her teeth, and hoped to sneak into the kitchen for a bottle of water and return to her room unnoticed.

"Is lover boy gone for the night?" Bree was genuinely happy for Kelsey, but at that moment she also knew why Kelsey looked so torn. "You're not ready yet for him to stay the night here, are you?"

"No… it just doesn't feel right. I don't want my kids to feel uncomfortable either. Something else is bothering me too and you're the only one I can talk to about it." Bree sat down on the couch barefoot, wearing lounge pants and white t-shirt. She wasn't wearing a bra and she was proud of it, in a thin see-through white tee and Kelsey had noticed and rolled her eyes. "I'm not sure how serious I can be with you sitting there showing me your boobies," Kelsey closed her eyes and Bree laughed at loud, "Oh come on, it's not like you haven't seen these girls before." They were giggling so hard that Kelsey had to take a minute to regroup, before she got serious with Bree.

Then, Kelsey kept her voice down and began to tell Bree what was weighing on her mind, that it might be time for her to own up to the truth. A truth that could bring her daughter and her daughter's biological father even closer together. Or the same truth that could tear their budding family apart.

"Are you absolutely sure that you want to do this?" Bree had seen all of them together, she was a part of that family too, and she hated to think about anything bringing any more pain into their lives. They had all been through enough.

"I saw Bailey interacting with Brady on the driveway today after she had driven his car home, with him. She loves him. She told him so. He held her so tight after hearing those words from her, and the look on his face hit me like a ton of bricks. He needs to know that she is his daughter. I need to give my daughter that gift as well."

"So how is the truth going to change how they feel about each other if they already feel so much love?" Bree had a point but Kelsey felt strongly about the two of them living the rest of their lives knowing they are also bonded by blood. It was time to tell them. "The only thing that will change is how they feel about you. Are you sure you're ready for the fallout from that secret?"

"This isn't about me anymore."

"The hell it isn't. That man wants to be your husband and you want to not only give Bailey a father but Miles too. He needs a man in his life. He needs Brady. You might not become a family if you tell them the truth now," Bree was worried about her. This wasn't going to be good. Bailey would lose respect for her mother, and Brady could walk away from her. For good.

"I hear what you're saying and I am terrified to do this."

"But you're going to do this anyway, aren't you…"

"Yes, I think so."

"Who will you tell first? Or will you tell them together?"

"I cannot tell them together. I plan to tell Brady first because if he chooses to walk away from us then I will not reveal the truth to Bailey. I will not have her feeling like another father has left her. She was devastated when Kyle died, and I will spare her that kind of pain again."

"He's not going to walk away from her. It's you I'm worried about, Kel."

"It's a risk I'm ready to take. For them."

CHAPTER 29

So she had his attention. A week had gone by with Kelsey tangled up at the newspaper office and juggling everything with her kids, while Brady was tied up more often than usual at the hospital. He had missed Miles' basketball game yesterday and Bailey's volleyball tournament all week. He made it to the house for dinner one night, but he was called back to the hospital for an emergency before they had finished eating.

Bree had teased Kelsey to get used to it, that was life with a doctor and then she added, *"Or maybe take it as a sign that you're not supposed to sit him down and fess up to a sixteen-year-old lie."*

Kelsey had been a bundle of nerves all week, and every time she had talked to Brady on the phone she wondered if he could sense the change in her. It was Saturday morning now and Bree was at the office, Bailey was at the mall with two of her friends in her class, and Miles had a sleepover across the street last night with Spence. Kelsey had asked Brady to come over after he woke up. He had worked until midnight the night before, but by eight o'clock he had been showered, dressed in old jeans with holes in the knees, and a royal blue Under Armour t-shirt. Kelsey had also slipped on a pair of jeans, a fitted yellow t-shirt, and she had her hair tied up in a knot on top of her head. Brady was sitting on her couch when she came down the stairs after telling him she would be right back. She had gone upstairs to look in the mirror and convince herself one more time that telling him the truth is the right thing to do.

"You look too cute today babe, I like the Saturday look on you."

He pulled her down onto the couch for a kiss after she walked barefoot into the living room and up to him. They kissed long and hungrily for a few minutes until Kelsey stopped. "Hey… I thought we were going to take advantage of the empty house," Brady was ready for some time alone with her again, and he had hoped she was open to them being together at her house.

"I like that idea but we need to talk first," Kelsey wondered if he would ever want to be near her again, once she told him the truth. A part of her wanted to ask him to make love to her, one last time, right now, just in case this would be goodbye.

"Something on your mind? I know it was a crazy week for both of us, but you just seemed distracted when we did touch base," Brady knew her and he worried about the way she was looking at him now. It reminded him of that day in his office when she found out he had medically induced Kyle's coma, and then walked out on him.

"Yes. You and Bailey."

"She's doing great with the career program at school. That girl knows what she wants and she's way ahead of the schedule I had originally planned to follow with the students in my group. She's an amazing kid, babe. You are so blessed to have her." Kelsey's eyes filled up with tears. She kept telling herself to *be strong* and now she was doubting she had the strength to do this. "We are both blessed to have her."

"Yeah, I agree. I really cannot wait to tell the kids we want to get married. I want to be their stepdad. I think they will be okay with that considering how we have taken this really slow and we all love each other, already."

"Yes my kids do love you. Miles worships you, like he did–"

"I'll never try to take Kyle's place babe, I promise, I will be me with them, I will not act like I'm running the show as their father."

"I know, and you have no idea how much that means to me. You get it, and you're not afraid to be honest with them about how you feel and what your intentions are."

"Well we both know that honesty is important in every relationship. I learned the hard way what a high price dishonestly can cost a man." This was the first time Brady had brought up that subject again, and this time Kelsey felt like *she* deserved to be abandoned. He thought she was an honest person. He watched her walk away from him, believing that she was the better person. What she did in the months and years that followed was equally as wrong, if not more so. "We don't have to relive that," Kelsey didn't know what else to say.

"Maybe we do in order for me to feel like I really am worthy of you and your kids."

"Brady, when I walked away from you that day and I went back to Kyle, I felt like he deserved better, I was not worthy of him. I had lied, I had cheated. I understood the path you were on when you chose to do what you did, and I forgave you. Call it desperation, maybe, but I've been there. After it was over for us, things got a little more complicated and I guess I just wanted to simplify it." Brady had a confused look on his face but he allowed her to continue talking. "I found out that I was pregnant. My doctor had told me how far along I was, and I calculated back to the weekend I had been with both of you." Kelsey felt ashamed, even after all these years, that she had slept with both men. And Brady knew when she left him, she had turned right around and accepted Kyle's marriage proposal. It had killed him then to know she was in his arms, and in his bed.

"I thought you told me in the grocery store parking lot, when you were six months pregnant, that you had known exactly when you and Kyle conceived your baby."

"I did know when my baby was conceived. I just didn't know which one of you was her father," Kelsey paused and watched Brady's face fall.

"So you're telling me that back when I asked you if you were carrying my child, because I had known there was a very good chance it was mine, that you weren't one hundred percent certain that it wasn't?"

"Yes. Kyle and I were married by then and we were having a baby."

"But the baby could have been mine?" Brady got up off of the couch and stood in front of her. Kelsey remained seated and looked up at him. "So tell me you somehow had a DNA test done, once she was born, without Kyle knowing about it? I mean you had to know for sure."

"No, I did not have any tests done on my baby."

"What? What the fuck are you telling me? You have gone by what you wanted to believe for the last sixteen years and that is your daughter is Kyle Newman's child when she could very well be mine?"

"She is yours." Tears sprung to Kelsey's eyes and she wiped them away as they fell onto her cheeks. Brady looked at her hard and cold and at that moment she almost felt frightened by the stare he was shooting at her. "I've known since the moment she opened her eyes. You had to have seen it, in all these months you've known her. Brady, she has your eyes. You are Bailey's father." Kelsey suddenly felt sick to her stomach. What had she done? And what would come of this lie now?

Brady just stood there not uttering a single word. He was shocked, he was hurt, and he was angry. But he couldn't move. He *did* know it. When he saw her for the first time at the high school and he found out who she, a Newman, belonged to, he had been struck by her eyes. They were familiar, they were his, but more so the young girl with those crystal blue eyes reminded him of his mother's. He thought it was a crazy notion and he tried to chase the idea out of his head. And then he couldn't take it anymore. He retrieved the address to their home and he went there, to ask her. If it were true, he had prepared himself to forgive her then and there. He wanted Bailey to be his. He felt an instant connection to her, they had bonded so quickly. She had his mother's name. He wasn't angry then. He was hoping and praying for it to be true - and he wanted Kelsey to be his again, too. He wanted this sweet young girl to bring them all together. Several months had passed since then and Kelsey continued to lie, to all of them. And now he was angry.

"Say something please…" Kelsey cried as she stood up to face him.

"You lied to me," his voice quivered and the tears stung in his eyes, "you, of all people, lied to me." Kelsey knew what he meant. She knew he had repented for lying to her all those years ago. She knew he had given up fighting for her because of what he had done. And now he knew that she had done something just as awful. "I had a right to know the truth. I had a right to love her. If you didn't want me, I still could have been her father. But, no, wait, that would have fucked up your plan to have a happy little family with him. Kyle Newman raised my baby. Kyle Newman loved my daughter. Yes, I love her now, but God, I've lost so much time with her. You robbed me of her childhood." Brady turned his back to her so she wouldn't see his tears freefalling. She touched his arm, and he jerked his body away from her. She was crying too and he didn't care. Her tears used to rip him apart inside, but now he wasn't feeling anything toward her except for anger.

"I know you're incredibly angry with me right now Brady, but please just listen to me."

"Yeah I'll listen… I want to listen to you tell me why you did it! Why did you pass off my baby girl as his? Because of what I did? So one lie, one cover up, deserves another? Was that my payback?" He was yelling at her now.

"No, of course not. I wanted her to be Kyle's. I didn't want him and everyone else to know what I did, with you. You and I were over."

"Stop making excuses!" he screamed and she jumped back.

"Okay. I did it for me. I did it for Kyle. I did it for the family I wanted after you disappointed me. But, then, when I saw her for the first time and I knew she was yours, I was comforted by the fact that she was yours. There, I said it. I had a part of you to keep forever. I didn't have to totally give you up. It broke my heart to walk away from you and what we shared. Despite your lie and your secrecy, I was torn and I still thought about you and about us and about what I gave up. Having Bailey, naming her after the mother you adored, gave me peace."

"So this was all about you - and your perfect storybook life. You had my daughter as a souvenir for the good time we had together, and you also had a good, decent, honest man by your side. Then you had a son with him and continued to live happily ever after in your beautiful home. Until he died and your world turned upside down, and now what the hell, Brady is back and he fell in love with you all over again - and with your children! Funny how things just work out, isn't it? So why now Kelsey? Why tell me the truth now? After all this time, you were on a roll with your well-kept secret!"

Kelsey knew she deserved his wrath, but his words were so hurtful she couldn't keep from crying. "Because watching the two of you together made me want to give you both more. You are blood and I want the two of you to spend the rest of your lives knowing you're father and daughter."

"Does she know yet?" Brady wanted to be the one to tell her, but he knew she needed to hear this from her mother. He wondered if their relationship would forever be severed. They were closer than close, but a lie this massive could change that forever. He wanted to be a real father to Bailey and nothing was going to stop him from doing that now.

"No. I wanted to tell you first."

"In case I wanted to run and never look back?" he knew her all too well, she was protecting her daughter.

"Is that what you want to do?" Kelsey held her breath, believing she already knew his answer.

"Of course not. She's mine and I want her to know that I will always be here for her. I had planned to do the same being married to you and being in your children's lives. I love all of you that much," Brady was no longer crying or yelling or feeling overwhelmed with anger. Kelsey could almost see his anger diminish. His body language changed. He was embracing the truth.

"You are a good man, Brady Walker," She wanted to take a step toward him. She wanted to fold up in his arms. She wanted him to tell her everything was going to be alright. With them. With all of them, together, just as they had planned. But that's when he walked away. Before he slammed the door, he said aloud, "Yeah, good enough now."

***

For three days, Kelsey had tried to call Brady on his cell phone. She didn't leave him a voicemail. She had just hoped he would pick up and talk to her. Bree had told her to stop trying to reach out to him, to give him time. He needed to process the truth and choose how to handle it.

Brady continued to work with Bailey at school and according to Bailey all was well. Nothing had changed. Kelsey knew he would not tell her the truth but she wondered how much longer he would wait for her to tell their daughter, everything. Kelsey had also heard that Brady was at Miles' basketball game at his grade school gymnasium. It was the night she could not make it. Two of her reporters had been out sick and she was handling all of their stories and doing her job as the editor to prepare the paper for publication. The fact that Brady was still very present in the lives of her children had made her realize he didn't want out. He was just shutting her out, and she had hoped that would change. Right now, however, she knew it was time to tell Bailey. That's what Brady was waiting for, and she owed him this. She owed him the chance to begin again with Bailey, this time as his daughter. She just had to prepare herself now. Telling her daughter the truth was not going to be painless.

***

Bree's job had consumed all of her time and Kelsey was missing her presence around the house. She left for work in the morning when Kelsey and the kids walked out the door, and she always returned long after dinner time. Kelsey knew that Bree needed to wrap herself up into her career because missing Max weighed on her mind, and on her heart, day and night. Bree seemed in control of her life and the loss of her son, but there were moments when she would lose herself thinking about him, talking about him, and crying.

Miles came up from the basement a few nights ago, after getting some Lego's in the playroom to add to the collection in his bedroom, and he had told Kelsey that Bree was crying in her room downstairs. When Kelsey found her, her heart broke. She was having a bad day, thinking about her son, missing her son, and she had gone down to the basement to be alone in her grief. She had told Kelsey she didn't want anyone to think she was weak. She was handling this. Kelsey reminded her that the pain is not going to go away, she had to allow herself to feel good and strong, and awful and weak sometimes, too. The two of them had spent the rest of the night talking about Max and looking at old pictures.

Kelsey was thinking about getting her through that rough time when the kitchen door opened up and Bree walked in. Kelsey had already tucked Miles into bed and Bailey was upstairs studying for a biology test.

"Coming from work this late again?" Kelsey asked her, wondering if maybe she had stopped at the gym or the mall or somewhere else.

"Yes, straight from work. I need to start going to the gym in the morning because I can't seem to get out of work at a decent hour, and by the time I do, I am beat and don't wanna work out."

"Are you hungry?" Kelsey had put some dinner leftovers in the refrigerator hours earlier in case Bree was looking for something to eat when she got there.

"No, Jack and I grabbed some take-out while we were working." Jack Logan had worked alongside of Bree for more than ten years at her office. They were both advertising executives and together they've been the masterminds behind numerous accounts. Kelsey had met him once at a party and he was a clean cut, handsome man. He was older than Bree, probably fifty by now, but could pass for being forty considering how well he took care of himself. Bree had mentioned running into him at the gym more than a few times over the years too.

"How's he doing? He's married right? But no kids?"

"No kids, and divorced for five or six years now. His wife left him for a younger man, younger than her too." Bree sat down at the kitchen table after Kelsey did the same.

"Oh, I don't remember you saying that."

"Yes he's been through a few things like we all have. No one gets by unscathed." Wasn't that the truth. Some people, however, were burdened with too much to bear. Losing a young husband, losing a child, counted as too much to bear.

"So you two talk a lot while you're working so closely together late at night?"

"Sure. He and I are the only two who are crazy enough to stay way past quitting time. No lives anymore to rush home to." Kelsey felt sorry for Bree and wanted her to have a life again. She was too young to be alone, and sad.

"It will get better for you, Bree. I'm sure of it."

"I'm sleeping with him."

"What? With Jack?" Kelsey couldn't believe it, at first. This was the old Bree, the Bree before Nicholas.

"Yes, with Jack. We are both incredibly lonely and working close and knowing each other so well after all these years, just led to sex in the break room last week."

Kelsey laughed out loud. "Nice, is he's doing you against the fridge or on the table?"

"Both, it's happened more than once," Bree had that familiar mischievous look in her eyes again, a look Kelsey had not seen in such a very long time.

"Oh my... so do you see this going anywhere or is it just great sex right now?" Kelsey didn't know what to think. Sex was all Bree used to care about in her previous relationships when she was younger and single, before Nicholas had been someone she thought she could love - and change.

"It's going somewhere, we both feel it and we've talked about it." Bree had always loved Jack like a friend, or even a brother. He had been her confidant when things were rocky with Nicholas, or when she was worried about her son for various reasons. Max had been sick with a flu virus when he was four years old and Bree had to take two weeks off of work to care for him, to get him well, and Jack had stepped in and taken all of Bree's accounts and covered for her without hesitation. He was that kind of friend to her. And now he had come to mean so much more. He felt the same way about Bree, and that gave her a comforting feeling she had never had before in a relationship with a man - especially not with her husband. Bree had been there for him too when his wife had an affair with and left him for a much younger man. He was heartbroken and she had helped him heal more than she knew. He had thought about her as more than a friend, and wondered if one day there would be a chance for them.

"What exactly have you talked about?" Kelsey was surprised this had happened almost overnight with them. Sure they had known each other for years, but Bree was vulnerable right now and she was concerned about her getting her heart broken. "He is sterile. He'll never be able to have any children of his own. That is why his wife left him. She's already had two babies in the last five years with her lover. Jack knows I want to have another baby, and he supports my decision to go the route of a sperm donor and he wants to raise the baby together." This was a lot for Kelsey to process. Bree was in way over her head, or so it seemed. Her grief, or her need to hurry up and get past her grief, was causing her to make very rash decisions. First, with a baby. And now, with a new man and a baby for them to raise together?

"Slow down sister. This is too much for you right now. Please reconsider jumping in with both feet. You need time to heal. You know what they say about not making any real decisions until one year after losing a loved one."

"Oh so what *they say* didn't pertain to you when you got involved with Brady again before that one year anniversary of Kyle's death?" Bree was angry and she was being hurtful because of it.

"Wow. I guess you wanted to kick me where it hurts with that comment," Kelsey got up from her chair at the table and walked over to the refrigerator. She needed to pour herself a glass of wine for this conversation.

"Okay, that was uncalled for. I'm sorry, but you're pissing me off. You know me, Kel. I am not going to wait around for something I know I want, something I know I need. Now."

"Then I say to do it." Kelsey poured herself and Bree a glass of wine, and she held her glass up and proposed a toast. "To you – and the future you deserve. I love you and I support you and I'm here for you for all of the good – and through all of the bad." The two women clinked their wine glasses together and drank to that beautiful toast, and then they sealed the deal with a hug. They had been through so much in their lives and they needed to support each other. Maybe taking risks is what they both had learned to do after overcoming grief.

When Kelsey was on her way upstairs to her bedroom to go to sleep for the night, she saw that Bailey still had light coming from her door. She knocked softly and pushed the door open. Bailey was laying across her bed on her stomach with her notes for the test scattered all around her. "I think you need to call it a night. You've been studying for hours. Trust that you know the information and give it another once over in the morning before we leave."

"Okay, but I don't know how much I trust myself for this one. It's gonna be tough. I almost wish Brady had stopped by tonight to help me study. He's good with answering my questions about some of this stuff." Brady, it was all about Brady for her daughter these days. She needed him."So where's he been? I mean he hasn't stopped by lately. Everything okay with you two?" Bailey, the perceptive one, suddenly made Kelsey feel uncomfortable. She couldn't continue with lying to her, especially now that Brady knew and he was waiting for her to come clean with *their* daughter. The mother in Kelsey didn't want to do this to her daughter, not the night before a big test. She needed her rest. But Bailey persisted. "You two are done aren't you? The dating thing didn't work out?" Kelsey didn't quite know how to answer that because she and Brady could very well be done.

"I wouldn't say we are done. We care about each other very much. Brady is just really upset with me right now." Upset seemed like such a mild word to use in this case. "It's time I told you something and I need you to do me a favor and listen to me and not just see me as your mother, but as a woman. I was young once and I made some choices that might not have been the best ones to make, I'm not calling them mistakes but I need to explain something to you." Bailey shook her head yes and continued to listen to her mother. "You know that Brady and I met more than sixteen years ago. You know that he and I were friends. We also got really close, really fast, and we fell in love."

"Wait, you fell in love? I thought you met him while you were dating dad when he ended up in the hospital in a coma?"

"Yes I was with your dad at that time. I…" Kelsey couldn't find the words. This was her daughter she was trying to explain her actions to. She had sex with one man while in a committed relationship with another. "This is the part where I need you to see me as a woman. I was attracted to Brady and he to me. We had an affair."

Bailey's eyes widened. "Mom! You did? Oh my God, did dad know this?"

"Let's just talk about Brady and me for a moment, okay? I ended our brief affair once your dad came out of the coma. It was over and remained over. I married your father and we had you."

"So you and Brady have sort of reconciled now after all these years? Why are you telling me this? I don't want to think of you two like that - especially not back then when dad was fighting for his life in the hospital. Mom, you loved dad, didn't you?"

"Oh yes, so much. But, there was a time when I loved them both. It was wrong, I know, and I was torn but I truly believe I made the right decision in the end. I know I did. I wanted to be with your father, I wanted to marry him and raise a family with him."

"Where are you going with this? What do you want me to know?" Bailey was feeling nervous watching her mom's face. She obviously had something important to tell her.

"I found out that I was pregnant with you after your dad and I got engaged, and after my affair with Brady."

"Oh my God, mom, please don't tell me this. You haven't raised me like that. You've taught me to respect my body. Were you sleeping with both of them?"

"No, but I had just ended things with Brady. I knew there was a chance for my baby's father to be either man. Bailey, there is no easy way to say this. Brady is your father."

Bailey gasped and yelled out, "No!" Kelsey held a finger to her own lips to remind Bailey that Miles was asleep in the next room. By now Bailey was up off of the bed and facing her mother standing at the foot of it. "What? You lied and passed me off as dad's baby? And he never knew? And you never planned to tell me? Why? Did Brady not want me? Oh my God I'm so confused right now!"

"I know honey, please, just listen." Bailey stood there with tears in her eyes and so much shock inside of her. "I did not know you were Brady's child. I married your dad, I gave birth to you, and when I saw you for the first time, I knew then that you had Brady's eyes." Bailey shook her head at the thought of it. She had noticed Brady's eyes and even her friend Emily had commented about the two of them having the same bright blue eyes. "I never told your dad. I never had any tests done to prove anything. You were Kyle's daughter in every way that counted." Bailey immediately began crying. She was his daughter. *He* was her father. And she missed him desperately and would always love him. She carried so many wonderful memories of him in her heart. She didn't want to believe it. She wouldn't believe it.

"No! Just stop it. I don't want to hear any more of your lies!" Bailey was screaming at her mother now and Kelsey had seriously been worried she would wake up Miles. He probably could sleep through a marching band stepping through his bedroom and she had hoped he was that sound asleep right now.

"I knew what I was doing when I kept this a secret from Brady, from Kyle, and from you. I wanted the life for you that you had as a baby, as a little girl, and as a teenager, all before your dad left us too soon. I do not regret my choice. I lied, yes, but I did it for a good reason."

"So you are at peace with this? Why? You don't think Brady would have been as good for me as a father?" Bailey was disgusted but she continued to press for more information from her mother.

"I think he is an amazing person and I want him to have the chance now to be a real father to you. I've hurt him very badly with this lie - and you too - and I'm so sorry. But you both need to realize that I am telling the truth now because of the two of you and the closeness, the bond, you already share. You both need each other, as father and daughter now."

"This is ridiculous. Dad was my father. I can't even call him Kyle. He was my dad. I don't want another dad. I want Brady to just be Brady to me."

"Yes, your dad was your father. I am not asking you to erase that. I am asking you to take this gift of Brady coming into your life and nurture your relationship with him. You both deserved to know the truth. Please treasure each other even more now that you know."

"I don't know what you're smoking mom, but that can't happen. This lie is just too much. You're screwing up my life!" Bailey was crying and choking on her sobs and Kelsey tried to comfort her. "Get away from me. Don't try to be the mother I've looked up to. Not anymore. You're such a slut!" Kelsey was taken aback by her daughter's harsh words and she slapped her across the face. "Don't you ever call me that again! I will tolerate your anger and all the pain I am causing you right now, but I will not stand here and allow you to judge me like that." Kelsey walked out of her daughter's bedroom and closed the door. This was far from over, but she had to walk away now before the two of them said, or did, anything more that they would regret.

Bree was waiting for her in the hallway when she walked out of Bailey's bedroom. "She knows," Kelsey said to her, and Bree responded, "So I heard." Bree was holding the wine bottle they were drinking from earlier and she walked into Kelsey's bedroom with her and the two of them sat on the bed and took turns taking swigs from it as Kelsey cried and Bree reassured her that Bailey was going to need time to sort all of this out in her mind, and in her heart. And then she told her to let Brady know what happened.

"He's not answering my calls."

"Then text him, tell him she knows."

And so she did. It was after eleven o'clock when she sent a brief text saying, *Bailey knows the truth.*

Less than five minutes later, he responded, by text. *I'm leaving the hospital now and I'm coming over to see her.*

***

Bree said she was going to bed, but really she was just going downstairs to give them some privacy. She had hoped, with all of her heart, that they would work this out.

Kelsey went into Bailey's bedroom and found her lying underneath her covers, with her bedside lamp on. Her hair was wet, and hanging loose, down onto her shoulders. She had showered and dressed in pajama bottoms and Kyle's gray POLICE shirt. Kelsey assumed she had worn that on purpose tonight, in order to feel close to him and to honor the man she knew and loved as her father.

Kelsey told Bailey that she had texted Brady, and he was on his way over to see her. Bailey got up and went downstairs and sat on the couch, to wait for him.

Less than a half an hour later, Kelsey heard his car pull up and there was a soft knock at the front door. It was already almost midnight and most people in their right minds were asleep on a weeknight. Kelsey opened the door to him, standing there still wearing his scrubs with his winter coat, she felt her heart flutter. He had a scruffy face. It was obvious he had not shaved in a few days. She was staring at the old Brady. Since he had been back, she had only seen him clean shaven. *Be still my heart,* she thought, as he made eye contact with her and then moved past her in the doorway. He looked to his right, into the living room, and he saw Bailey sitting there.

Kelsey closed the door, and walked up the stairs. She knew the two of them didn't need her there, not right now.

CHAPTER 30

Kelsey had waited in her bedroom and never heard any raised voices, or doors slamming inside the house or outside in Brady's car. It was after four in the morning when she must have dozed off while lying on her bed wondering what was happening downstairs in her living room. When her alarm sounded at five-fifteen, she looked and felt like she only had an hour of sleep. She grabbed her robe off of the chair in her bedroom, slipped it on, and went downstairs. The living room was empty and when she looked outside the window, there was no car on the driveway. She went back upstairs to see if Bailey was in her bed and that's when she heard the shower water running in the hall bathroom. Whether she had gotten any sleep or not, her daughter was awake now and getting ready for school.

When they met in the kitchen an hour later, both Bailey and Kelsey were showered, dressed and ready to start their day. Miles was sitting in front of the TV in the living room eating a bowl of Cheerios, and Bree was already gone for the day. Kelsey wanted to know what happened between Bailey and Brady, but the silence the two of them were sharing in the kitchen right now had made her feel hopeless about gaining any ground.

"So, are you going to speak to me?" Kelsey was not used to this awkward feeling with her daughter.

"I didn't get any sleep last night so I don't really feel like talking right now. I am just hoping to get through the day, I have a biology test remember?" Kelsey felt awful, dropping a bomb on her last night when she needed to get her rest for the test she was hesitant she would do well on.

"I'm sorry, I know you must be exhausted, but I have no worries that you will do fine on the test. I didn't sleep either. I wanted to give the two of you time alone to talk. What time did Brady leave?"

"Four-thirty."

"What did the two of you talk about for more than four hours?"

"The weather, mom. What the hell do you think we talked about?"

"Excuse me? Watch your language and the way that you speak to me. I am still your mother!" Kelsey was watching her pour some Cheerios into a bowl and then add milk before she grabbed a napkin and a spoon and sat down at the table to eat her breakfast.

And that was the extent of their morning conversation.

***

Kelsey drove both of her kids to school, and went on to work. It was making her crazy not knowing what she had caused. Did the two of them embrace the truth? Or was the shock too much for both of them to handle? She knew that Brady wanted her in his life, as his daughter now, but she was skeptical about how accepting Bailey would be. She had worn another POLICE t-shirt, this one was black, to school today. Kesley didn't know if Bailey had room in her heart to love another father the way she had Kyle.

After work, Kelsey skipped the gym and drove directly home. It was Tasha's day to pick up the kids and when the front door flew open after Kelsey was already home and in the kitchen trying to plan what to have for dinner - it was only Miles who walked in.

"Hey buddy," she kissed him on the cheek and gave him a squeeze, "Where is your sister?"

"She didn't come home with us. Tasha said she had something to do after school."

"Who told Tasha that?" Kelsey asked, grabbing her cell phone off of the kitchen counter. "Did Ari tell her mom that?" Ari, Tasha's daughter, is Bailey's age and the two of them aren't close friends but they get along and do talk a little while riding to school together. Ari didn't have her driver's license yet but she would be getting it, next month. Kelsey worried about not having Tasha to help out with driving her kids to or from school because Ari was getting a car and wanted to drive herself and her brother to school. Kelsey had already told Tasha that her kids wouldn't be going along. Not after what had happened to Max, with Savannah at the wheel, and Tasha had understood.

Kelsey had already dialed Tasha's number as Miles started rummaging through the cabinets looking for a snack. "Tasha? What is going on with Bailey?"

"She told Ari that she had something to do after school and wouldn't need a ride home. She said to tell me it was squared away with you."

"I had no idea," Kelsey was livid, but not toward her friend and neighbor. This was unacceptable behavior from her daughter.

This was unusual territory for Kelsey. She had a good girl, teenager or not, who was responsible and trustworthy. When Kelsey hung up the phone, after promising to let Tasha know what was going on when she herself found out, she tried calling Bailey's cell phone. And she got her voicemail. She left a message for her to call her as soon as possible. Then she called Brady and repeated the same process. Neither one of them had answered her call, and she prayed that it meant they were together.

An hour went by and Kelsey had just called Tasha back and asked her if she could send Miles over for a little while. She was going to go look for her daughter. As she was standing outside on her front porch, watching her son walk across the street, Brady's car was pulling up on the driveway – with Bailey in the passenger seat. She walked out onto the driveway toward them as they both got out of the car. "Where in the hell have you been?" At the moment she directed her words and her anger at Bailey.

"I was with Brady."

"Yes I can see that," Kelsey snapped as she glared at Brady, "How nice of you both to make me worry sick. I left you both messages."

"Let's go inside," was all Brady said in response and the three of them filed into the house.

They ended up sitting down at the kitchen table. Kelsey felt like she was following their lead. She was no longer holding all of the cards. This wasn't her game anymore. It was theirs. Would they love her or leave her? And were the two of them on the same team now?

Brady spoke first.

"We are sorry that we worried you. I picked up Bailey early from school this morning, right after her biology test." Kelsey could not believe the school had allowed her to leave with him. Then she remembered he was her career mentor and he had probably drummed up an excuse for her to be excused. "And we both turned off our cell phones. There was something that we needed to do together, without any interruptions." Kelsey sat there, looking at him and then over at her daughter. Their daughter. Something in Bailey's eyes had changed from last night, and especially from this morning. She had looked like she desperately needed sleep, yes, but she also seemed at peace. "We went to the hospital and swabbed the insides of our cheeks." Kelsey had seen that done in the movies. It was for DNA testing. "We wanted to know, for sure, that we are blood. And, I wanted to be the one to give Bailey her first experience in a hospital lab. We did the test and I put a rush on the results." What Brady didn't say next was while the two of them were in the lab, working and then waiting, he had seen Bailey feeling anxious for the first time. He watched her chew the inside of her lip and the inside of her cheek. There was only one other person who he had seen do that when she was nervous about something. His mother. He didn't need that test result. He already knew. She was his. Kelsey remained silent and very touched about what the two of them had agreed to do, together. She had never wanted or needed a test for proof. She had just known.

"So how long before you get those rushed results?" Kelsey asked them, knowing it must be important to them to have solid proof before they could move on and maybe share a life-long relationship.

"She's mine," Brady said. He couldn't help himself. He was smiling so big and so sweetly. His dimple was deep and vivid on his left cheek and Bailey got up from the table and hugged him. Kelsey was crying as she watched the two of them embrace - and bond. This is what she had wanted. This was why she risked their love for her.

"Oh my God… please tell me this is exactly what it looks like, that the two of you are going to be okay. I need this more than you both know," Kelsey was still crying as Bailey sat back down.

"We went to the cemetery after the DNA test," Bailey said, causing a surprised look on her mother's face. "Brady went with me, and held my hand, while I told dad how much I love him - and always will." Tears were streaming down Bailey's face and onto her lips as she was speaking. Kelsey reached across the table for her daughter's hand - and Bailey responded by taking it and then getting up and rushing into her mother's arms. They both cried, for Kyle's loss, and for Brady's gain. Kyle had the best years raising and loving his little girl. And now Brady would pick up where he left off and see this young girl grow into a woman. She had her whole life still ahead of her, and he knew she would do amazing things. And he felt so privileged to know she was accepting him to take that ride with her, by her side, as her father.

Last night they had talked endlessly about this change and what it would mean for them. Bailey's biggest worry was feeling as if she was betraying her father. To her, Kyle Newman was her father, and always would be. And that is when Brady suggested that they take this news one day at a time. He offered to do the DNA test, with her, to ensure the truth. He also mentioned how he thought she should get some closure with Kyle - and he wanted to help her do that.

When the two of them had stopped crying in each other's arms, Brady watched them part and smile at each other, both of their faces blotchy and red and wet with tears. "I love you, mom. I have had some crazy feelings running through my body since last night, but please know that I am very sure I will always love you and I don't want to live my life without you in it."

Her daughter's words had her in sobs again. "Oh baby girl… thank you… you are my world and loving you - and your brother - has been the greatest joy of my life." More tears and more hugs followed and then finally Bailey said she was skipping dinner to take a shower and go to bed. She was physically and emotionally spent. Kelsey told her she was making a huge breakfast in the morning since she didn't want to eat tonight. Bailey agreed to eat it, and said an early goodnight to both her mother and Brady before she left the kitchen.

She didn't know what to say to him. She felt so relieved but flustered at the same time. Should she ask *what he was thinking, what came next for them?*

She chose to walk over to her cell phone on the counter. "I need to call Tasha and tell her she can send Miles back home. I needed her help when I was worried and on my way out to find Bailey." Kelsey was fidgeting with the touch screen on her iPhone when Brady stood up, walked over to her, and took the phone out of her hands. He set it back down on the counter and looked at her. "That can wait a few more minutes."

Kelsey only nodded her head as she stood facing him. She was still wearing her heels from work and in heels she had always almost met his height, give an inch or two. She was thinking how she may have to spend the rest of her life forcing herself to ignore her feelings for this man. Hadn't she done that to some extent already? She was a happily married woman for fifteen years, but she had still thought about him. Now her lie might have cost her this man. Forever.

"I wish I knew what you are thinking," he said to her and her face flushed.

"I'm thinking about how grateful I am for my daughter. She was so hurt and so angry with me last night. I didn't know if I'd ever get her back."

"She's still hurt and angry and those feelings are not going to just go away. But, she loves you, and she's willing to move forward with you. It will all work out." Kelsey didn't know if Brady had been talking entirely about her relationship with Bailey. It had seemed more like Brady was speaking for himself. For them.

"And what about you? Are you ever going to be able to forgive me for all of the time you've lost with her?"

"I've spent the past four days full of anger and bitterness. I can't live like that, I have to live by example now. I have a daughter," Brady couldn't help but smile at the sound of those words coming out of his mouth, and straight from his heart. "Last night, and again just a few minutes ago in this kitchen, she showed me how to choose love over hate. I hate what you did, but I love you. I don't want Bailey to live her life watching this secret, your lie, destroy any of us."

Kelsey's eyes were tearing up again. She had hurt him, she had hurt their daughter, and there was a time she had hurt Kyle - and she had never been aware of it. Kyle had known and he became the bigger person after learning the truth. He hadn't let anything get in the way of happiness. All of their happiness.

"I will spend the rest of my life making up for our lost time. There is nothing I can do to get that back, and after talking to Bailey all night last night and spending that moment with her today, at Kyle's graveside, I'm not so sure I could have been the kind of father that he was to her. She adores that man, and as strange as it may sound, I will be forever grateful to him for loving her and raising her so flawlessly when I was not there."

Kelsey was crying. She didn't know what she had ever done to deserve the unconditional love of two wonderful men. Kyle was her first, and now Brady would be her last. She wanted to spend the rest of her life with him, and now she knew - after everything - he had still wanted her.

As she was crying, Brady pulled her close. She folded herself into his arms like she never had before. She felt safe with him. She felt loved by him. And forgiven by him.

He pulled her closer and she didn't want him to ever let her go. When they finally parted, she stepped back and wiped her tears away.

Then Brady placed both of his hands on her face and he held them there. His own face was inches away from hers. And then he kissed her.

CHAPTER 31

Six months later, Kelsey and Brady were again standing in front of each other, flanked by Bree at Kelsey's left, and Bailey at Brady's right. Miles had just walked his mom down the aisle and then took a seat in the church pew next to Jack Logan. Jack gave him a high five and then looked up at Bree standing there in her royal blue maid of honor's gown, looking every bit of six months pregnant. He had hoped one day soon, maybe after their baby was born, that it would be the two of them. Getting married.

Kelsey looked stunning in an ivory, off-one-shoulder, full-length, silk dress. The dress had a side slit revealing almost her entire leg, which looked remarkable in ivory stilettos. Some things had not changed for her, even in her mid-forties, she still looked incredible.

And Brady had been thinking the same thing about her as he faced her, holding both of her hands in his, while the minister spoke to them about loving, honoring, and cherishing each other all the days of their lives.

Brady had asked Bailey to be his best girl, and she had accepted believing how perfect it had felt to be on his side, watching him vow to love her mother - and to be a family with her and Miles. She never thought she would be content seeing her mother with another man, married again, but she was. She knew what a blessing it was for her to have two parents in her life again.

After the ceremony, the six of them went out for a special dinner to celebrate Mr. and Mrs. Brady Walker and family. And then they all went home.

Bree had moved out of Kelsey's house the day after she found out the first uterine implantation had been successful. She was pregnant. Biologically she had a sperm donor, but the baby was hers and Jack's. The two of them would raise *their* son together. She was having another boy, and his name already was Sam Maxwell Logan. Max would always be a part of her heart and now he would forever be a part of her baby as well. Bree had taken Kelsey's advice and she met with a lawyer, Tasha's husband, who lived directly across the street. That is where they had lived, however, until they put up a For Sale sign in their front yard and sold their house on the very same day. Tasha's husband had been offered and accepted a job transfer to become a partner in a law firm in Baltimore, Maryland.

Kelsey was heartbroken to say goodbye to her dear friend and neighbor. Tasha had kept her afloat so many times. But now that very same house had a special new home owner. Bree bought the house, and she and Jack had moved in. And soon their baby would, too.

To all of them, it had felt like they were beginning a new chapter in their lives. A chapter, which God willing, would only bring happiness, fulfillment, and that seamless feeling – to each of them. There had already been too much loss. And too many secrets.

Kelsey had never regretted her critical choice all those years ago. She still had no regrets. She did feel sorrow for the pain she had caused her loved ones – but their hearts harbored forgiveness and love for her, and they all were moving on now. Together, and as a family. There was nothing else to hide.

Brady walked up the stairway from the basement. Kelsey had done some remodeling and rearranging in her home over the course of the past few months. Bree's room downstairs, the guest room, was now the bedroom she would share with Brady, her new husband. Bailey had moved into Kelsey's master bedroom across the hall upstairs and Miles had chosen to keep his same bedroom but wanted to turn Bailey's old room into a playroom since Brady had wanted an office downstairs in the old playroom. Life was coming together inside the Newman-Walker house. They were making it *their* home now. When Brady reached the living room, he spotted Kelsey setting down her luggage by the front door. The two of them were going on their honeymoon. He couldn't wait to be alone with her, for an entire week. The love of his life. His wife.

He stood there thinking about all that had happened. All that he had done to get to this point in his life. He remembered seeing Kelsey for the first time that night in the hospital. He remembered their brief affair so full of passion and dreams. He didn't want to chance losing her then so he had administered the drug to keep Kyle Newman in that coma for as long as it would take to ensure Kelsey would be his. Forever.

And when the truth surfaced, she couldn't handle it. She walked away. Brady had lost her. He remembered that last day in the hospital when he had ordered a precautionary CAT Scan for Kyle because he had still been having headaches. Kelsey had stayed behind in the examining room to wait for Kyle - and to finalize her goodbye with Brady. She had made it perfectly clear that she was moving on with her life. She loved him, and always would, but they were not to have a future together. Brady hid his pain and heartache, but both were deeply severing him to his very core. He walked into the lab and consulted with the technician. There appeared to be a bulge or ballooning in a blood vessel in the brain. It had not shown up previously. On this scan, it was visible and had looked like a berry hanging on a stem. The technician and Brady both had diagnosed a brain aneurysm for the patient.

Most of the time an aneurysm will not rupture or create health problems or symptoms. Sometimes, however, an aneurysm will leak or rupture and this can be life threatening. Every aneurysm was different and every person responded differently to them. It depended on the size, the location, and the blood pressure of the individual.

Some people lived full and complete lives never knowing they had an aneurysm. Kyle Newman never knew that he had one because when the technician left the lab, Dr. Brady Walker deleted the file. He also retrieved the hospital's back-up file and deleted it. Nothing had shown up on the CAT Scan, Brady had told Kyle. And then he wondered just how long that man would be fine. And just how long he would have to wait until Kelsey was his again.

He walked over to his wife and kissed her by the front door of *their* home. He knew he was not flawless, but he believed he was a good man. He would spend the rest of his life proving that to his wife. And protecting her and their children. And safeguarding their love from the one thing he knew could destroy it.

ABOUT THE AUTHOR

Lori Bell lives in Trenton, Illinois with her husband, Mike and two children, Bailey and Connor. She has a bachelor's degree in journalism and is a former newspaper reporter. Seams is her first published book.

Made in the USA
Charleston, SC
28 December 2014